Journal of Beat Studies

Volume 3, 2014

PACE UNIVERSITY PRESS • NEW YORK

ISSN 2165-8706
ISBN: 978-1-935625-17-9 (pbk: alk.ppr.)

Member

Council of Editors of Learned Journals

Journal of Beat Studies

Volume 3, 2014

Letter from the Editors

We are excited and proud to state that this is the third volume of the *Journal of Beat Studies*. As many of you no doubt realize, initiating a scholarly journal, especially in the humanities in the early twenty-first century, is a challenge on multiple levels. Particularly in the United States, academic presses are finding it increasingly difficult to achieve a profit margin for scholarly publications. Add in the mounting pressure on graduate students and new Ph.D.s to publish in order to secure a viable teaching/research position, and it becomes even more difficult to solicit and vet high quality research that contributes substantially to the scholarly field. Editors of academic journals are also faced with the reality that their home institutions often cannot provide release time or administrative support for them. In this troubling context, we thank Pace University Press for its faith in and support of the *JBS*, particularly our new editor at Pace, Walter Raubicheck. His familiarity with the field and his congenial approach to scholarly collaboration has gone a long way to promote what we hope will be a long life for the *JBS*. We also thank our editorial board members and others who have contributed a great deal of *pro bono* time to the mentoring and promoting of scholars published in the *JBS*.

Volume Three of the *JBS* features two long essays focused on Beat artists' interactions with the Boston/Cambridge community. This area of Beat art and history has been given short shrift, but deserves more critical attention. So we welcome both Maria Damon and Marian Janssen's recognition of the importance of this topic. Damon's essay "John Wieners in the Matrix of Massachusetts Institutions: A Psychopoeticgeography" uses the life and art of poet John Wieners as a touch point to explore how the Beats were among the first U.S. writers to take on the city as, Damon states, "a serious site of ambiguous magic in which subjectivity could undertake its own experiments and undergo those imposed upon it." The essay provides a virtual walking tour of sites familiar to both Wieners and Damon, including the north and south sides of Beacon Hill, demonstrating the sharp class divisions existing in the early 1970s.

Janssen's essay "The Enigmatic Relationship of Poets Isabella Gardner and Gregory Corso" turns an historical eye to the relationship between Boston poet Isabella Gardner, grand-niece of Isabella Stewart Gardner, and Gregory Corso, bringing into the Beat mix the internecine controversies between avant garde and mainstream poet/editors Allen Tate and Paul Carroll. Janssen, author of *Not at All What One Is Used To: The Life and Times of Isabella Gardner* (2010), argues that at mid-century the lives of the Beat poets "touched those of the established poets more intimately and diversely than is usually assumed."

Taking an historical approach to the Beat canon, Dustin Griffin follows the long and vexed history of the stabbing death of David Kammerer by Lucien Carr in August 1944. In the wake of the 2013 movie *Kill Your Darlings*, Griffin takes a different tack, investigating the early lives of William S. Burroughs, David Kammerer, and Lucien Carr as friends in St. Louis, Missouri; eastern prep schools; and New York City. Working with heretofore unavailable manuscripts from the personal archives of the Kammerer family, Griffin does not definitively answer the question of Kammerer's sexuality or the reason Carr stabbed him, but rather fashions complex human portraits of the three young men, revealing how myth-making has directed and distorted histories of early Beat lives.

In keeping with the focus on early Beat works and lives, Todd Giles in his essay "Entering the 'Gate of Nondualism': Gary Snyder's 'On Vulture Peak' and Mahāyāna Shūnyatā," provides the first ever comprehensive reading of Gary Snyder's poem that decades later developed into *Mountains and Rivers Without End*. Giles takes into account Snyder's evolving identity as a Buddhist and as an American poet, the essay ultimately filling in a critical gap in Snyder scholarship and serving as an effective introduction to Buddhist-Beat connections in general.

Journal of Beat Studies Volume 3 also includes reviews of five recent works of Beat scholarship. Matt Theado incorporates reviews of *The Beats: A Very Short Introduction* by David Sterritt and *The Beat Generation: A Beginner's Guide* by Christopher Gair to assess the overall state of introductory texts on Beat writers. There are a plethora of introductions to Beat writers and artists, which demands that we ask: Do we really need another one? But Theado, himself the author of two well-respected introductions (*Understanding Jack Kerouac* and *The Beats: A Literary Reference*), skillfully delineates the diverse and distinct audiences for a number of these texts, "A Discussion of Introductory Texts on Beat Writers" providing useful guidelines for both scholars and classroom instructors seeking appropriate vehicles for those beginning to learn about Beat artists.

Simon Warner's *Text and Drugs and Rock 'n' Roll: The Beats and Rock Culture* is reviewed by David Sterritt, who finds the book to be "a goldmine for anyone fascinated with the particulars of Beat and rock in the all-important postwar era, which exerts an uncanny sway over pop culture even now."

Scientologist! William S. Burroughs and the "Weird Cult" by David S. Wills helps to clarify a Burroughs claim about cut-ups that has bothered Oliver Harris for three decades: Burroughs' statement that there is no connection between Scientology and the cut-up method. Harris' review points out the limitations of taking on such a huge project but stresses the value of Wills' findings that caution against any of us taking as facts Burroughs' on-the-record assertions.

The latest work by veteran Beat scholar Gregory Stephenson, *Pilgrims to Elsewhere: Reflections on Writings by Jack Kerouac, Allen Ginsberg, Gregory Corso, Bob Kaufman and Others*, is reviewed by Todd Giles. The book, introduced in 2013 at a European Beat Studies Network conference in Aalborg, Denmark, does not function as a scholarly sequel to Stephenson's *The Daybreak Boys*, published in 1990, but stands more fully as personal reflections and a guide for those new to Beat writing.

Finally, we present our inaugural "Beat Index 2013," an annual summary of Beat Scholarship, which we hope will provide scholars with a single and reliable "super-source" for scholarship, allowing both neophyte and accomplished scholars to assess more accurately the work we draw upon to advance Beat scholarship. For this section of the *Journal of Beat Studies* we extend a huge thank-you to our editorial assistant, Scott Mclellan, an undergraduate women's, gender, and sexuality studies major at The College of Wooster. If you have a publication to include in the 2014 Index, send it to Nancy Grace (Ngrace@wooster.edu).

We welcome your response to the issue, as well as your submissions. If you would like to serve as a reviewer for us, please let us know that as well. And continue to pass along to other scholars the good news about the journal.

Onward!

Ronna C. Johnson and Nancy M. Grace

The St. Louis Clique: Burroughs, Kammerer, and Carr

Dustin Griffin

"The whole thing really begins in St. Louis." That's what Jack Kerouac said in a 1960 interview about the beginnings of what was later known as the "Beat Generation" (Aronowitz). Most accounts of the origin of the Beats focus on the meeting of Kerouac and Allen Ginsberg in New York in early 1944, but Kerouac said it in fact began with the "St. Louis clique."[1] By that term he meant three friends—all of whom had grown up in St. Louis—who brought Kerouac and Ginsberg together: William S. Burroughs, David Kammerer, and the much younger Lucien Carr. Burroughs, then 30, would go on to write *Junky* (1953), *Naked Lunch* (1959), and many other novels. Kammerer, 33, had taught English at Washington University in St. Louis for a couple of years. Carr, 19, was a sophomore at Columbia University. Ginsberg later said that "Lu" Carr—who introduced Ginsberg, his floor-mate in a Columbia dorm, and later Kerouac, to his St. Louis friends—was "the glue."[2]

"The St. Louis clique" ended abruptly early on August 14, 1944, when after a night of drinking, Carr stabbed Kammerer to death on the banks of the Hudson River near Columbia, reportedly (according to Carr) after the older man had made an unwanted sexual advance. Both Burroughs and Kerouac were called as material witnesses. As Ginsberg wrote in his journal the next day, "The libertine circle is destroyed with the death of Kammerer" (*Martyrdom* 63). A month later Carr pleaded guilty to first-degree manslaughter.

The killing[3] of Kammerer is an oft-told tale.[4] It received another fictionalized telling last year in the independent movie *Kill Your Darlings*, directed by John Krokidas from a screenplay by Krokidas and his Yale roommate Austin Bunn, and starring Daniel Radcliffe as Allen Ginsberg. Ginsberg is the central figure, with the entire story told from his point of view. Burroughs and Kammerer play secondary roles. The presentation of Carr is not flattering, and his account of the killing is called into question. The appearance of the filmed version of the story, which includes some invented episodes, makes it timely to take a closer look at the verifiable facts in the case.

All printed accounts of the killing derive ultimately from the same sources, primarily the contemporary newspaper reports—eight stories about the killing of Kammerer appeared in the *New York Times* from August 17 through October 10, 1944. The other major sources for the story of the "St. Louis clique" in 1944 are Ginsberg's journals from that period, but they have less evidentiary value: he tended to write his journals as if they were on their way to being fiction.[5] Kerouac wrote several accounts of the episode, including his novel *The Vanity of Duluoz* (1968), but they too were fictionalized and lack documentary status. Equally fictionalized is the novel he and Burroughs composed about the event, *And the Hippos Were Boiled in Their Tanks*, written in 1945 but not published until 2008. The account in Joyce Johnson's recent biography of Kerouac, *The Voice Is All* (2012), is colored by its point of view: it looks at the St. Louis trio through the eyes of Kerouac and Ginsberg.[6] Ted Morgan's 1988 biography of Burroughs, though largely an imaginative reconstruction of events (and dialogue), was at least based on 100 hours of interviews with Burroughs in the 1980s. The story as told in Barry Miles' *Call Me Burroughs: A Life*, published earlier this year, like that in his earlier *William Burroughs: El Hombre Invisible* (1992), depends on Ginsberg's journals, the memories of Lucien Carr (not a disinterested witness), and interviews with Burroughs some forty years after the event. Miles also candidly concedes that Burroughs was not always a reliable reporter on his own past (see, for example, *Call Me* 175, 633). There are also a few memoirs with brief, and usually tendentious, sketches of Carr and Kammerer. Journalists and bloggers depend on these few primary sources and continue to retell the story, playing up the more sensational elements of sexuality. It is commonly reported, for example, that Burroughs at the time "was gay," but it is more accurate to say that he was bisexual. He was twice married; when Ginsberg and Kerouac introduced him to his future wife, Joan Vollmer, in 1944, they assumed he was straight, and Carr later told Miles that he thought Burroughs was actively heterosexual in the 1930s (*Call Me* 130, 642). His friends thought Kammerer had homosexual inclinations (and some had no doubt that he was gay), but it is not certain that he ever acted on them, even on the night in August 1944—Carr was the only witness. Kammerer's pursuit of Carr seems obsessional and might have had a sexual element, although just what he proposed to Carr on that fateful night remains unclear. Carr himself was a golden boy, apparently ready for almost any kind of experiment. But despite the fact that both Kerouac and Ginsberg were attracted to him, and despite his presentation in *Kill Your Darlings*, there is no hard evidence that he was bisexual. In addition, Carr had a series of girlfriends (unmentioned in the film) and was later married.

Biographers of Beat writers disagree about Carr and Kammerer: was Carr, as some have described him, a "campus Rimbaud" (Campbell 11),[7] an intellectually precocious student of Lionel Trilling, or, as others have suggested, a seriously unbalanced and disturbed young man? Did he welcome Kammerer's company or try to push him away, or both? What explains his post-1944 transformation to responsible adulthood and long career as a respected editor for the United Press? Was Kammerer, as some have written, a pitiful, clumsy, obsessive hanger-on, a homosexual stalker? Or, with two degrees in English literature, was he, as others claim, a hearty, boisterous, intellectually powerful, well-read magnetic conversationalist, and at least occasionally heterosexual? Was he, in fact, the intellectual heavyweight of the three St. Louisans?

There is a stronger biographical consensus about Burroughs: that at age 30 he was alienated from his St. Louis upbringing; already a "literary outlaw" in the making; a brilliant and well-read man quoting Shakespeare, who steered Carr and Ginsberg to Yeats while dazzling Kerouac; and on his way to becoming the American Jean Genet. But this view of Burroughs is largely derived from his own later reports and from the reactions of the young and impressionable Ginsberg and Kerouac. In fact, in 1944, the beginning of his writing career was still more than five years in the future, and it is not at all clear that he had figured out what he wanted to do with his life or what he wanted to make of his past. Like Carr and Kammerer, Burroughs was at loose ends in wartime New York City, all of them exempt from military service,[8] without any clear purpose or commitments, two of them without even the need to work for a living.

One way to cut through many of these journalistic half-truths and the mythmaking is to collect more evidence. Materials that biographers have not yet discovered or have overlooked— including unused "out-takes" from Ted Morgan's biography of Burroughs, now at the Arizona State University Library[9]; school records for Lucien Carr; and letters to and from David Kammerer (including thirteen letters from Burroughs to Kammerer), now in the possession of the Kammerer family—shed new light on the members of the "St. Louis Clique." The picture that emerges suggests that most of those who have written about the beginnings of the Beat Generation in 1944 have to some extent misrepresented these three central figures. It is still not possible to give a clear answer to why Lucien Carr killed David Kammerer or to provide an unequivocal account of just what happened on that fateful night. But the exploration of the St. Louis background of Burroughs, Kammerer, and Carr in the 1920s and 1930s does provide a fuller picture of who they were, how they interacted, and how they influenced each other. Two points, in particular, emerge from a new reading to qualify received judgments about a key moment in the founding of the Beat generation. The first point is that the conclusions to be drawn are biographical rather than literary or critical: they make claims not about the writings of William S. Burroughs or other Beats but about the writers themselves. The second is that new evidence does not solve any of the mysteries associated with the founding of the Beats, but it challenges some of the myths that have grown up over time, some of them traceable to the participants themselves.

St. Louis

Most journalists and even biographers of Beat writers do not know St. Louis well and have contented themselves with reproducing a few clichés about the provinciality of Midwestern cities. Many have also taken Burroughs at his word, parroting what he wrote in the foreword to a 1988 edition of adventurer Jack Black's autobiography: that he was "stultified and confined by middle-class St. Louis mores" (v). However, when Chandler Brossard, later a novelist but then a young "Talk of the Town" writer for *The New Yorker* magazine, first met Burroughs, Kammerer, and Carr in New York in 1943–44, he was struck by their attractive "style," which was, he thought, at the same time "provincial" and "elegant" in a slightly old-fashioned way. Burroughs had a "certain upper-middle-class quality about him." Kammerer, he remembered, was "charming" and "sophisticated." He came from a "good family," was a "person of quality," and had a "very nice accent and speech patterns" (Morgan, Box 4 Folder 15). Brossard's report does not suggest that the St. Louis they came from was a bastion of Babbitry.

In fact, in the early twentieth century, St. Louis was a major metropolitan center. In 1910, it was still proud of being the fourth-largest city in the country, cosmopolitan, and culturally oriented toward the northeast, where its wealthy families often traveled, sent their sons and even their daughters to college, and where some had summer homes. In 1914, the year Burroughs was born, the city was still basking in the afterglow of the 1904 World's Fair. It had a major national newspaper, the *St. Louis Post-Dispatch*, founded by Joseph Pulitzer. It had a major regional university: Washington University, founded in 1853, was one of the first private universities west of the Mississippi. The city had a vibrant musical culture[10] and strong literary traditions. In his later life Burroughs often referred to St. Louis' most famous writer, T. S. Eliot, or alluded to his work. But even as a young man he might have heard about Eliot, who came from the same social milieu as he and lived in the same neighborhood.[11]

There is no evidence, however, that Burroughs was aware of the many other writers active in St. Louis during his own formative years, including Tennessee Williams (whom he finally met in 1960).[12] This might seem surprising, given Burroughs' later literary career, but in his early years Burroughs was not yet thinking of himself as a writer. By comparison, Williams, who lived in St. Louis from 1919 until the late 1930s, had literary ambitions in his early years; admired the St. Louis poet Sara Teasdale;[13] had his plays performed by the St. Louis Mummers (founded in 1929) at the Wednesday Club, a fashionable association of women who met regularly and sponsored literary contests and programs; developed a friendship with the poet William Jay Smith at Washington University's Poetry Club; and in 1935 won the short-story contest sponsored by the St. Louis Writers Guild. Burroughs seems not to have encountered writers associated with Washington University in the 1930s and '40s (e.g., Josephine Johnson, A. E. Hotchner, and William Inge), or the group of proletarian writers, such as Jack Conroy, associated in the 1930s with the leftist Union of Artists and Writers.

Burroughs, however, did have some contact with the European-based intellectual culture in St. Louis, especially in the Central West End, where a number of assimilated German Jews settled. It is sometimes noted that one of the Burroughs' neighbors on Pershing Avenue was a hardware dealer, representative of the bourgeois business elite, but not that on the other side was Dr. Gustave Lippman, whom Burroughs later remembered vaguely as an "old Jewish doctor who painted" (Morgan, Box 4 Folder 3). The doctor and his wife, who were early benefactors of the St. Louis Art Museum, held literary salons for visiting intellectuals, including the poet Witter Bynner (1881–1968) and the psycholanalyst Gregory Zilboorg (1890–1959) (Morgan, Box 4 Folder 3). Burroughs' parents must have made Bynner's acquaintance, since while Burroughs was at Los Alamos Ranch School in New Mexico, he and his mother went to see Bynner in Santa Fe (Morgan, Box 4 Folder 19).

That Burroughs was sent to boarding school is consistent with the mores of the social world in which he, Kammerer, and Carr were raised. Education was taken seriously, even if it was as much about socializing with the right people as it was about learning. The educational backgrounds of their parents were similar. At a time when few men (and fewer women) graduated from college, five of the six parents had college degrees, and two of them graduate degrees. Burroughs' father had a bachelor of arts degree from Washington University and a bachelor of science degree from the Massachusetts Institute of Technology. Kammerer's father had a bachelor of science degree from Washington University and a doctorate from the University of Pennsylvania—his mother also had two degrees from Michigan. Carr's father graduated from the University of Virginia and his mother from the University of Illinois. All three families sent their sons to Community School, a private primary school founded in suburban Clayton in 1919, and then to John Burroughs School, for which Community was a kind of feeder school, both schools founded on progressive educational principles. After Carr was dismissed from Andover in 1941, he spent a final high school year (1941–42) at the very small private academy, Taylor School, in Clayton, where Burroughs had spent his own final year in 1931–32 after withdrawing from Los Alamos Ranch School.

Burroughs would sometimes make it sound as if the schools to which he was sent were clubs for future capitalists, but the world of St. Louis private schools was, in fact, more diverse than has been generally understood. For instance, John Burroughs School, founded in 1923, was not a venerable institution. Granted, it soon enough attracted the children of the city's elite, but students did not all come from families with large fortunes, nor were they all "WASPs." And while a number did acquire personal fame, they were not all destined for careers as captains of industry or for safe berths in their families' businesses. During the years that the three St. Louisans attended John Burroughs School, the student body included the future novelist and war correspondent Martha Gellhorn (1908–98), her brother Alfred Gellhorn (1914–2008), who became a distinguished oncologist, and Rebekah (Betty) West (1915–82), a free spirit from a wealthy family who later married Standard Oil heir William Harkness and founded the Harkness Ballet in New York City. Burroughs' classmates at John Burroughs also included Anne Russe Prewitt (1915–2012), in later life a politically active Democrat; and Florence Steinberg, later an important St. Louis art collector. In the same years, students at St. Louis Country Day School (the *other* leading private day school and favored by most of the business elite because it was single sex) included another Gellhorn brother, Walter (1906–96), later a distinguished law professor, and the Pulitzer-Prize winning novelist and short-story writer Peter Taylor (1917–94).

Biographers who have written about Burroughs, Kammerer, and Carr sometimes assert that they were all from "upper class" or even "aristocratic" families. Some journalists have thought Kammerer's family of much lower social rank than Carr's, accentuating the melodramatic story that the pitiful Kammerer was fatally attracted to somebody beyond his reach. It is more accurate to say, as did the *New York Times* when on August 17 it first reported the story of the killing, that Kammerer's family was "socially prominent" (Adams 13). All three families were more or less on the same social level, and all part of the upper middle class. The Carr family money was oldest, made by his great-great-grandfather (in dry goods) beginning in the 1840s. The Burroughs money was made by his grandfather in the late 1890s. David Kammerer's family's money was newest—made by his father, a professional engineer, although according to Kammerer's nephew Richard Kammerer, his mother reportedly brought some money into the marriage. They all belonged to old-line Protestant churches. Both the Kammerers and the Carrs were Episcopalians, the Burroughses were Presbyterians and Methodists, with Burroughs' maternal grandfather the head of the most prominent Methodist church in the city. Both Kammerer's parents and Carr's were listed in the 1922 edition of the *St. Louis Social Register*, along with Carr's mother's family and Burroughs' grandparents, but not Burroughs' parents. The Carr family probably enjoyed somewhat higher social access: Lucien's maternal grandfather, Benjamin Gratz, was a member of both the elite St. Louis Country Club and Bellerive Country Club, and president of the Commercial Club; neither the Burroughs nor the Kammerer family belonged to these clubs. All three families buried their dead in the same elite Protestant cemetery, Bellefontaine.

Families in the St. Louis business elite often intermarried. Children grew up to marry their neighbors or their school classmates. However, this was generally not the case in the Burroughs, Kammerer, and Carr families: the St. Louis natives, (Burroughs' father, Kammerer's father, and Carr's mother) all found their future spouses out of town, as did Burroughs and Carr themselves. But Burroughs' brother Mort would later marry one of his Community School classmates, Margaret (Miggie) Vieths, who was, in fact, distantly related to Lucien Carr.[14]

Like other members of their social class, the three families all lived in the same neighborhoods. The Central West, developed in the 1880s, was a compact and fashionable area west of "Midtown" and adjacent to Forest Park (the site of the 1904 World's Fair), and only about eight blocks north-to-south, and ten blocks east-to-west. The district included several private "places" where impressive mansions were erected, most from about 1890 to 1910. The Burroughses, Kammerers, and Carrs lived not in the private places, but in the handsome nearby streets, lined with substantial three-story brick houses. Burroughs' father grew up on McPherson Avenue; after he married, he moved to nearby Pershing Avenue, which at the time was called Berlin Avenue but in 1918 was renamed Pershing after the American Gen. John J. Pershing, head of the American Expeditionary Forces. The Kammerers lived on Lindell and then West Pine. Carr's mother also grew up on West Pine, and after her marriage she and her husband lived with her parents on Lindell. All were just a few blocks apart. The Central West End was the home not only of the business elite but also of literary St. Louis: Eliot and Teasdale lived in the Central West End, as did Tennessee Williams. The Wednesday Club was located there, as was St. John's United Methodist Church, where Burroughs' grandfather presided; the Second Presbyterian Church; and St. George Episcopal Church.

In the 1920s, many comfortable St. Louis families decided to try to escape the city's famously dirty air by moving west, either to suburban Clayton or, a little further west, to what would later become the separate township of Ladue (now one of the wealthiest suburbs in the country). The Kammerers moved to Clayton by 1925. The Burroughs family moved out to Price Road, in an unincorporated area (later incorporated as Ladue) adjacent to Clayton, in 1926. The Carrs, when they returned to St. Louis in 1930 after several years in New York, bought a house in Clayton.

The Burroughs, Kammerer, and Carr families were relatively unaffected by the Depression, which hit St. Louis very hard. For example, there was a major riot at City Hall in July 1932. The local unemployment rate reached thirty-five percent in 1933, and eighty percent for African Americans. Hooverville camps also sprang up along the Mississippi River. Grown and married children who lost their jobs moved back in with their parents, even in the Central West End. But the children in the Burroughs, Kammerer, and Carr families continued in private school. Burroughs' father sold his remaining shares in the Burroughs Corporation in July 1929, three months before the Crash, for $276,000, and took the family on a European tour (Morgan, *Literary Outlaw* 24). (The family had traveled to Paris and Cannes in the summer of 1927, and in the summer of 1932 went to Majorca [Miles, *Call Me* 37, 49]). The money was enough to carry the family through the 1930s. In September of 1929, Burroughs was sent to one of the most expensive boarding schools in the country. In 1932, he was sent to Harvard and went to Europe in the summers of 1933, 1934, and 1936. Apparently, he felt no need to begin a career, or even take a job: after he graduated from Harvard, his parents provided him an allowance of $200 per month that continued into the 1950s. Burroughs bristled when he read in John Tytell's *Naked Angels* [1976] that he had a "trust fund" (Hibbard 98). But the allowance he received was the equivalent of the income from a $50,000 trust fund. David Kammerer did not go east to college but probably not for financial reasons: in September 1929 he was already enrolled as a freshman of Washington University, where his father had gone before him. However, he lived at home, as did most Washington University students in those days. The Carrs had enough money, even after Lucien Carr's father, apparently devolving into drink, abandoned the family about 1930 and disappeared into Wyoming and Colorado: during the 1930s Lucien and his sister spent summers with their mother in Vermont.

None of the three young men showed much interest in the devastating effects of the Depression, the Marxist thinking that spread through the intelligentsia, or the rise of the Nazis in Germany. Burroughs encountered both Germans and left-wing ideas at Harvard, where communism was fashionable, especially with the faculty. A classmate, Robert Miller, reported that Burroughs read the *Communist Manifesto* but didn't think communism would work in practice. Other classmates disagree about student interest in communism. Miller remembered that "if you weren't a Communist sympathizer you were a reactionary" (Morgan, Box 4, Folder 14). Roger Scudder thought the faculty were very political and the students apolitical (Morgan, Box 4, Folder 19). Burroughs himself seems to have regarded strong political sentiments in other people with detached suspicion: on one occasion at Harvard he claimed to have flown planes for Franco, but only to show up another student who claimed that he had flown for the Republicans (Morgan, Box 4, Folder 8).

Miller remembered that at Harvard Burroughs had "no interest in politics, the election of FDR and impact of the New Deal" (Morgan, Box 4, Folder 14). In Vienna in 1938, Burroughs saw fascism first hand: "The students I knew were almost all pro-Nazi, and many of them violently anti-Semitic." Miller, too, remembered that while in Vienna, they ". . . were conscious of the political context because it was shortly before the Nazis took over. . . . They were beginning to be obvious . . . . We went up to Salzburg and there was a parade with a lot of Nazi sympathizers" (Morgan, Box 4, Folder 14). However, Burroughs' reaction, at least in memory, was curiously detached—sardonic. He read the pro-Nazi *Volkische Beobachter* and later remembered the "rising note of hysteria. Jews were all criminals. You could see it coming" (Morgan, Box 4, Folder 14). He was evidently interested in the manipulation of symbols and the ways in which Jewish people were linked to homosexuals but seems to have held back from any political engagement (Morgan, Box 4, Folder 14). He married a Jewish refugee, Ilse Klapper, enabling her to escape from an increasingly Nazi-dominated Europe, but there is no reason to resist the conclusion of most biographers that the act was more personal than political: Burroughs had told his parents that he was "just trying to help a refugee" (Morgan, Box 14, Folder 14). Less is known about the political interests of Kammerer and Carr during the 1930s, but no evidence has survived to indicate that they were strongly engaged in domestic politics or in international affairs, although one of Kammerer's and Burroughs' St. Louis friends, Rex Weisenburger, was vehemently anti-Semitic in the early 1930s, and inclined, so he said, to take Hitler's view of the Jewish people.[15]

After Pearl Harbor, none was stirred by patriotic sentiment or caught up in the war effort. Burroughs was drafted in 1942, but after basic training managed to be re-classified 4F and to secure an early discharge, later referring to himself as a "furtive anonymous 4F" (Morgan, Box 4, Folder 3). Kammerer apparently tried to join the Merchant Marine; at that time, service in the Merchant Marine qualified him for a draft deferment. In a March 3, 1944, letter to his parents, Kammerer's account of an attempt to join the Office of War Information (OWI) makes it sound as if, unhappily employed as a window washer in the middle of winter, he simply wanted a dry and warm office job (Kammerer Collection).[16] Carr's attempted suicide in Chicago in 1943, when at age eighteen he became eligible for the draft, has struck most observers as an attempt to be classified 4-F. But D–Day, June 6, 1944, came and went without diverting the "libertine circle" of Burroughs, Kammerer, Carr, and their new Columbia friends from their private concerns. A June 8 letter from Kammerer to his mother makes no mention of the Normandy invasion, which had been front-page news for three days (Kammerer Collection). Carr's abortive plan (with Kerouac) to ship out with the Merchant Marine in August of 1944 appears to have been driven primarily by the idea of adventure: namely, reaching Paris in time for the expected liberation and celebration.[17]

William S. Burroughs

Burroughs' own memory of St. Louis was not always reliable. He seems to have thought, for example, that Kammerer and Carr met in 1936, when Carr was only eleven-years old, but most evidence suggests that the meeting was not until 1939 (Burroughs and Kerouac, *Hippos* 187). He repeatedly mined his early days for material to be recast in his fiction and once said that every word he had ever written was autobiographical, and every word was fiction (Bockris 28). Clearly, then, one needs to be cautious in reconstructing Burroughs' own St. Louis days from the fictionalizations of his childhood in various of his novels. By the time he was granting interviews, Burroughs had become a self-consciously avant-garde writer with an interest in representing himself as an outcast from a staid, conventional, and uncomprehending world. And like many people, he sometimes chose to edit his own history, eliding episodes that seemed irrelevant. For instance, when he applied to a workshop at the Institute of General Semantics in Chicago in 1939, he omitted reference to the Los Alamos Ranch School and claimed he had attended Taylor School from 1927 to 1932, when the dates were actually 1931–32; he also reported that he was single instead of married. So one needs to be cautious in drawing on Burroughs' own published statements, if only because they sometimes contradict each other and because they are inconsistent with statements he made in personal letters in the early 1930s and with statements made about him at the time by his close friends. Granted, self-descriptions in personal letters can be disguises or deceptions, and friends can be mistaken in their judgments. But, other things being equal, evidence from private letters at the time generally may carry more weight than statements made to interviewers many years after the fact.

Burroughs in his later years liked to say that his family had been "outcasts" from St. Louis society. He recalled that his parents were not part of the "in group" and told interviewers that he shared their sense of not belonging: "This feeling I experienced from early childhood, of living in a world where I was not accepted. . . I was searching for an identity denied me by the WASP elite" (Bockris viii). But, in fact, he and his family were nothing if not "white Anglo-Saxon Protestants," comfortably enmeshed in the upper social and financial strata. A number of his childhood friends, neighbors, and classmates were sons and daughters of the "WASP elite" that he claims rejected him. Others were professional men: the father of one friend was a lawyer, horticulturalist, and book collector; the father of another a professor at the Washington University medical school—he took out Burroughs' tonsils. His classmate "Sis" Francis' grandfather, David R. Francis (1850–1927), had been governor of Missouri. The father of Kells Elvins, his friend at John Burroughs School, had been a congressman and chairman of the Republican State Committee. True, his parents did not belong to the St. Louis Country Club, but his father belonged to a "duck club" whose members included Joseph Pulitzer, publisher of the *St. Louis Post-Dispatch*, as well as O. K. Bovard, its editor (Miles, *William Burroughs* 23–24). Their close friends included Eugene Angert, a prominent Harvard-trained lawyer and bank director and first president of the Garden Club of St. Louis. Burroughs later reported that in his youth he went to the "country places" of friends on weekends—his aunt and uncle had a "farm" in rural Chesterfield.

In 1919, Burroughs' father bought an old farm just west of Chesterfield, near the Missouri River and the little town of St. Albans, where he built a weekend house: although Burroughs never mentioned the farm to interviewers until his final years, he drew on his experience there in both *The Place of Dead Roads* (1983) and *The Western Lands* (1987) (Miles, *Call Me* 28–29). In the summer, the family went to a clubby resort on Lake Huron, where he would have known St. Louisan Franklin Ferriss, who sat on the Missouri Supreme Court and lived nearby in the Central West End. At Los Alamos Ranch School, he met the sons of the heads of national companies, and among the St. Louisans who accompanied him to Harvard was Joseph Pulitzer's son. Burroughs' Harvard classmates also included David Rockefeller.

Interestingly, Burroughs said that when his family moved to 700 Price Road in 1926, he felt "cut off" from the social world of St. Louis. In fact, the Burroughs family was following other friends, including the Pulitzers, the Angerts, and the Bovards, who had also moved from the Central West End to what would become the socially prestigious town of Ladue. A John Burroughs classmate, Bill Turner, says that Burroughs was well liked: as class president, Turner wrote amiably to him after their 50th high school reunion in 1981, which Burroughs declined to attend. His name appears with some frequency in the "class history" published in 1931, after he had left the school, mostly for minor trouble-making: throwing a teacher's briefcase out the window, getting into fistfights with another student, causing an explosion with his chemistry set. One fellow student, Marjorie Capel Sheldon (John Burroughs, class of 1930), in a conversation with the author in 2012 remembers that Burroughs was "weird" and "wild" (Sheldon). Nonetheless, his friends at the school—Gene Angert, Kells Elvins, and Anne Russe—were class leaders, Russe remembering that after Burroughs left school she still saw him "at big parties," suggesting that his name was "on the list" of socially presentable young men (Morgan, Box 4, Folder 14).

Fellow St. Louisan Rogers Scudder remembers that at Los Alamos Burroughs "rather throve . . . [and] was quite popular." Looking back on Los Alamos during their Harvard years, Scudder recalled that Burroughs "seemed rather fond of it" (Morgan, Box 8, Folder 19). Another friend, Rex Weisenberger, reported to Kammerer in a letter dated March 18, 1931, that Burroughs' letters from Los Alamos were "very jolly and conducive to mirth" (Weisenberger). Neither of them may have noticed Burroughs' depression and his loneliness, which seems in part to have led to his withdrawal from the school in the spring of 1931. (It may also have had to do with a frustrated "romantic attachment" he formed for one of his schoolmates. Miles, in fact, declares that this was "the cause" for Burroughs' departure [*Call Me* 46].). But Burroughs had a sociable side: he compensated for that loneliness by frequently writing letters to his old St. Louis pals, including David

Kammerer (Kammerer's younger brother, Richard, was Burroughs' classmate at John Burroughs School.) In one of the letters, dated March 1931, he reports to Kammerer that after he "finishes writing to everyone I know I am going to start in on perfect strangers" (Burroughs). During the summers and holidays of his Harvard years, Burroughs, so Scudder remembers, also got together with their mutual friends in St. Louis, several of whom Burroughs had known since childhood, including Jack Senseney and Jay Rice, who had been at Los Alamos with Burroughs (Morgan, Box 8, Folder 9).

Reports of his "alienation" from the world he grew up in only surfaced decades later, when Burroughs, by then an avant-garde writer, gave interviews. Lucien Carr took his word for it: Burroughs, he said, was "rejected by St. Louis society, appointed a misfit" (Morgan, Box 6, Folder 8). But Carr was only eleven years old when Burroughs graduated from Harvard and did not meet him until about 1940, or spend much time with him until the 1950s. He would not have been able to make an independent judgment about the relationship between the young Burroughs and the world in which he was brought up. Scudder, who knew Burroughs at Los Alamos Ranch School and at Harvard, reported that the Burroughs family "were [sic] very much in the upper strata" (Morgan, Box 8, Folder 19). If anybody "appointed" Burroughs a "misfit," it was Burroughs himself, from the perspective of later years, when he had chosen (and later rejected) a life of drugs and then of avant-garde writing. As Carr may not have realized, in the 1940s Burroughs had not yet burned his bridges: he belonged to the University Club in New York from 1942 to 1949 and actually lived there for a time.[18]

When the Burroughs family lived at 4664 Pershing Avenue, they had a cook, a string of Irish governesses, and a black yardman named Otto Belue. But in later years, Burroughs resented being described as coming from a "wealthy" family. He tended to minimize the family's assets and said almost nothing about the Burroughs Glass Company that his father started in 1918 with the proceeds of the sale of some of his Burroughs Corporation stock, mentioning the company only once in his many interviews with Ted Morgan (*Literary Outlaw* 25). It was only on a few occasions that he admitted that his family was "very comfortable, uppermiddle class," such as the interview he gave in 1981 to *The Bloomsbury Review* (*Burroughs Live* 499). But even on those occasions, he emphasized that his family was not wealthy: "My parents were in fairly good circumstances, but they were not at all in the millionaire class. Money means everything in the class system of a middle-western town like that, and we were very much outsiders as far as the really big money in St. Louis was concerned" (*Conversations* 98). He tended to exaggerate the wealth of other families, dwelling on that handful that had "ten, twenty, fifty million dollars," focusing on the top 1/10th of one percent. As it happened, the family of Daniel Catlin, which had that kind of money, lived just a block or two from him in Westmoreland Place when Burroughs lived on nearby Pershing.[19] It may have been the close proximity of greater wealth that made him feel poor by comparison, and living across Price Road from the entrance to the St. Louis Country Club might have made him feel excluded.

Just as Burroughs in later years liked to describe his alienation from the "solid citizens" of St. Louis—his term, in the prologue of *Junky*, for the parents and children at Community School—so too he liked to describe himself when a young boy as a writer in the making. This is by no means surprising: James Joyce's portrait of himself as an "artist" when he was still a young man was the prototype for a now-familiar story that finds the writer in the child and helps biographers tell an appealing story that confirms reader expectations. Like many bright children, he was an avid reader, but his tastes seem to have been formed by the wider popular culture rather than the intellectual milieu of the Central West End. He read "boys' books," including *Biography of a Grizzly* (1900) by the popular writer Ernest Thompson Seton (author of *Wild Animals I Have Known* and later co-author of the *Boy Scouts Handbook*). He later became interested in stories about gangsters—perhaps not surprising in the 1920s when Al Capone was at the height of his fame and the "Hogan Gang" and other criminal groups were active in St. Louis. As Burroughs himself noted, "In the 1920s, gang war was box office, year after year . . . it was front page news" (*The Adding Machine* 36). In his "Literary Autobiography," written in 1972, he remembered being "fascinated by gangsters and like most boys at the time [he] wanted to be one because [he] would feel so much safer with [his] loyal guns around [him]" (*Word Virus* 74). Looking back, he did not see this fascination as darkly predictive of a future "literary outlaw" but as a sign that he was "like most boys at that time." [20] About 1928, he read Jack Black's *You Can't Win*, the autobiography of a reformed petty thief. This was not an underground or cult book but rather a well-reviewed best-seller, a lively and detailed report of twenty-five years "on the road" written in an accessible, straightforward style. Burroughs could have seen ads for the book, with blurbs from Carl Sandburg ("as exciting as the most thrilling fiction") and Clarence Darrow ("a marvelous story"), in *Overland Monthly* and *Out West* magazine (December 1926). Such magazines were a staple of his early reading: "I read all the outdoor magazines; it was a sort of hunting and fishing culture" (*Conversations* 97).[21] In such magazines, he could have pursued his interest in guns. It is easy to assume that his interest amounted to an obsession, but Burroughs himself said that it was "no special or noteworthy interest, because in the 1920s everybody was brought up with guns. It was a very widespread thing" (*Conversations* 97).

At about the age of sixteen, at Los Alamos Ranch School, Burroughs experienced a change in his tastes in reading. According to an undated 1931 letter that he wrote to Kammerer, he read a *Manual of Occultism* by a popular English theosophist (Burroughs). He also developed an interest in modern French writers. He had been performing poorly in his French classes, but then discovered the "Little Blue Books," a series of 5-cent "modern classics" published by E. Haldeman-Julius. It was here that he read, in English translation, Anatole France's *The Wisdom of the Ages*, and writings by Baudelaire, de Maupassant, and Remy de Goncourt, as well as Oscar Wilde's *Dorian Gray*.

As with many young people, reading led to an interest in writing. In an often-cited passage from his 1972 "literary autobiography," he remembered that as

> a young child I wanted to be a writer because writers were rich and famous. They lounged around Singapore and Rangoon smoking Opium in a yellow pongee silk suit. They sniffed cocaine in Mayfair and they penetrated forbidden swamps with a faithful native boy and lived in the native quarter of Tangier smoking Hashish and languidly caressing a pet gazelle. [22] (*Word Virus* 16)

This is, of course, not to be taken literally, since it is highly unlikely that at the ages of ten to twelve he represented to himself the life of a writer in this stylized and caricatured way, evoking the world of Somerset Maugham, whose books Burroughs would read in the late 1930s [Miles, *Call Me* 63).

Burroughs wrote "stories" when he was a young boy, but so do lots of children. None of these stories has survived: one, "The Autobiography of a Wolf," allegedly written when he was nine, was manifestly an imitation of Seton's *Biography of a Grizzly*. But Burroughs' own description makes these early stories sound like parodies of genre fiction: "English period," sketches about "gangsters," a "hard-boiled detective story," "a short beau geste," "crime stories" (Morgan, Box 4 Folder 3). His short essay on "Personal Magnetism" for his high school literary magazine in 1929 does not suggest any particular talent, even for an adolescent. The brief essay is a mocking review of an unnamed book, probably Edward Shaftesbury's *Instantaneous Personal Magnetism* (1926), dismissed by the young Burroughs as "a mass of scientific drivel cunningly designed to befuddle the reader, and keep him from realizing what a fake it was" (*John Burroughs Review*, February 1929, repr. in *Word Virus* 23). By his own account, Burroughs abandoned writing stories about 1930, at the age of sixteen, and except for an abortive attempt or two did not resume writing until the late 1940s. One project, not reported by his biographers, was a novel based loosely on his trip to Europe in the summer of 1933 with his friend David Kammerer. (Two letters from Kammerer reveal that he and Burroughs toured London and southern England in July, before crossing to France at the end of the month [July 15, 1933, to his brother Richard; July 24, 1933, to his mother, Kammerer Collection]). The novel was to be written in collaboration with Kammerer, and by February 1934 Burroughs had written "about fifty pages" (Morgan, Box 8, Folder 19). But according to a February 8, 1934, letter that he wrote to Kammerer, it seems that Burroughs soon abandoned the project.[23] His Harvard classmate Richard Stern says he knew of no "literary aspirations" on Burroughs' part at Harvard—if he had them they were kept "well hidden." "It never occurred to me that he would write anything" (Morgan, Box 4, Folder 14).[24] By contrast, Roger Scudder remembered that their mutual friend Gene Angert "had literary leanings" (Morgan, Box 8, Folder 19).

Burroughs had never been much of a student, and at Harvard he did not develop into one (Miles' recent claim in *Call Me* that Burroughs got all A's and graduated with honors is undocumented). In the fall of his first year, however, he worked hard, especially on his German; he enjoyed history, and found geology easy. In his letters back to David Kammerer he reports taking part in the round of traditional college activities: rowing every day, drinking whisky, and even attending the Yale-Harvard football game in New Haven.[25] But as time went on, he may have found studies and collegiate life less engaging: by the spring of his first year, his letters to Kammerer suggest he was more interested in experimenting with marijuana, visiting local "speakeasies," and planning summer travel, although he sent a full report about Gide's autobiographical novel *Si Le Grain Ne Meurt* (1924), which he had just read, noting in particular Gide's candid report of his homosexual encounters. He reports without enthusiasm that a fellow student "writes plays 'in the school of Ibsen'" and that another reads his "terrible" poetry aloud—Burroughs said he had "severed connections with him permanently."[26]

His Harvard friend Robert Miller noted that Burroughs had a "casual attitude" to his studies and "wasn't terribly interested in the courses" (Morgan, Box 4, Folder 14). Burroughs later said that he "majored in English literature for lack of interest in any other subject" (*Word Virus* 48). But he was interested enough in Shakespeare to audit George Lyman Kittredge's famous course (Morgan, Box 4, Folder),[27] and in later years scattered allusions to Shakespeare in his conversation and writing.[28] He reports having attended one of T. S. Eliot's Norton Lectures on Romantic poetry at Harvard: Eliot delivered "Wordsworth and Coleridge" on December 9, 1932, and "Shelley and Keats" on February 17, 1933, as part of "The Use of Poetry and the Use of Criticism," his Norton Lectures (Morgan, *Literary Outlaw* 61–62). In later years, Burroughs would remark on the importance for a writer of reading widely in English literature, but it is not clear that he in fact did such reading at Harvard, or how wide reading in the standard works of English poetry and prose had any deep influence on *Naked Lunch*.[29] Burroughs also looked back on Harvard as a time when he was lonely and bitter, but, in fact, Burroughs had a number of friends in addition to Miller and Stern (Miles, *Call Me* 55–56).

After Harvard, he seems to have been looking fitfully for something that might engage him intellectually. While traveling in Europe, he decided to try medical school in Vienna. This lasted about six months in 1936–37. He spent a month at the Diplomatische Akademie in Vienna (Miles, *Call Me* 65). He also began courses in psychology at Columbia—Miles states without documentation (*Call Me* 67) that Burroughs had by then read "most of Freud" and was now reading Jung, Otto Rank, and Theodore Reik—but soon dropped out. When he heard that his friend Kells Elvins was studying psychology at Harvard, he moved to Cambridge in 1938 to join him, taking courses in archaeology. Egyptian hieroglyphics seemed interesting, and he went to Chicago to seek out a professor in the Department of Egyptology at the University of Chicago (*Queer* xix–xx). This too came to nothing, but while on the campus he heard about a weeklong workshop in "General Semantics" to be given by Count Alfred Korzybski at the Institute of General Semantics, which Korzybski had founded the previous year. Burroughs had read Korzybski's book *Science and Sanity*, published in 1933. He enrolled and attended but seems not to have undertaken any further study or reading of Korzybski's writings at the time. He did read some popular fiction, including Felix Riesenberg's *Left-Handed Passenger* (1935), and it was about this time that he encountered Oswald Spengler's much-discussed *Decline of the West* (1917, 1923),[30] a book he would later give or recommend to Kerouac or Ginsberg (Morgan, *Literary Outlaw* 91). He acquired a copy of Djuna Barnes' *Nightwood*, first published in the United States in 1937.[31] In the early 1940s, he seems once again to have been reading French literature, including Rimbaud and Céline,[32] presumably *A Season in Hell* and *Voyage to the End of the Night*, in English translations. He later claimed to have read all of Proust while awaiting his discharge from the army in 1942 (Miles, *Call Me* 84). But apparently he was not yet seeking out the writers then living in New York. Morgan, for instance, claims that in 1940 Burroughs was taken by a mutual friend to meet W. H. Auden in Brooklyn but did not find either Auden (then at the height of his fame) or his poetry to be interesting (*Literary Outlaw* 72).

However, the young Columbia students who would go on to become Beat writers were very interested in meeting *him*. When Lucien Carr introduced his new friends Allen Ginsberg and Jack Kerouac to Burroughs in 1944, Ginsberg was impressed with the books he saw in Burroughs' apartment. Most accounts of what Burroughs was reading at the time derive from Ginsberg and Kerouac, and may reflect what they later found influential on their *own* writing.[33] Ginsberg, thinking that an older sage—Burroughs was all of 30—might impart wisdom, ventured to ask a naively youthful question of him: "What is art?" Burroughs' prompt answer, "A three-letter word" (*Literary Outlaw* 90), may have simply been designed to deflate the sophomoric Ginsberg, or, as Morgan, who reports the story, suggests, Burroughs might have been invoking Korzybski's famous dictum that "words are not things" from *Science and Sanity* (*Literary Outlaw* 90). In any case, it is difficult to conclude that Burroughs was thinking seriously about art. Nonetheless, Carr and his friends were apparently dazzled by Burroughs, listening intently when he told them that "literacy was the greatest curse of man, but if you were cursed with it you should read Spengler, Korzybski" (Morgan, Box 6 Folder 8).[34] Likewise, when Kerouac met him that same year, he thought Burroughs and his St. Louis friends were "decadent intellectual types, *fin de siecle enfants terrible* types" (Aronowitz), but this most likely reflects more on Kerouac than Burroughs, who may have appeared "decadent" because of his formal way of dressing; his dry, eccentric manner; and his worldly experience, all of which may have come across as "intellectual" because he (and the other St. Louisans) had read more than had the young Kerouac. What emerges, then, from a fresh look at Burroughs is recognition that in the early 1940s he had not yet formed an identity as a writer; that is, he was not yet the "literary type" that Carr thought he was. Other commentators have conceded as much, and Burroughs confirmed it as well, stating that "[d]uring and after the war I did no writing" (Morgan, Box 4, Folder 3). Perhaps more importantly, it seems too that Burroughs was not yet formed *intellectually*: He was still trying to work out who he was and where he came from. As Miles observes, Burroughs as late as 1942—and I would say 1944—was "adrift" and "bored": "there was no direction to his life, he had no ambition, no drive" (*Call Me* 92).

In time, he decided that although he grew up in St. Louis, he had left it behind him and moved on. In later years, he told an interviewer that "my whole past is something I have nothing to do with. I am now a completely different person. Anything in the past as far as I'm concerned is of no importance" (Miles, *William Burroughs* 30). We should make some allowance here for rhetorical overstatement, especially since he elsewhere hinted that he shared something with Eliot and Williams, two other St. Louis writers. But this statement may have been tactical, part of the impression he now wanted to create. As commentators have noticed, it is clear from his novels and interviews that Burroughs retained a few strong impressions of his St. Louis childhood, especially his pre-teen years. He repeatedly refers, for example, to the house on Pershing Avenue and its back garden, and to sitting on the banks of the River Des Peres, a polluted stream, later enclosed in culverts, that then flowed through his neighborhood. Perhaps these images were indelibly imprinted on his imagination, or perhaps he found them suitable for literary recycling. With his gaunt frame, sallow skin, and cadaverous face, he refers too to being described by the parents of his friends as looking like "a sheep-killing dog" or a "walking corpse," wounding words for an adolescent that resurfaced more than once in his fiction decades later (Bockris xviii). Even by 1944, when he met up in New York with his old friend David Kammerer and his new friend Lucien Carr, he had not cut his ties with his hometown. Indeed, he had spent part of 1942 in

St. Louis, recovering from mononucleosis, doing his military training until he was discharged from the army, and then working briefly as a reporter for the *St. Louis Post-Dispatch*. After the killing of Kammerer in August 1944, he would travel to St. Louis in the company of his father, before returning to New York later that year.

David Kammerer

David Kammerer remains the least known of the three St. Louisans, and the most elusive, partly because he died at 33, partly because the only reports that have reached print are by those who knew him in New York during the last year of his life. The primary accounts, from Burroughs and from Lucien Carr, were carefully edited for their own purposes. Unpublished material, however, helps to construct a more complete and complicated picture.

Kammerer was born in 1911, which made him two years older than Burroughs and fourteen years older than Carr. Kammerer's younger brother, Richard, was a classmate of Burroughs at both Community School and John Burroughs School, and it was through Richard that David Kammerer and Burroughs met and became close friends no later than 1928–29, Kammerer's senior year in high school. At John Burroughs School, Kammerer showed no special signs of intellectual power or promise; he was not a varsity athlete or a distinguished student. But he had some talents. In his first year at the school (seventh grade), he had been elected class president—the class historians suggest that he got many votes from girls who thought him good looking. He published a facetious but literarily sophisticated essay "On the Pleasures of Eating" in the high school literary magazine in 1928. The essay, presented as "Somewhat after the manner of Joseph Addison," effectively parodies the arch tone of Addison's *Spectator* essays. His senior-year speech, in December 1928, on the history of marionettes, was judged by his classmates as "the most interesting talk so far."[35] Kammerer enrolled at Washington University, as did many of his John Burroughs classmates. He lived at home with his parents, only a few minutes away in Clayton and within easy commuting distance by streetcar. He exchanged letters with Burroughs when the latter was at Los Alamos Ranch School and probably saw him when he returned to St. Louis in the spring of 1931 to finish high school (1931–32) at Taylor School, which was just a couple of blocks from Kammerer's home.

He also exchanged letters with Rex Weisenburger, a John Burroughs School friend (and friend of William Burroughs) who by September 1930 was at Yale. They debated the merits of the Episcopal church to which Kammerer belonged and Roman Catholicism to which Rex had just converted, discussed their shared interest in classical music (Rex was an aspiring composer), and exchanged reports about girlfriends—Kammerer had apparently been seeing "Sis" Francis, a former classmate of Burroughs and still a senior in high school. In the spring of his sophomore year, Kammerer's letters to Weisenburger suggested that he was dissatisfied with his life in St. Louis—going to college but living at home, when friends like Rex were enjoying the cosmopolitan "East" and especially New York—and with himself for not achieving "anything in any line." Kammerer's despondency was perhaps little more than what many introspective college students go through from time to time, since Rex told him to buck up.[36] In the summer of 1932 Kammerer was able to gratify his desire for experience of "the East": he traveled to Durham, New Hampshire, where he took summer courses in English literature at the University of New Hampshire (see three letters from July and September 1933 to his Aunt Eva Eames, Kammerer Collection). His parents joined him, renting a house in Durham and touring New England with him on weekends. Kammerer and Burroughs resumed their correspondence when Burroughs went off to Harvard in the fall of 1932. Burroughs teased Kammerer about attending "club dances," the Veiled Prophet Ball for St. Louis society and a debutante party for his classmate Sis Francis – confirming that Kammerer was still moving in high social circles (October 16, 1932; December 2, 1932, Kammerer Collection). Rex, however, in a February 2, 1932, letter to Kammerer had been sterner about Kammerer's time spent on the debutante circuit the previous winter—"so sterile, so inane" (Kammerer Collection).

While Kammerer was apparently attracted to the high life, he also had a more serious side. For instance, in the spring of 1932, he became interested in mental illness and made visits to a local mental hospital. He also wrote poems and showed them to friends, including Burroughs, who jokingly called them "an assemblage of morbid poetry" (Burroughs to Kammerer, February 2, 1932, Kammerer Collection). In the fall of 1932, his senior year, he was still committed enough to his own education that he made up a reading list of books that an educated person should have read, including ancient classics and modern European "masterpieces" (Weisenburger to Kammerer, February 2, 1932; October 20, 1932, Kammerer Collection). An English major, he graduated on time in 1933, and then spent the summer in Europe, traveling with Burroughs and others. It was reportedly during this summer that he and Burroughs visited clubs in the Parisian rue de Lappe, one of the standard stops for tourists in search of raffish night life (Lawlor 167). Because he ran out of money, Kammerer returned on his own earlier than he had planned, as he explained in an August 25, 1933, letter to his aunt, Eva Eames (Kammerer Collection). He sailed back from Cherbourg, arriving in New York on August 29. It also appears that he had been sexually active as a heterosexual. In a September 27, 1933, letter to Kammerer from a young Englishman whom he met in Europe, the young man inquires, "How do you succeed with those young damsels?" (Cottrell, Kammerer Collection). Other letters hint that Kammerer got a girl pregnant and that she "threatened" to expose him "if he wouldn't marry her" (Celine Young to Allen Ginsberg, September 1944, reporting what she says Carr told her. Allen Ginsberg Papers, Series 1, Box 2, Folder 23). That this 1944 letter refers to an episode in 1933 is suggested by a May 1933 letter from Burroughs to Kammerer, which speaks elliptically to "the blackmailers," and his February 1934 letter to Kammerer reporting that he had invented a character for their "prospective novel" to be "a victim of the blackmail plot" (Burroughs to Kammerer, May 18, 1933; February 8, 1934, Kammerer Collection).

How Kammerer spent his early twenties is unknown, but as late as December 1934 he was still living at home. His nephew, Richard Kammerer, Jr., thinks he may have returned to Europe, especially to Paris, where he thought about being a writer or an artist. The September 27, 1933, letter from Cottrell expresses hope that "your work of writing will prosper" (Kammerer Collection). It appears that in December 1933 Kammerer put on some kind of marionette show, perhaps the Nativity story, and in January 1934 was making plans for another theatrical production. In a January 14, 1934, letter Weisenburger tells Kammerer that he "enjoyed the marionettes" and jokes that since the show featured the Virgin Mary it can properly be called a "*marionette*" show. On the envelope, Kammerer made what appear to be a series of notes—on music, curtain, lighting, chairs, changing scenes—for a forthcoming "play." At a time when work was hard to find, he evidently also held a series of short-term jobs, including factory worker, sales clerk, filling station attendant, shipwright, liquor salesman, electrician, wood carver, stock clerk, farm agent, and book store manager. In fact, on the back of a December 1943 letter to his mother, Kammerer self-deprecatingly listed the various jobs he had held since he left school, some of them most likely from 1933 to 1936 (Kammerer Collection). He also wrote to Burroughs that he had met a "spiritualist"; Burroughs, as evidenced in a February 8, 1934, letter to Kammerer, had already investigated spiritualism. In the meantime, Kammerer continued corresponding with Rex Weisenburger, who in a January 14, 1934, letter thanked Kammerer for recommending that he read Proust (Kammerer Collection). In the fall of 1936, while still living at home, he enrolled in the master's program in English at Washington University. During the course of his study, he attended the 1937 summer session at Columbia Teachers College with the thought that he would apply for a teaching job in a secondary school.[37] As part of the requirements for the degree, which he took in June 1938, he wrote a 263-page master's thesis on "The Boy in English Fiction to Defoe."

Given the reputation Kammerer later acquired in New York as a homosexual pursuer of Lucien Carr, it is tempting to assume that Kammerer's sexual interests in young men led him to the topic. But his discussion in the master's thesis of literary representations of "the boy character" will mostly disappoint anybody looking for hints of a homosexual sensibility. His manner of proceeding is scholarly, and his prose reproduces the style of literary histories of the early twentieth century: artificial and elevated diction, a leisurely pace, mostly quotation, plot summary, character description, and not much close analysis, which did not become academically fashionable until a decade later. His work is thoroughly grounded in English prose fiction from the Middle Ages into the seventeenth century. Kammerer does reveal some interest in "pretty" and "beautiful" boys, remarks on the "paederastic inclinations" of a pirate in one early story, and startlingly alludes to himself at one point in the thesis as a "literary paedophile." What might he have meant by this? He may have invented the word: the editors of the *Oxford English Dictionary* have not recorded any use of *pedophile* (or *paedophile*) prior to 1941, and the word was not used outside specialist academic journals until 1976. It is, of course, unlikely that Kammerer would report any sexual attraction to children in his master's thesis, and it's possible that he was making a learned philological joke, intending by the made-up pseudo-Greek word simply "one who delights in the literary representation of children, esp. boys."

Of equal interest in Kammerer's thesis, because they suggest his literary tastes, are the comparisons he makes with modern books. They include Romain Rolland's *Jean-Christophe* (1904–12), Faulkner's *Sanctuary* (1931), Steinbeck's recent *Of Mice and Men* (1937), and the poems of Francis Thompson. This is a rather more ambitious reading list than Burroughs was following during his college years, suggesting a deeper interest in serious literary fiction and poetry. The two might have shared an interest in one book Kammerer notes, the British writer Mark Benney's *Low Company: Describing the Evolution of a Burglar* (1936), published in the United States the following year as *Angels in Undress*. Kammerer compares Benney's account of a young petty thief with Daniel Defoe's *History of the Remarkable Life of the Truly Honourable Col. Jacque, Commonly Called Col. Jack.*

After taking his master's degree, Kammerer was hired as an assistant in the Washington University English Department and in the fall of 1939 was promoted to instructor. He was still living at home, and, to eke out what must have been a modest academic salary, took a job as counselor of a once-a-week youth group at John Burroughs School. The nature of this group remains unclear: Morgan thought it an after-school "play group" (*Literary Outlaw* 85), while Tytell suggested a Saturday group (*Naked Angels* 59), and although the John Burroughs School had an organized Boy Scout troop, there is no evidence that this group employed Kammerer. However, it is probably at the youth group that he met fourteen-year-old Lucien Carr in the spring of 1939. While there are no documented reports of the activities of the group, Carr did tell Morgan that he had enrolled in a series of "nature hikes" that Kammerer conducted (Box 6, Folder 8).[38]

Despite lack of evidence regarding specific youth group activities, clearly Kammerer and Carr hit it off, and in the summer of 1939, with the blessing of Carr's mother, they took a trip together to Mexico. Evidence surviving in a series of postcards suggests that the trip was less "wild" than has been imagined. Kammerer, for instance, planned and budgeted carefully, and insured the luggage. He and Carr spent some time with Kammerer's uncle in Mexico City, and Kammerer wrote regularly to his mother (and once to Lucien's mother) about their activities —attending a bullfight, renting bicycles, horseback riding, and sailfishing. All apparently went well until, while surfing in Acapulco, Kammerer dislocated his neck. Placed in a cast, he was advised to take ten days of rest before trying to drive back to St. Louis. Because of the unscheduled delay, Carr apparently traveled back to St. Louis on his own shortly after the accident. Kammerer stayed on and while recuperating went twice to the opera with Mexican friends.[39] Miles states that during the Mexican trip Kammerer "revealed his feelings" and Carr "rejected" him (*Call Me* 79), but the report is third hand—based on what Ginsberg (who got it from Carr) told Miles more than forty-five years later—but neither Carr nor Ginsberg was a disinterested reporter, and Miles himself concedes that there are "differing accounts."

Whatever happened during that Mexican trip, Kammerer remained close to both Carr and his mother. In January 1940, Kammerer and Carr's mother saw Lucien's train off to Andover at St. Louis's Union Station. Kammerer was then twenty-nine, and life seemed full of promise. He was employed, had over the Christmas break attended "more parties than usual" (so he told his brother), and had been invited to take part in an informal salon organized by a young Princeton graduate a few years his senior.[40] During the upcoming semester break, he was planning to drive east to visit both his brother in Pennsylvania and Lucien Carr at Andover. At this distance, it is impossible to characterize the relationship between Carr and Kammerer any more precisely than to say that they evidently enjoyed each other's company.

Kammerer continued as an instructor at Washington University through January 1941. Undocumented reports claim that he lost his job after being involved in a student prank (Morgan, *Literary Outlaw* 86). He also quickly made arrangements to take graduate courses in English at Princeton, where he was enrolled for spring semester 1941. Two March 1941 letters to his mother report on his studies and on the "Prom Weekend" with his date, "Nancy," evidently a St. Louis girl (March 24 and 27, 1941, Kammerer Collection). It may have been later in 1941 that he served in the merchant marine and held several defense-related jobs, since in a December 15, 1943, letter he refers to "most of the defense jobs I've had" as "tedious and repellent" (Kammerer Collection).

In the summer of 1942, he drove to Maine, where Lucien Carr had enrolled in summer school at Bowdoin but was preparing to drop out. They met in Bath, near Bowdoin, and drove together back to St. Louis. In January 1943, when both Burroughs and Carr were in Chicago, Kammerer joined them there for a couple of months. While in Chicago he met a couple of young women—and with one of them went to a lecture on the psalms "at a Jewish College."[41] In the late spring of that year, Carr left Chicago for New York, and Kammerer's nephew, Richard, believes that Kammerer may have then taken another trip to Mexico, this time on his own (private communication with the author). Late in 1943, Kammerer went to New York, where Carr was now enrolled at Columbia and Burroughs was living in Greenwich Village. He found a room near Burroughs, in the West Village at 48 Morton Street. The building was by no means a dreary refuge for the down-and-out: another tenant, for example, was gainfully-employed Chandler Brossard, who remembered his own apartment as "fabulous" (Morgan, Box 4, Folder 15).

The remainder of Kammerer's life is well documented by a series of letters from Kammerer to his mother in St. Louis, with whom he was very close, written nearly every week and preserved by the Kammerer family, and now made available for the first time. Although a man of thirty-two does not tell his mother everything that's going on in his life, the letters present a granular idea of what Kammerer was doing and thinking, and the people he was seeing, during the last nine months of his life. What they suggest is that he was neither the pitiful homosexual hanger-on and psychologically-crumbling derelict that the New York City District Attorney's office, Carr's lawyers, and lazy journalists have described,[42] nor—except for a few weeks in the summer of 1944—was he the dazzling host of an ongoing Greenwich Village salon described by Patricia Harrison, who knew him during his New York City year.

Harrison, then a Barnard student, was married to the Irish writer Thomas Healy and living in the Village. In a letter to *New York Magazine* in June 1976, she responded indignantly to an article by Aaron Latham about the Kammerer killing, which appeared in the magazine earlier that spring, depicting the victim as a "decadent old queen," obsessed with young and brilliant Lucien Carr, living hand-to-mouth from a series of jobs that were beneath him. Latham, she claimed, had borrowed his picture from old "Beat Generation" myths deriving ultimately from Carr, whom she regarded as overrated, and Kerouac, whom she called a "self-serving mythomaniac."[43] Kammerer, she insisted grandly, was the genius, "possibly the most significant talker of his generation . . . a born teacher." He was, she said, a powerful intellect, widely read in literature (she mentions Meredith, Hardy, and Arnold Bennett) and in religion (Buddhism and Anglican mysticism), and insisted that the men who would become Beat writers learned from *him*. Not only that, he was good-looking, "robust, red-bearded" (before he shaved it off in late

May 1944), with a "gargantuan sense of fun," and he was on at least one occasion (apparently New Year's Eve of 1943), she confided, actively heterosexual.[44] In her account, it was he who pushed Carr away, not the other way around.

The truth about Kammerer is probably somewhere in between, but rather closer to Harrison's view than Latham's. There is corroborating evidence that he talked about modern novels: Ginsberg remembered discussions of *Anna Karenina*, Thomas Mann, and "the German mind," as well as Kammerer's "affability" (*Martyrdom* 64), and it has been established that he had read the Anglican mystic Francis Thompson and was reading Indian philosophy. Lucien Carr's girlfriend, Céline Young, liked Kammerer and thought him "charming, helpful, informative"—an unlikely opinion if she thought Kammerer was her rival for Carr's affections. But she also told Kerouac that Kammerer was "an incorrigible liar." She says nothing about his sexuality but declares that he was a "distorted and ruined man."[45] John Cherry, a St. Louis friend who knew Kammerer in New York, told Ted Morgan that Kammerer was "high-spirited . . . well-liked . . . bi-sexual . . .healthy, exuberant, . . . funny and not square," but for reasons unknown Morgan did not use the report in his biography (Box 6, File 8). Burroughs later said that Kammerer was "always very funny, the veritable life of the party, and completely without any middle-class morality" (Morgan in Lawlor, 167)[46]—he seems to have recognized Kammerer as a kindred spirit. Chandler Brossard said that Kammerer was "one of the very few people I liked in this city. . . . we were the tightest of friends." Kammerer, he was certain, was "totally homosexual," but Brossard, who was straight, "didn't mind" (Morgan, Box 6, File 8).

What Kammerer's letters home do confirm is that he stayed in close touch with his mother and his extended family of aunts and uncles; that he led a lively social life, much of it lived quite apart from the Columbia campus; that he attracted the attention of a number of young women; that he avidly sampled the cultural offerings of New York City—theater, opera, film, concerts; that he had a highly developed literary sensibility, was actively reading, and even doing some writing; that he spent as much time with Burroughs as he did with Lucien Carr; and that he got on well with his landlady. On the other hand, they show a frustrated young man who was unable to find work that suited his education; that he was often behind in his rent, borrowed money from friends, and was partially supported by checks from his mother; that he had difficult relationships with his father and brother; that he was plagued by dental problems; and that his relationship with Lucien Carr sometimes left him feeling lonely and depressed.[47]

By December 1943, shortly after arriving in New York, he had quickly gotten a job as a deck hand on a harbor dredge, but he was soon fired for coming to work late. Bouncing back, he was hired a few days later as a freight handler for Railway Express. He spent time with old friends from St. Louis—among them a "Dick

Rubinstein" (possibly the poet Richard Rubinstein) and Peter Cohen, who was then taking classes at the Art League, and with relatives, including his married first cousin whose husband was off at war. He reported to his mother about various girls he knew: a Vassar graduate from Wisconsin now working as an editor at Doubleday and trying to help him get a job in publishing; a girl from Binghamton, New York, whom he had met in Chicago, who invited him to lunch; and a couple of Lucien Carr's girlfriends. His pointed references to girls, of course, catches one's attention, given claims that he was homosexual. It is possible that he was, in effect, trying to reassure his mother that he was straight. But it's clear from recurrent allusions in his letters to "Lucien" that Kammerer was not trying to hide his close relationship with Carr, and that his mother knew and liked him, and approved of their friendship. One might then conclude that Kammerer's attachment to Lucien Carr did not preclude his being attracted to—and attractive to—young women.

Kammerer's letters home also enable us to follow his life from week to week. He reads the newspapers regularly and almost immediately gets word from a friend about the Cairo Conference (a meeting of Allied leaders)—the final communiqué was issued on Nov. 27, 1943. He is thinking about applying for a teaching job at Columbia, writing to a Washington University professor for a recommendation. He has seen a Russian film, *The Siege of Stalingrad*, and heard the New York Philharmonic at Carnegie Hall. He is working on a story, for which he rereads Isaiah, the psalms (he finds them to be "great poems"), and the old Episcopal hymnal. He goes to church. He spends time over Christmas with Lucien Carr and his girlfriend.[48]

In January, he reports going to the opening of *Jackpot*, a Broadway musical in which a St. Louis friend, Mary Wickenhauser, performing under the name of Mary Wickes, had a major role.[49] He found it "commercial" and "boring," and much preferred the *Otello* at the Metropolitan Opera, with Paul Robeson in the title role. He is writing poems in the strenuous style of Donne and Hopkins and showing them to friends, who think them good, as he reports in a January 15, 1944, letter to his mother. In February he continues to see Lucien and has been reading Arthur Koestler's new novel, *Arrival and Departure* (1943), as well as the well-reviewed debut novel by Gladys Schmitt, *The Gates of Aulis* (1942). He pursues his interest in Eastern philosophy by reading *The Wisdom of China and India* (1942), a collection of parables and sketches edited by Lin Yu Tang. He also reports on seeing Russian and French movies. But his job at Railway Express has ended, and he is now cleaning windows part-time, working off his back rent by "taking care" of the furnace in his landlady's house, and at the end of the month trying, without success, to get a job with the Office of War Information.[50]

In March he lets his mother know that he is going through a rough patch. It has been a difficult winter: working outside can be invigorating but the cold gets to him; he sometimes does not have enough to eat, and his gums are bothering him.

He would like to move, but he is behind in his rent. What is worse, he has "no sense of self-realization or achievement or satisfaction and no security and no future." To illustrate his "terrors," he quotes a passage from "No Worst, there is None," one of Hopkins's "terrible sonnets": "O the mind, mind has mountains; cliffs of fall / Frightful, sheer, no man-fathomed. Hold them cheap / May who ne'er hung there." But he also reminds himself that Hopkins wrote sonnets on patience. What may have caused his depression is that he had not seen Lucien for nearly two weeks. On March 3, 1944, he writes his mother that Lucien "felt we were too dependent on each other and might each do better independently. I feel he is perhaps right until I get on my feet, but I miss him terribly."

In April he has Easter dinner with Burroughs and "Jack" (probably Kerouac) and spends time with Lucien Carr. He is unemployed and looking for work as a writer. He cannot pay his rent, but his landlady agrees to keep him on; he thinks about moving uptown "to be nearer Lu," but "for some reason" Carr "doesn't want me to." He attends an Easter performance of the *Messiah* with "Alf," a young German emigré friend of his landlady's, and a performance by the Ballet Russe with Chandler Brossard (Kammerer to Mrs. Alfred Kammerer, undated but datable as April 9 and May 1, 1944, Kammerer Collection). But this period of depression does not last. In May he has a good visit with his parents in St. Louis. He has been painting his landlady's house to make up back rent—he had paid nothing since January. He has also done some tutoring through a "tutoring school" and continued with window washing. He sees another French film and a production of Shaw's *Major Barbara*. On June 6, he attends the Columbia commencement. He and Burroughs spend a great deal of time together at Kammerer's apartment, and Burroughs takes him to the University Club for dinner several times. Lucien Carr leaves town for a couple of weeks of vacation, planning to return for summer school. But Kammerer has numerous "visitors" to his apartment, "too many," he writes, and even Burroughs is "getting on my nerves a little." He has quarreled with his brother and is not invited to his wedding in Gettysburg, Pennsylvania. By the middle of the month, he and Burroughs are getting on better: they cook dinner together.[51]

By July life seems to be looking a good deal more promising. He has paid off all his back rent and redecorated his own room. He continues to tutor and takes steps to get a full-time high school teaching job in the fall. He is seeing Lucien occasionally, but "for some psychotic reason" Lucien generally stays away. Kammerer finds him conflicted: "he seems to be fonder of me than ever but afraid to see too much of me." Meanwhile, Kammerer is "constantly besieged by callers or visitors at all hours." This is probably what Patricia Harrison described as "those long evenings . . . when David would talk extemporaneously and uninterruptedly to the seven or eight people crowding in . . . on whatever was preoccupying his extraordinary, discursive mind." Kammerer tells his mother that he finds it "flattering," but "most of the people bore me and inconvenience me." In his final letter, dated August 4, Kammerer reports that he saw Lucien a few nights earlier and that he himself has recently spent Sunday "at the shore with a girl." Ten days later he was dead.[52]

David Kammerer (standing, front left); unidentified man (standing, center); and Lucien Carr (standing, right) in Mexico in the summer of 1939, when Lucien Carr was fourteen years old. It is from the collection of Richard Kammerer.

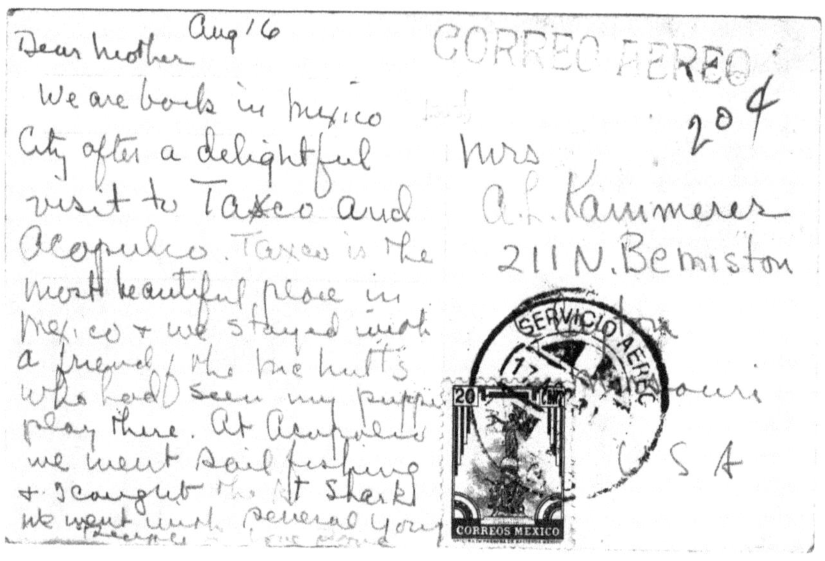

Lucien Carr

The Carrs, an older St. Louis family than were the Kammerers and the Burroughs, had been in St. Louis since the 1830s, and Lucien was the fourth in his family to bear the name. The most distinguished of his forebears, Lucien Carr I, born in Troy, Missouri, was an anthropologist and archaeologist at Harvard's Peabody Museum. The second became a gentleman farmer in Virginia, the third an engineer who died in the First World War. Carr's father, Russell Carr (brother of the engineer), married St. Louis money, seems to have adopted no career, and by age forty, about 1930, abandoned his wife, Marion, and two small children. It was apparently at this point that she moved back to St. Louis and enrolled her children in Community School. Lucien was one of the youngest in his class and small for his age.

Marion Carr and the children spent time in the summers in Underhill, Vermont, where they rented a house (a converted barn). Lucien and his sister ran free and, apparently playing Indian, wore sheath knives at their belts. A summer resident who knew the family recalled that Lucien was "extremely quick and intelligent" but was temperamental and "emotionally very unstable": he would "go berserk . . . fly off the handle and chase people with his knife when he was crossed," which caused "some alarm" in the summer colony. This report was procured by Carr's lawyers in 1944 but did not emerge at his trial.[53]

In 1936, when he was eleven, Lucien was sent on from Community School to John Burroughs School. His grades, like those of William S. Burroughs, were mediocre, mostly B's and C's. Both his mother and the headmaster were concerned that although he was clearly intelligent "his achievement has not been commensurate with his ability." He was unwilling to make a "steady effort" and was merely "satisfied to pass" (Archives, Andover). But he made friends—especially with John Lionberger, who attended Country Day School and was Carr's neighbor on Aberdeen Place in Clayton—and was apparently comfortable with adults. During Carr's third year at John Burroughs School, his mother, who seems to have been unable or unwilling to discipline her son, thought about sending him to boarding school, which was a not uncommon step to take for a family in St. Louis in her class when it was found that a child was not doing well in the local private day school.[54] She selected Andover, where Lucien's first cousin, Godfrey Rockefeller, was in attendance. Marion had also become acquainted with an Andover master during her summers in Vermont, and there may well have been an earlier family connection since a copy of Lucien Carr I's *Missouri, A Bone of Contention* (1888) is in the Andover Library. In January 1939, she applied to Andover for a place for Lucien the following September. In describing her son, she reported that he was "hard to divert when determined to proceed in an unsocial direction . . . [and] tends to resist authority perhaps excessively"; however, her St. Louis neighbor, John Lionberger Sr., assured Andover that Carr was "a very attractive and enterprising boy" (Archives, Andover).

As already noted, it was probably in the spring of 1939, when Carr was fourteen and before he entered Andover, that he met David Kammerer. In the opinion of his John Burroughs headmaster, Carr seemed to lack a male presence in his life, and Marion Carr may have felt that Kammerer might fill the need—although there is little reason to think Lucien consciously regarded Kammerer as a father figure. When Kammerer suggested that he take Lucien on a summer trip to Mexico, she agreed. After Kammerer's accident, even though she was anxious that Lucien return home on schedule, she gave no sign that she was troubled by the relationship between her son and a man twice his age.[55] It was not until sometime in 1940, so it was later claimed, that she discovered a cache of fifty love letters from Kammerer to Carr (Miles, *Call Me* 91).

At Andover, in addition to his cousin Godfrey, Carr's new classmates included William Sloane Coffin and George H. W. Bush. Carr enrolled in a traditional curriculum: English, math, history, French, Latin, religion, biology, and art. His best subject was art; his weakest math. He was also reported to be an avid reader (Archives, Andover). In this milieu, his academic performance improved, and in his junior year he was ranked fourteenth out of 224 students (Archives, Andover). But he was not working hard. His housemaster, Hart Day Leavitt, remarked in an August 25, 1940, report that Carr had "creative imagination" but not much "intellectual vigor" and thought Carr got "fairly good marks without straining his energy." He added that Carr seemed "fundamentally aimless right now, and needs a purpose" (Archives, Andover). Another housemaster at Andover reported that Carr's self-confidence was "low"; he "tries to cover it up by showing off – craves popularity and attention and tries to get it by swaggering, would-be daring actions." Using the psychological language of the day, the housemaster suggested that an "inferiority complex" gave Carr an "asocial attitude" (Archives, Andover).[56] His "asocial" attitude was in evidence outside school as well. When he returned to St. Louis for the 1940 summer vacation, he saw Kammerer. One friend from John Burroughs School, Kennett Love, remembered getting drunk at Carr's house, along with Kammerer and Burroughs. Carr, he said, was "a bad drunk who insulted people and punched them out" (Morgan Papers, Box 6, Folder 8).

As one might expect, Carr bridled at the discipline at Andover and by March 1941 was on probation. It was during this period that Kammerer visited Carr at Andover at least once or twice during the 1940–41 school year (one of the occasions was probably late January/early February, before the opening of the spring term at Princeton), and by late April, Carr was expelled for leaving campus and going to nearby Lawrence, Massachusetts, without permission (Archives, Andover). After the expulsion, in a confidential report dated January 6, 1942, his housemaster Frederick Allis stated that he thought Carr's "close association" with Kammerer since the trip to Mexico was "most unfortunate" (Archives, Andover).

Carr returned to St. Louis, where he contacted the Taylor School (where Burroughs had graduated a decade earlier), and the headmaster, Edgar Taylor, arranged for Carr to enroll in the fall for his high school senior year (Archives, Andover). He did well at Taylor, ranking first in a class of fourteen, as well as winning the Faculty Cup for the highest grade point average in the Upper School, the annual speaking contest prize, and a medal for excellence in French. It was also during this time, 1941–1942, that, as Carr told Ted Morgan, he saw Burroughs "maybe four or five times," going so far as to borrow Burroughs' 1936 Ford (Carr would have been just old enough to drive legally in 1941.), which ended up breaking down in East St. Louis (Box 6, Folder 8).

In June 1942, having graduated from Taylor School at age seventeen, Carr immediately enrolled at Bowdoin College. Edgar Taylor was a 1920 Bowdoin graduate and had given Carr a strong recommendation: "Lucien Carr is a youth of very superior intelligence"——tests showed an IQ of 138–140—and "is a much more stable youth now than he was" (Bowdoin Special Collections). On June 20, Carr registered for summer school and was doing "good work." However, for breaking a number of rules, he was called before a student committee, a group of sophomores charged with enforcing "Freshman Rules," a kind of institutionalized hazing. He was given the penalty of what the director of admissions later called "a somewhat grotesque haircut." But Carr continued to ignore the "Rules"—displaying the resistance to discipline that his mother and his Andover housemasters had remarked on for the previous three years—and was called before the committee again on July 15, whereupon he voluntarily left the college that same day (Letter to Edgar Taylor, July 21, 1942, Bowdoin Special Collections).

Records indicate that he met David Kammerer in nearby Bath—officials at Bowdoin thought it was someone named "Cameron" (Bowdoin Special Collections)—and that the two of them drove to New York, where they stayed with an Andover friend, later stopping in Princeton to see their St. Louis friend Kennett Love. Bowdoin wanted him back, but Carr wrote to the college on July 21, 1942, stating that he had "always wanted to go to a large university where more emphasis is placed on intellectual development than on college life" (Bowdoin Special Collections). Carr then returned to St. Louis. As of December, he was living not with his mother but at the Hotel Bristol, a residential hotel in the Central West End. He asked Bowdoin to send his transcript to the University of Chicago and transferred there for the winter quarter of 1943, which ran from January 4 through March 27. A story from the *New York Times* dated August 18, 1944—and after the killing—states that, according to Carr's attorney, Marion Carr arranged for the transfer to the University of Chicago after she had found, and then burned, a cache of fifty love letters from Kammerer to Carr "a few years ago." But she reportedly discovered the letters in 1940 (Miles, *Call Me* 91), and, as already noted, Carr did not begin his studies at Chicago until January 1943, more than two years after she allegedly discovered the letters and only twenty months prior to the killing. The story about the letters, with its dubious chronology, has not been corroborated. There is also little evidence that Marion Carr was able to manage her son, much less control his movements, such as a college transfer.

Why then would Carr choose Chicago? Granted, the University of Chicago was "large" and placed emphasis on "intellectual development." Perhaps Carr also knew that Burroughs was then living in Chicago and thought it would be interesting to be able to see him. The reality, however, is that we simply don't know. What we do know is that he went to Chicago in time for the beginning of the winter quarter on January 4 and that Kammerer soon appeared on the scene, spending some alcohol-fueled evenings with both Burroughs and Carr (Morgan, Box 6, Folder 8). One episode led to Burroughs being thrown out of his rented room; another led to what sounds like Carr's attempt at suicide: he put his head in an oven and turned on the gas. Psychiatrists at Cook County Hospital in Chicago, where he spent a month, treated him for mental instability and depression. But Carr later claimed, according to Allen Ginsberg, that he had simply intended to construct a "work of art" (*Martyrdom* 98; also Campbell 12). On another occasion he said it was just a "drunken impulse" (Miles, *Call Me* 92). It has also been suggested that Carr was trying to get out of the draft, since in early March he had turned eighteen, which would have qualified him for military service. Subsequently, Carr was, in fact, classified 4-F, "on medical grounds."

After his release from the Cook County Hospital, he returned to New York, where his mother was then living at 419 E. 57th Street. If Miles is right in saying that Carr had acquired "seaman's papers" from a summer job on New York Harbor (*Call Me* 108), it must have been during that summer of 1943. In September, he applied to Columbia and was admitted as a sophomore for the fall semester, which, during that wartime year, did not begin until November. It was in the student dorm on West 122nd Street, during Christmas vacation of 1943, that, according to the familiar story, Carr met Allen Ginsberg and quickly dazzled him with what Ginsberg thought was "genius." It was during the same month that Kammerer arrived in New York and made contact with Carr.

Carr spent three terms at Columbia, from November 1943 to August 1944, where, according to the *New York Times*, he was majoring in English and anthropology. Accounts of his work as a student are inconsistent. He was enrolled in Lionel Trilling's Humanities A class, where, as reported by a fellow student, Ed Gold, he was a precocious contributor to class discussion and engaged with Trilling in what seemed like a "private conversation." Gold also considered Carr to be "an intellectual spur and catalyst" for both Ginsberg and Kerouac (1–7). Although Columbia will not release his transcript, it seems likely that in addition to "Humanities A" and anthropology, he took a French literature course—he had already studied French for five years—and it is here that he may have encountered Rimbaud's poetry, to which he would later introduce Ginsberg (*Martyrdom* 50). He also made time to study, often at Kammerer's apartment in Greenwich Village, where Kammerer helped him with his geology. Carr did very well in his first semester: Kammerer wrote proudly to his mother on February 23, 1944, that Carr got 4 A's and a B+. In addition both Carr and Ginsberg were members of Philolexian, one of Columbia's literary societies.[57] Immediately after the killing, on August 16, 1944, the *New York Times* reported that Nicholas McKnight, associate dean of Columbia College, thought Carr "definitely a superior student," a "quiet, well-behaved intellectual type." Although some have scoffed at the idea that Carr was a "genius," and have suspected that by commending him Columbia was simply attempting to suppress unfavorable publicity, it seems clear from Carr's academic and public records that his teachers thought him intelligent and that he could produce good work when he chose to.

But other evidence suggests that he did not follow through in his written work, actually persuading Kammerer, who contacted him in New York in late 1943, to write a term paper for him (Morgan, *Literary Outlaw* 9). In addition, Patricia

Harrison claimed in the *New York Magazine* (June 7, 1976) that when Carr returned to Kammerer for another term paper, Kammerer knocked him down. And if the stories told by Kerouac and Ginsberg about him are to be believed, Carr spent a number of drunken nights in the bars in Morningside Heights and the Village. Some people also didn't like him. When Kerouac first met him, for instance, he thought Carr a "mischievous little prick" (*Vanity of Duluoz* 223). John Cherry called him "a nasty piece of work" (Morgan, Box 6, Folder 8). Chandler Brossard took Kerouac's view: Carr was "a shallow little prick" who "wouldn't admit he was homosexual" (Morgan, Box 6, Folder 8).[58] But he could clearly be charming: he had a string of girlfriends before settling on Céline Young, a Barnard student who was half French. And he found time for long conversations with Ginsberg and Kerouac about "art" and "life," and about their ambitions to be writers. They both considered him a fascinating figure. In a long journal entry in August 1944, entitled "Essay in Character Analysis. Lucien Carr," Ginsberg attempted to understand his new friend:

> Carr is strangely limited by subliminal repressions . . . he declares that he cannot write . . . It all seems to be a result of inquietude from the usual reasons – no parents, no standard, no security, intellectual or moral; most important, an inquietude coming from a comparison not with the world around him . . . but with his higher imagined self. . . He confesses he fears sterility at the bottom of everything. . . .He really fears that he is not creative. . . he adopts the postures and attitudes of the intellectual with which he is familiar – the bohemian. (*Martyrdom* 47)

Ginsberg, as he went on, was primarily interested in defining himself as a budding artist by means of the difference between himself and Carr: "I am satisfied by no forms of poetry any more. There must be some new way, some new visionary method to deal with art and beauty. . . [Carr] takes refuge in life, in exhibitionism" (48–49). Ginsberg's journals, of course, need to be read critically, especially since he tended to turn them into "scenes" for future art. However, although largely self-absorbed and perhaps projecting his own fears of "sterility," he may have been on to something about Carr, in particular his affecting a bohemian manner. Carr's Andover housemaster, H. D. Leavitt, had suggested four years earlier that Carr was "inclined to achieve a decided individuality, evidenced by doing unusual and somewhat unpleasant things." Leavitt also suspected that "his sloppiness in dress is affected" (Archives, Andover). Patricia Harrison as well seemed to think that Carr's "*épater-le-bourgeois* manner" was an affectation.

While Ginsberg thought that what Carr's affected manner was covering up was his fears, Kerouac thought it was self-hatred. In an October 1944 letter to

Ginsberg, Kerouac declared that Carr "hates himself intensely. . . . Hating himself, as he does, hating his 'humankindness,' he seeks new vision, a post-human post-intelligence. He wishes more than Nietzsche prescribed. He wants more than the next mutation—he wants a post-soul. . ." (Columbia, Box 11, Folder 11; Kerouac, *Selected Letters*, I, 81–82). Like Ginsberg, Kerouac was primarily concerned to define the difference between Carr and himself.

The court and the journalists did not or could not see any of this: they simply saw a disturbed young man. After Kammerer was killed, and Carr turned himself in, the district attorney was puzzled, noting that Carr struck him as "emotionally unstable," a phrase that Carr's attorney had also and previously used in speaking to *New York Times* reporters (August 17, 1944). This is perhaps not surprising: anybody likely to be put on trial for murder might well feel and act "unstable." But it is the same phrase that an Andover dean used to describe Carr when he was a young boy of seven or eight. The district attorney and reporters covering the case also thought Carr behaved in a bizarre manner, clutching a copy of Yeats' *A Vision* and reading it during pauses in his interrogation and arraignment.[59]

Which brings us to the question many have asked for decades: Why did Carr kill Kammerer? He told police that after a night of drinking together Kammerer, a homosexual, had made what the newspapers euphemistically reported as an "improper," "indecent," and "offensive proposal." Most writers on the topic assume that Kammerer proposed sex. For instance, in *Call Me*, Miles bluntly reports that Kammerer insisted that Carr let him fellate him (109). Carr said he resisted but could not fend off the much bigger Kammerer, and then stabbed him with a Boy Scout knife he happened to have in his pocket. In the legal proceedings that followed, Carr was represented by the Wall Street firm of Parker and Duryee (later Spence, Hotchkiss, Parker and Duryee). Carr was represented in court by Vincent J. Malone and Kenneth M. Spence, and the legal team also included Franklin E. Parker Jr., who gathered background information on Carr from Andover.

The police and the district attorney were apparently dubious about Carr's story, and proceeded with the prosecution, securing an indictment for second-degree murder. At a pretrial hearing the judge suggested a psychiatric evaluation and—over the protest of the assistant district attorney—conferred privately with Carr's attorney (*New York Times*, August 18, 1944). Early press reports suggest that reporters accepted Carr's story. At the trial, however, Carr's attorneys argued that the killing of Kammerer was justifiable homicide. A number of character witnesses testified on Carr's behalf, including a family friend from his Vermont summer days, a housemaster from Andover, and a dean from Columbia.

But little-known evidence suggests that there may have been other motives for the killing. Although almost all of those who knew the two men apparently accepted Carr's account, his close friend Kennett Love told Morgan years later that

Lucien told him that Kammerer "had threatened to go after Céline, which is what led to the killing"; presumably this meant "pursue her romantically." Morgan, did not use the detail (Box 6, Folder 8). Miles' understanding of the story (*Call Me* 109), also derived from Carr, is that Kammerer threatened to "injure" her. A letter from Céline Young to Kerouac suggests that the real story was even more disturbing: she thought that while Carr showed some remorse, he still had some "pride" in "doing away" with Kammerer, and thought that he had done "a messianic service by ridding the world of Dave" (Ginsberg, Stanford, Subseries 1, Box 1, Folder 23).

On September 15, Carr pleaded guilty to a reduced charge of first-degree manslaughter. The assistant district attorney later told the press (*New York Times*, October 7, 1944) that he didn't think he could make a charge of second-degree murder stick because he lacked an eyewitness and a murder weapon. Céline Young was in the courtroom that day. So too was a woman dressed in the uniform of the Canadian Women's Army Corps and later identified by Carr as someone who had eleven years earlier threatened to expose Kammerer "if he wouldn't marry her." Not present at the trail—at least not reported in the New York papers—were any members of David Kammerer's family. On October 6, Carr was sentenced to an indefinite term at the state reformatory at Elmira, New York, rather than at Sing Sing Prison, because the judge thought that Carr could be rehabilitated and recommended that he be seen by a prison psychiatrist. But he warned Carr that bad conduct at Elmira could send him to Sing Sing for fifteen years. Carr was apparently a model prisoner. When he came out in 1946, he went to work for United Press as a copyboy, applied himself, and over several decades rose through the ranks. What accounts for his transformation into a responsible journalist? As he wrote to Ginsberg on September 21, 1944, "One thinks in jail" (*Martyrdom* 75).

Afterword

The St. Louis clique did not end on August 14, 1944. Burroughs and Carr remained friends, and both stayed in close touch with Ginsberg and Kerouac. In October 1944, Ginsberg began a novel about Carr and Kammerer, although he only sketched a few scenes, including what he called the "Death Scene" (*Martyrdom* 85–116). About the same time, Burroughs and Kerouac wrote their thinly-veiled version of the Kammerer killing but could not find a publisher. Carr provided the paper for the famous typescript of *On the Road,* and he was the initial dedicatee of "Howl."

Burroughs also stayed in contact with his St. Louis friend Kells Elvins until Elvins' early death in 1961, and he kept in touch with the yard man on Pershing Avenue, Otto Belue, with annual Christmas letters, as late as 1970 (William S. Burroughs Papers, Berg Collection, New York Public Library, Berg Collection,

Box 87, Folder 19). He returned to St. Louis several times in the 1940s, then again in 1964–65. After he killed his wife, Joan Vollmer, in a game of William Tell, his son William S. Burroughs Jr., born in 1947, was raised primarily by his St. Louis grandparents. Burroughs returned to St. Louis again in March 1983 for his brother's funeral and again in April–May 1984.

Burroughs mined his St. Louis childhood for much of his writing in the 1970s and 1980s, especially in *The Wild Boys*, *Exterminator!* and *Port of Saints* (from the early 1970s) and what one critic has called his "St. Louis trilogy" (*Cities of the Red Night*, *The Place of Dead Roads*, and *The Western Lands*, from 1981, 1984, and 1987). A reader in search of autobiography finds a few glancing allusions, some fairly autobiographical, some fictionalized. By the 1960s, when he was producing literary "cut-ups," Burroughs began to claim T. S. Eliot as a predecessor: one of the cut-ups was of Eliot's *The Cocktail Party*. *The Waste Land*, he said in 1960, was the "first great cut-up collage" (Bockris 93). In 1963, he told an interviewer that he was born in St. Louis, "like T. S. Eliot," and in *The Western Lands* (1987), his published account of the 1964–65 trip to St. Louis, he made several allusions to *The Waste Land*.

I have found no evidence that Carr returned to St. Louis after he was released from prison. But he visited Burroughs in Mexico and kept in touch with his old Columbia friends. Carr died in Washington D.C. in 2005, having long abandoned any connection to St. Louis. But his great-great grandfather, Wayman Crow, is buried in Bellefontaine Cemetery in St. Louis, and both Burroughs and Kammerer are buried there too. There is a substantial Burroughs family monument, but the name of William S. Burroughs is not on it.

In his final years Burroughs was a literary celebrity. Seventeen years after his death, he continues to enjoy a significant afterlife: many of his books remain in print, and new biographical accounts re-introduce readers to a life that even today has the power to shock. He remains prominent in the accounts of the origins of the Beat Generation in 1944 because he formed friends with two of the leading Beat writers, Kerouac and Ginsberg, already on their way to literary careers, and because he himself went on some years later to become a writer of equal reputation. Lucien Carr, though he spent a career editing other people's writing, never published anything under his own name, tried to keep that name out of the papers, and discouraged interviewers from digging up his past. David Kammerer faded from memory, except as the central figure in a scandalous episode.

Carr's account of the events of August 1944 has up until now largely defined the story of the St. Louis clique because it was not challenged during his trial and because it was he who survived and remained friends with the leading Beats for another forty years. Kerouac, Ginsberg, and Burroughs all predeceased him, and after Carr died in 2005, very few of those who knew the St. Louisans in 1944 were left. The last of their friends who might have shed new light, Kennett Love, died last year. But on the basis of new documentary evidence—particularly Carr's school records, letters from Kammerer and Burroughs, and material that Morgan gathered but declined to use—there are grounds to conclude that Carr's account of the event was carefully editing so as to exculpate himself, and therefore open to challenge. So too is his account of Kammerer, who by the summer of 1944, as his letters suggest, seems to have pulled himself together. At the time, of the three St. Louisans, Kammerer was no less likely to make some kind of significant literary mark in the future than was William S. Burroughs.

Notes

[1] Not to be confused with an earlier "St. Louis clique"—a term used disparagingly by journalists to refer collectively to St. Louis politicians who controlled Missouri politics in the first half of the nineteenth century (see W. Stephen Belko, *The Invincible Duff Green: Whig of the West* [2006], 54).

[2] Ginsberg's remark is often misquoted as "Lou was the glue." In an interview with Ted Morgan, Carr later described himself as "Lucien the introducer": "my importance in that whole little circle was that by happenstance I was the guy that introduced them all" (Box 6, Folder 8).

[3] Many accounts of Kammerer's death use the term "murder" to describe Carr's actions, but since Carr was not found guilty of murder (a legally-defined crime), that term cannot be accurately applied to the event. Thus throughout this essay, I use the terms "kill" and "killing." On the Certificate of Death, the Manhatten Examiner declared the death a "homicide" and the cause of death "hemorrhage following stab wound of left chest, pericardium and heart." Some factual details (e.g., date of burial) are incorrect as well.

[4] Most recently by David Krajicek, in "The Last Beat," published in the Winter 2012–13 issue of *Columbia Magazine*, and by Ronald Collins and David Skover, in *Mania: The Story of the Outraged and Outrageous Lives That Launched a Cultural Revolution* (2013). Krajicek, who writes for the *Daily News*, focuses on Carr and on the killing, and relies on a number of old half-truths and journalistic labels. Collins and Skover, who recycle the standard story of the killing in their "Prologue," did little original research of their own and rely heavily on Kerouac's fictionalized version of events. James Fritz's *The Beat Killer: A Biography of the Beat Writer Lucien Carr and the Riverside Park Murder* (2012) is a brief (fifty-eight pages) and wholly derivative e-book with many factual errors. Barry Miles' *Call Me Burroughs:*

A Life (2014), while it produces much new material about Burroughs' youth, largely draws on his own account of the killing in his *William Burroughs: El Hombre Invisible* (1992).

[5] See his extended 1944 entries on Carr and Kammerer in *Martyrdom*, esp. 55–68 and 93–116. A dramatic account of the killing, complete with invented dialogue, is entitled "Death Scene" (112–14).

[6] Her chapter on the killing (155–70) repeats a number of minor errors and clichés about Carr and Kammerer.

[7] Rimbaud's name was invoked loosely: Ginsberg in his journal says Kammerer once told him Burroughs had described him, Ginsberg, as "the bourgeois Rimbaud" (*Martyrdom* 56). The idea of Carr-as-Rimbaud is taken furthest by R. Blank, in a 1998 undergraduate honors thesis at Columbia, in which Carr is treated as a serious philosophical thinker.

[8] By contrast, several of their St. Louis friends, including Kennett Love and Rex Weisenburger, were serving in the armed forces.

[9] One scholar who has made use of Morgan's papers is William Lawlor, author of *Beat Culture: Lifestyles, Icons, and Impact* (2005). Another is Barry Miles, who cites his own transcriptions of Morgan's taped interviews in *Call Me Burroughs* (2014).

[10] The St. Louis Symphony Orchestra, second oldest in the country, was founded in 1880. Josephine Baker (1906–75) began her career in St. Louis—she was dancing in a local vaudeville show by 1921—as did Miles Davis, born in 1926, who grew up in East St. Louis.

[11] Eliot had left St. Louis before Burroughs was born, but returned in 1933 to lecture at Washington University, an institution founded by the poet's grandfather, William Greenleaf Eliot.

[12] While living in St. Louis, Burroughs may not have had occasion to hear much about St. Louis-born Kate Chopin, who died ten years before he was born, or Marianne Moore, who was born in suburban Kirkwood and graduated from Bryn Mawr in 1909.

[13] She grew up and was married in a house a few blocks away from Burroughs, published her first collection of poems in 1907, and won the Pulitzer Prize for poetry in 1918. It is not clear when Burroughs learned about Teasdale. Miles (*Call Me* 26) repeats an unlikely story from Burroughs that a schoolmate of his at Community School read Teasdale's (and Millay's) poems.

[14] Her great-great-grandmother, Anne Wayman Crow, was the sister of Lucien Carr's great-great grandfather, Wayman Crow.

[15] Rex Weisenburger attended John Burroughs School and then Yale. His father, Walter Weisenburger, was head of the St. Louis Chamber of Commerce and later executive vice president of the National Association of Manufacturers

(Weisenburger, Rex to David Kammerer, September 28, 1934, Richard E. Kammerer Collection).

[16] The OWI's activities were both foreign and domestic. Many writers worked for the OWI, but by 1943 its funds were cut and the agency was refocused on foreign operations.

[17] See Morgan's recreation of the episode, based, he reports, on his interviews with Burroughs: *Literary Outlaw* 98–102.

[18] Burroughs' name appears in club directories during those years, first as a resident member, then as an Army/Navy member, and finally as a non-resident member. Richard Stern saw Burroughs "around '46, [when] he was living at the University Club" (Morgan, Box 4, Folder 14).

[19] His grandson, Daniel Catlin, III, took his medical degree from Harvard the same year Burroughs took his bachelor of arts degree.

[20] He was also fascinated with *literary* violence: about the age of 13 or 14 he memorized Thomas Hood's popular 1831 ballad, "The Dream of Eugene Aram," about a murderer, and recited it to his class at John Burroughs School ("The Name is Burroughs" from *The Adding Machine* 7, 24).

[21] Decades later, Burroughs devised cut-ups from the *Boys Magazine* of his youth, including the September 1, 1920, issue (William S. Burroughs Papers, New York Public Library, Folio 81, items 35–40). In his last years he continued to read gun magazines (Miles, *Call Me* 610).

[22] Cf. a somewhat earlier memory: ". . . as a very young child I had wanted to be a writer" ("Remembering Jack Kerouac," 1969, repr. in *Word Virus* 323 and a later one: "I had always wanted to be a writer" (1981, repr. in *Burroughs Live* 499).

[23] Burroughs possibly refers to this novel in his "Literary Autobiography" as one of the "satirical novels about the people I met" during summer trips to Europe (*The Adding Machine* 6).

[24] Although Henry Miller was published in an issue of the *Harvard Advocate* in 1935, a comprehensive review of Burroughs and Miller, published in 2007 on a Burroughs website, did not uncover any evidence that Burroughs knew anything about Miller until many years later (See RealityStudio.org/scholarship/henry-miller-and-william-burroughs).

[25] Burroughs to Kammerer, October 7, 1932; October 16, 1932; November 28, 1932. Kammerer Collection.

[26] Burroughs to Kammerer, October 7,1932; October 16, 1932; November 28, 1932. Kammerer Collection.

[27] He thought Kittredge, the medievalist, dull but was very impressed with J. Livingston Lowes, who as a lecturer taught a famous course on Romantic poets (Hibbard 96).

[28] Burroughs sometimes misquoted: his quip in response to a report on a fight between two lesbians, "'tis too starved an argument for my sword" (during a December 1943 incident, quoted in Morgan, *Literary Outlaw* 89), conflated "I cannot fight upon this argument. / It is too starved a subject for my sword" (*Troilus and Cressida*, I. 1. 92–93). Miles writes that it was "one of Burroughs' favorite expressions, one he used frequently" (*Call Me* 102). Burroughs' introduction of the quotation with a cliché, "In the words of the immortal bard," suggests that his allusions to Shakespeare were designed to be ironic or mock-pompous.

[29] The literary allusions in *Naked Lunch* consist mostly of parodies of familiar tag lines in a popular poem by Sir John Suckling ("Why so pale and wan, fond lover"), familiar lines from Coleridge and Housman, a well-known song from *The Beggar's Opera* ("Over the hills and far away"), "The Midnight Ride of Paul Revere," and occasionally echoes of *Macbeth and Hamlet*.

[30] The 1928 translation of Spengler's second volume was heralded in a *Time* magazine review dated December 10, 1928.

[31] Nearly fifty years later Burroughs reportedly said that he read *Nightwood*, by Djuna Barnes, "back in the 1930s, and was very taken with it," and even tried imitating her style (a 1985 letter to Mary Lynn Broe, transcribed in Broe's *Silence and Power: A Reevaluation of Djuna Barnes* [1991] 206).

[32] Burroughs added Céline's name to a list of writers that an interviewer told him he had recommended to Kerouac and Ginsberg (*Burroughs Live* 248). For a skeptical survey of various "mythological" accounts of Burroughs' books in 1944, see Thom Robinson, "Burroughs' Library," *European Beat Studies Network*.

[33] A c. 1944–45 entry in Ginsberg's journal describing Burroughs' "reading" suggests that Burroughs' taste was eclectic: both modernist writers (mostly European), including Kafka, Cocteau, Rimbaud, Baudelaire, Gogol, Barnes, and some recently-published novels (mostly American) by William Maxwell, Charles Jackson, Denton Welch, and Richard Brooks (*Martyrdom* 78). Many years later, Burroughs later claimed that he was more influenced by Denton Welch than any other writer (Thom Robinson).

[34] Burroughs had perhaps encountered Pareto's *The Mind and Society*, the 1935 translation of a work first published in Italian in 1916. Both Spengler and Pareto are on Ginsberg's c. 1944–45 list of Burroughs' "reading."

[35] See *The John Burroughs Review*, vol. V, no. 3 (Feb. 1928), pp. 42–43; *The John Burroughs World*, vol. 1, no. 4 (Dec. 7, 1928), 3.

[36] Rex Weisenburger to David Kammerer, December 1, 1930; March 18, 1931; March 25, 1931; November 17, 1931; November 30, 1931. Kammerer Collection.

37 Five letters from July and August 1937 report mostly on his extracurricular activities, such as visiting the Museum of Modern Art and The Cloisters Kammerer Collection.

38 At trial in 1944 Carr's lawyer stated that Carr's association with Kammerer began "five years ago in a St. Louis private school" (Special to the *St. Louis Globe-Democrat*, September 16, 1944).

39 Fourteen letters and postcards postmarked July, August, and early September 1933 (Kammerer Collection). One performance was a production with marionettes of *Don Giovanni*. There is some evidence in one letter that Kammerer had traveled to Mexico with his own marionettes during a previous summer and presented a show in Taxco.

40 David Kammerer to Richard Kammerer, January 8, 1940. Kammerer Collection.

41 Kammerer to Mrs. Alfred Kammerer, December 7 and 15, 1943. Kammerer Collection.

42 Assistant District Attorney Jacob Grumet accepted Carr's report that Kammerer's personality had "steadily deteriorated . . . until he was little more than a derelict, barely keeping himself alive" as a janitor (the *New York Times*, Frank S. Adams, August 17, 1944, 13).

43 Many years later Latham wrote a play about the killing, titled *Birth of Beats: Murder and the Beat Generation*, produced in Brooklyn in April 2012.

44 Burroughs' literary executor, James Grauerholz, picks up the theme of intellectual prowess. Kammerer, he said, was a "brilliant conversationalist" and "one of the overlooked sources of Burroughs' personal philosophy" (*Word Virus* 10).

45 Céline Young to Jack Kerouac, October 1944, in Allen Ginsberg Papers at Stanford's Department of Special Collections, M0733, Series 1, Box 2, Folder 23.

46 When Morgan wrote up this part of the interview for the book, he toned it down to "he was . . . funny and unconventional. He had a friendly, open, and exuberant manner" (*Literary Outlaw* 85).

47 Twenty letters from Kammerer to his mother, written from December 3, 1943, to August 4, 1944, have survived in the Kammerer Collection.

48 The letters are dated December 3, 7, 14, 15, and 25.

49 She was a St. Louis debutante, the daughter of Frank Wickenhauser, a wealthy banker. She graduated from Washington University in 1930. She died in 1995, leaving part of her estate to establish in the memory of her parents a fund for television, film, and theatre arts at Washington University. A devout Episcopalian, she could also have met Kammerer at St. Michael's and St. George's Church. She never married.

50 The letters are dated February 7, 12, 23, and 28.

[51] Letters dated May 31, June 8 and 20.

[52] Letters dated July 7, July 12, July 25, and August 4.

[53] Grenville G. Benedict (dean of students at Andover) to Franklin E. Parker, Jr. (one of Carr's lawyers), August 25, 1944 (from Carr's student file at Andover, in Archives and Special Collections, Oliver Wendell Holmes Library, Phillips Academy, Andover, Massachusetts).

[54] Carr was little remembered by his John Burroughs classmates when they graduated in 1942. For instance, his name does not appear in the class history. However, at least one classmate, Kennett Love, remembered him well. Love (1924–2013) was born in St. Louis and graduated from John Burroughs School in 1942. He spent a year at Princeton, and after serving as a pilot in World War II graduated from Columbia in 1948, becoming a foreign correspondent for the *New York Times* and later a freelance writer. He remained a friend of both Carr and Ginsberg. See Morgan, Box 6, Folder 8.

[55] At Carr's trial, Allis testified that Carr was of "good character" (photocopy of an AP story, dated New York, October 6, 1944, that appeared in an unidentified newspaper under the headline "P. A. Grad Pleads Guilty in Slaying" [P.A. stands for "Phillips Andover."] Andover Library).

[56] The substance of the Leavitt and Allis reports was also incorporated in a report dated August 25, 1944, and sent by Dean Grenville Benedict to Carr's lawyers. This evidence did not appear at the trial.

[57] See the *Columbia Spectator*, vol. LXVIII, no. 1, September 1, 1944.

[58] Morgan did not use the second of the remarks.

[59] The *New York Times*, August 18, 1944; August 19, 1944. The August 18 story reports in addition that Carr also carried a copy of *The Third Morality* (1937) by the philosopher Henry Fitzgerald Heard. In the Burroughs-Kerouac *And the Hippos Were Boiled in their Tanks*, "Phillip Tourrian" (a stand-in for Carr) talks about Heard's book. Columbia's Philolexian Society, at its August 24, 1944, meeting chaired by Ginsberg, voted to send to Carr a copy of Eliot's just-published *Four Quartets*, according to the *Columbia Spectator*, vol. LXVIII, no. 1, September 1, 1944.

Works Cited

Adams, Frank, "Columbia Student Kills Friend and Sinks Body in Hudson River," *The New York Times* August 17, 1944: 1 and 13. Print.

Archives and Special Collections, Oliver Wendell Holmes Library, Phillips Academy, Andover, Massachusetts.

Aronowitz, Al. www.blacklistedjournalist.com. Myles, Brett, and Joel Roi Aronowitz. Web. 22 Feb. 2014.

Belko, Stephen W. *The Invincible Duff Green: Whig of the West*. Columbia, Missouri: U of Missouri P, 2006. Print.

Benney, Mark. *Low Company: Describing the Evolution of a Burglar*. London: P. Davis, 1936. Print.

---. *Angels in Undress*. New York: Random House, 1937. Print.

Blank, R. *Lucien Carr and the Origins of the Beat Generation*. Undergraduate thesis, Columbia University. 1988. Print.

Bockris, Victor. *With William Burroughs: A Report from the Bunker*. New York: St. Martin's, 1981, rev. ed. 1996. Print.

Broe, Mary Lynn. *Silence and Power: A Reevaluation of Djuna Barnes*. Champaign-Urbana: U of Illinois P, 1991. Print.

Burroughs, William S. *The Adding Machine: Selected Essays*. London: John Calder, 1985. Print.

---. *Junky*. New York: Penguin, 1977. Print.

---. *Naked Lunch*. Paris: Olympia, 1959. Print.

---. *Quee*r. New York: Viking, 1985. Print.

---. *The Western Lands*. New York: Viking, 1987. Print.

---. *The Wild Boys: A Book of the Dead*. New York: Viking, 1971. Print.

---. with Jack Kerouac. *And the Hippos Were Boiled in their Tanks*. New York: Grove, 2008. Print.

---. *Burroughs Live: The Collected Interviews, 1960–1997*. Ed. Sylvere Lotringer New York and Los Angeles: Semiotext(e), 2000. Print.

---. *Conversations with William S. Burroughs*. Ed. Allen Hibbard. Jackson: UP of Mississippi, 1999. Print.

---. *Word Virus: The William S. Burroughs Reader*. Ed. James Grauerholtz and Ira Silverberg. New York: Grove, 1998. Print.

---. *MS letters to David Kammerer, 1931–34*, Richard E. Kammerer, Jr. Collection, St. Louis, Missouri.

---. William S. Burroughs Papers, Berg Collection, New York Public Library.

Campbell, James. *This is the Beat Generation*. New York—San Francisco—Paris London: Secker & Warburg, 1999. Print.

Carr, Lucien I., *Missouri: A Bone of Contention*. New York: Houghton-Mifflin, 1988. Print.

Carr, Lucien IV. Student file, MS and TS, Special Collections, Oliver Wendell Holmes Library, Phillips Academy, Andover, Massachusetts.

---. Student file, MS and TS, George J. Mitchell Dept. of Special Collections & Archives, Bowdoin College Library, Brunswick, Maine.

Collins, Ronald, and Skover, David. *Mania: The Story of the Outraged and Outrageous Lives that Launched a Cultural Revolution*. Chicago: Top Five, 2013. Print.

Defoe, Daniel. *History of the Remarkable Life of the Truly Honourable Col. Jacque, Commonly Called Col. Jack*. London: J.M. Dent, 1895. Print.

A Descriptive Catalogue of the William S. Burroughs Archive. London: Covent Garden, 1973. Print.

Fritz, James. *The Beat Killer: A Biography of the Beat Writer Lucien Carr and the Riverside Park Murder*. ebook, BookCaps, 2012.

Ginsberg, Allen. *The Book of Martyrdom and Artifice,* Ed. Juanita Liebermann-Plimpton and Bill Morgan. Cambridge, Massachusetts: Da Capo, 2006. Print.

---. Allen Ginsberg Papers, MSS, 1944, Columbia University Library, New York City, New York.

---. Allen Ginsberg Papers, MSS, 1944, Special Collections and University Archives, Stanford University, Stanford, California.

"Guilty Plea Made by Carr in Slaying: Columbia Student's Admission of First Degree Manslaughter Is Accepted by Court." *New York Times* September 16, 1944: 15. Print.

Johnson, Joyce. *The Voice is All: The Lonely Victory of Jack Kerouac*. New York: Viking, 2012. Print.

Kammerer Collection. *Letters to and from David Kammerer, 1932–44*. MS. Richard E. Kammerer, Jr. Collection.

Kerouac, Jack. *Selected Letters, Vol. 1, 1940–1956*, Ed. Ann Charters. New York: Viking Penguin, 1995. Print.

---. *The Vanity of Duluoz*. New York: Coward-McCann, 1968. Print.

Kill Your Darlings. Dir. John Krokidas. Perf. Daniel Radcliffe, Dane DeHaan, and Michael C. Hall. Killer Films, 2013. Film.

Korzybski, Alfred. *Science and Sanity: An Introduction to Non-Aristotelian Systems and General Semantics*. Brooklyn, New York: Institute of General Semantics, 1933. Print.

Latham, Aaron. "The Columbia Murder That Gave Birth to the Beats." *New York Magazine*. Vol. 9 No. 16 (April 19, 1976), 41–53. Print.

Lawlor, William. *Beat Culture: Lifestyles, Icons, and Impac*t. Santa Barbara, Denver, and Oxford: ABC-Clio, 2005. Print.

Miles, Barry. *William Burroughs: El Hombre Invisible*. London: Virgin, 1992. Print.

---. *Call Me Burroughs: A Life.* Boston and New York: Twelve, 2014. Print

Morgan, Ted. *Literary Outlaw: The Life and Times of William S. Burroughs.* New York: Henry Holt, 1988, rev. ed. 2012. Print.

---. Ted Morgan Papers. Special Collections. Arizona State University Libraries. Tempe, Arizona.

Pareto, Vilfredo. *The Mind and Society.* New York: Harcourt-Brace, 1935. Print.

Robinson, Thom. "Burroughs' Library." European Beat Studies Network. 27 Aug. 2012. Web. Sept. 2012.

Sheldon, Marjorie Capel. Private communication to author, December 19, 2012.

"Student Is Indicted in 2d-Degree Murder." *New York Times* August 25, 1944: sec. Amusements15. Print.

"Student is Silent on Slaying Friend: Held Without Bail After He Listens Lackadaisically to Charge in Stabbing Case." *New York Times* August 18, 1944:14. Print.

"Student Slayer Sent to the Reformatory." *New York Times*. October 7, 1944, sec. Amusements15. Print.

Tytell, John. *Naked Angels: The Lives and Literature of the Beat Generation.* New York: McGraw-Hill, 1976. Print.

"Young Slayer Goes to Elmira." *New York Times* October 10. 1944: sec. Business Financial 38. Print.

Entering the "Gate of Nondualism": Gary Snyder's "On Vulture Peak" and Mahāyāna Shūnyatā

Todd Giles

In 1956, soon after Gary Snyder left the United States to study Zen Buddhism in Japan, Jack Kerouac, Philip Whalen, and Snyder himself each composed three important multi-section, mid-length American poetic explorations of Mahāyāna Buddhist philosophy: "Desolation Blues," "The Slop Barrel: Slices of the Paideuma for All Sentient Beings," and "On Vulture Peak," respectively. At the time, these poets were deeply engaged in reading and discussing texts such as Dwight Goddard's *A Buddhist Bible*, D. T. Suzuki's essays on Zen, and Lin Yutang's *The Wisdom of China and India*, as well Kenneth Rexroth's Japanese and Chinese translations that were published in 1955 and 1956, not to mention his own unique Buddhist-American explorations in *The Signature of All Things*. Buddhism provided them with a new way of thinking about issues of identity, being, and interconnectedness in a postwar world of gray flannel suits, McCarthyism, sprawling Levittowns, and thermonuclear detonations.

One of the most striking aspects of the poetry and philosophy these poets were exploring is the ways in which the intersections of these disciplines clarify and cut through to the present moment of experience. What Whalen said of Zen in a 1972 interview holds true for the poetry itself: "Zen seemed to cut away many extravagances and get down to the point of emancipation and energy and cutting loose from all your emotional problems. . . . There is also the problem of right now: what are you doing right this minute and how do you get through that and how can you make it alive, vivid, solid?" (*Off the Wall* 59). In turning away from some Western poetic and philosophical traditions, Snyder, his friends, and other Beat-associated writers such as Diane di Prima, Joanne Kyger, and Lew Welch worked to create a poetic discourse enabling them to move past the historical moment to arrive at a deeper, ever-present immediacy, much like the poetry of ancient China and Japan, something that even Rexroth's poetry seldom achieved because of its politico-anarchist undergirding.

Though lighter in tone than Kerouac's soul-searching struggle with identity and impermanence in "Desolation Blues" and Whalen's exploration in "The Slop Barrel" of the aggregates of attachment that collectively make up one's personality, "On Vulture Peak," which has received no critical attention by scholars to date, explores some of the most complex and allusive concepts of Mahāyāna Buddhism in Snyder's poetry. Snyder scholars focus on either book-length works such as *Myths & Texts* and *Mountains and Rivers Without End (MRWE)* or approach his work conceptually by exploring several poems dealing with larger topics such as Buddhism, shamanism, or ecocriticism. Both of these approaches have led to a growing body of serious, engaging, and insightful interdisciplinary criticism, opening the way for lesser-studied writers such as Whalen and Kyger. However, the lack of attention given to "On Vulture Peak" might have more to do with the fact that, as Timothy Gray points out, Snyder "gave little attention to his own writing during his stay in Japan. The poems Snyder did write in late 1956 and early 1957 are few in number, modest in scope, and uneven in quality" (129–130). Gray's assertion is backed up by Snyder himself in the March 8, 1957, letter he sent Whalen from Kyoto, which included "On Vulture Peak" along with the "Dullness in February: Japan." Neither poem, he claimed, was intended "to be considered final statements on anything, just ways of passing time."[1] Likewise, Snyder stated that "'On Vulture Peak' is a light-hearted poem and [should not be taken] too seriously."[2] Whatever the reason for its lack of attention—lightness of content or "uneven quality"—the poem merits inclusion in the critical discussion for two reasons: 1) "On Vulture Peak" is unlike any poem written by Snyder at this important juncture in his practice and poetics—it is the longest, most experimental, humorous, and philosophically challenging; it is also the only one written as a dialogue; and 2) if we take Snyder at his word that the poem is in fact not a "final statement," we can think of it as a dry run for what was to become his magnum opus nearly forty years later, *Mountains and Rivers Without End*, which he began one month before composing "On Vulture Peak." Indeed, whereas Anthony Hunt suggests that the correspondence of early 1957 between Snyder and Whalen about *Mountains and Rivers Without End* is the "earliest documented indication that the poet had distinct ideas about the form his long poem might take," I suggest that Snyder's "On Vulture Peak" is itself the initial poetic working out of that very evidence (10).

The content of "On Vulture Peak" was largely inspired by the Japanese theatre Snyder was exploring upon his arrival in Kyoto. As he wrote Whalen in the same letter that included the poem, "I am fascinated by the kabuki & noh [sic] recitation technique. . . . [and] can imagine a very jolly creative sort of modern poetry-modern-dance music shot built around the reading of one long dramatic-type poem with musicians & possibly a dancer."[3] Snyder later addresses this "fascination" in the endnotes of *Mountains and Rivers Without End*, saying he "became an aficionado of Nō [sic] history and aesthetics." Noh, like "On Vulture Peak," is, according to Snyder, "a gritty but totally refined high-culture art that is in the lineage of shamanistic performance, a drama that by means of voice and dance calls forth the spirit realms" (155). Its content is also, as Anthony Hunt says of *Mountains and Rivers Without End*, "associated with a particular kind of Nō play wherein a wondering monk or lay pilgrim encounters a spirit, first in the guise of an ordinary person . . . and later as an awesome . . . spirit of the place" (6). In combining two non-Western artistic forms and complex Buddhist philosophy, "On Vulture Peak" marks a pivotal transition between *Myths & Texts*, Snyder's "first venture into the long poem"—on which he put the finishing touches in the spring of 1956 prior to leaving for Japan—and *Mountains and Rivers Without End*, a fact that perhaps speaks to the seemingly playful light-heartedness of "On Vulture Peak" (*MRWE* 156).

While drawing substantially upon Japanese classical theatre, the poem fundamentally follows the conventions of the *sūtra*, allowing Snyder to grapple with notions of emptiness (*shūnyatā*), wisdom (*prajñā*), and compassion (*karunā*). The word *sūtra* means "thread," or the stringing together of a series of discourses. The purpose of *sūtras* is to communicate the way to enlightenment, doing so not by providing readers with a how-to manual, but through an eternal truth or revelation transmitted from the depths of transcendental wisdom. These lessons are conveyed through an unobtrusive first-person narrator—generally thought to be Ananda, a disciple of Buddha—before the often lengthy and complex setting forth of the core teachings of Buddhism. These *dharma* talks, which are presented in the form of parables and allegories, begin with a question posed by Buddha or one of the disciples, and are usually divided into philosophically content-specific sections which are numbered or have headings, which is precisely what both *Mountain and Rivers Without End* and "On Vulture Peak" do. Kerouac too, in dialogue with "On Vulture Peak," wrote his own multi-section *sūtra* during this time called "Poems of the Buddhas of Old." His *sūtra* of forty-five stanzas, which is not as complex stylistically and philosophically as Snyder's, merits mention here as an example of the playful, yet philosophical way in which Snyder, Whalen, and Kerouac were bouncing Buddhist concepts back and forth while at the same time experimenting with non-western poetic forms.

Sūtras traditionally open with a brief description of the setting, the occasion, an acknowledgement of those present, and occasionally a reference to the time of year. Snyder's does the same but with a contemporary twist. While the ancient Vulture Peak is located near the city of Rajgiriha in the Satna district of Madhya Pradesh, India, Snyder who "never lost [his] sense of belonging to North America," set his *sūtra* on the California coast (*MRWE* 155), where a teacher and his disciple sit around a beachside campfire discussing the dharma, both participants "creative" and "jolly."

As a poetic *sūtra*, "On Vulture Peak" also opens with Snyder's version of a classical Chinese *shih* prologue. Dating back to 1000–600 B.C.E., *shih* were originally written as song lyrics; they generally employ rhyme, alliteration, parallelism, onomatopoeia, and end-stopped lines that create a series of tight, single syntactic units, with the final couplet often ending the poem with a run-on line. Snyder wrote his *shih* in six rhyming iambic tetrameter couplets, both of which he has rarely used. When he does, he does so very pointedly: in this case, the opening stanza acts not only as a précis of what is to come in the *sutra* but also as a general introduction to Mahāyāna Buddhism through a highly-condensed retelling of the *Vimalakīrti Sūtra*. As with this second century C.E. text, set during Buddha's lifetime, Snyder's *shih* prologue is set in Vimalakīrti's time, for in the realm of nonduality, space and time no longer exist because all distinctions between here and there, then and now, have been theoretically obliterated. Writing in and about emptiness thus allowed Snyder to shuttle back and forth between Buddhist concepts, the present moment, and Native American lore.

However, it is important to note that the *Vimalakīrti Sūtra* is unusual in the Buddhist canon in that the central figure is not Buddha, but rather a layman whose understanding and practice, as Burton Watson puts it in the introduction to his translation of the *sūtra*, "epitomizes the lay ideal" (1). This concept of the "lay ideal" highlights one of the fundamental differences between Theravāda and Mahāyāna Buddhism, the latter of which took root in America in the form of Zen. Mahāyāna Buddhism broadened the earlier teachings of the Theravāda school by reinterpreting the ideals, rewards, and practices of Buddhism to include everyone, not just monks and nuns, as well as distinguishing its practitioner's goals for achieving enlightenment. For Theravāda Buddhists the goal is to achieve the state of the *arhat*, or one who is released from the suffering from the cycles of existence, whereas for Mahāyāna Buddhists, their ideal figure is that of the *bodhisattva*, one who vows not only to achieve enlightenment for him or herself, but also to assist all sentient beings in doing likewise.[4]

The *Vimalakīrti Sūtra* opens with a large number of laity, *bodhisattvas*, and various devas and other nonhumans who are gathered in the Amra Gardens to hear Sākyamuni Buddha discuss the *dharma*. One key person is missing, though: the wealthy Vimalakīrti, who, as Snyder describes him, "was an enlightened Buddhist layman from North India who fell sick" (note "The Mountain Spirit," *MRWE* 163); he was considered by all who knew him to be a paragon of Buddhist practice. When Buddha learns of Vimalakīrti's supposed illness-induced absence, he asks which of his major disciples will visit him. All decline to do so because in the past each has been castigated for his lack of understanding of the *dharma*. Mañjuśrī, the *Bodhisattva* of Wisdom, finally agrees to go see Vimalakīrti in his bedchamber, where "[n]o matter how many keep arriving, they all fit into his one small room, 'ten feet square'" (163). Eventually Vimalakīrti , Mañjuśrī, and the others return to the Amra Gardens to continue their conversation with Buddha.

The playfulness of "On Vulture Peak," like that of the *Vimalakīrti Sūtra* Snyder riffs on in the prologue, comes not from the concepts explored but through its sense of musicality, familiarity, and, at times, silliness. Snyder's "long dramatic-type poem" begins: "All the boys are gathered there / Vulture Peak[5], in the thin air / Watching cycles pass around / From brain to stone and flesh to ground . . ." (*Left out in the Rain* 70).[6] For comparison, Kerouac's "Poems of the Buddha of Old," which rhymes throughout, opens: "The boys were sittin / In a grove of trees / Listening to Buddy / Explainin the keys" (*Pomes All Sizes* 123). The "cycles" that open Snyder's *shih* are the stages of existence sentient beings traverse through the *samsāra* world of birth, death, and rebirth until reaching enlightenment, a state "arrived at" ("the other shore") through the eradication of suffering and desire that comes with understanding nonduality. Seeing the "cycles pass / From brain to stone and flesh to ground" implies the nonduality of the subjective ego "I" and the external "other" world. In other words, the gist of Mahāyāna philosophy—that "form is emptiness, emptiness is not different from form"—suggests that if the aggregates of attachment (*skandhas*), which collectively make up one's personality (form, sensation, perception, discrimination, and consciousness), are impermanent, then it follows too that physical phenomena such as our bodies and the object world ("flesh," "stone," "ground") are also impermanent, thus implying that the concept of "self" must also be a delusion. In watching the "cycles pass," then, "the boys" learn that "love and wisdom are the same" (70). "Love" here means compassion (*karunā*); "wisdom" (*prajñā*), which comes with understanding the concept of nonduality, refers to the immediacy of intuitive knowing without the fetters of intellectualization. Recognizing that love and wisdom work in tandem like yin and yang is a key characteristic of Mahāyāna Buddhism, a concept Julia Martin suggests is the primary concern of *MRWE* ("Seeing a Corner" 58). As Snyder says in his 1990 *TriQuarterly* interview, "Buddhism holds that the universe and all in it are intrinsically in a state of complete wisdom, love and compassion; acting in natural response and mutual interdependence" (Martin 90). It is in the concept of mutual interdependence that one realizes that embracing emptiness, as paradoxical as that sounds, leads to wisdom, which is the "starting place for true compassion" (Hunt 197).

The casual nature of Snyder's setting and language lends itself well to the more relaxed and inclusive nature of Mahāyāna doctrine, allowing Snyder to shuttle back and forth between Beat vernacular and highly esoteric philosophy throughout "On Vulture Peak." For example, the prologue continues with the line "But split like light to make the scene," which initially looks like it modifies the preceding line about "Love and wisdom," but in fact modifies the next line: "Ten million camped in a one-room shack" (70). This "one-room shack," like Vimalakīrti's bedchamber mentioned above, is an image Snyder probably first encountered in the poetry of Rexroth, such as "Hojoki," which appeared in Rexroth's *The Signature of All Things* in 1949, or "Empty Mirror," which was included in the

1952 *The Dragon & the Unicorn,* a collection that had a marked influence on Snyder's own poetics. We also see a connection in a 1954 letter to Whalen: "My room is small for human beings, but like Vimalakīrti's ten-foot-square-hut, it will accommodate ten thousand Bodhisattvas."[7] Those who "split" to "make the scene," as this earlier quote suggests, are the disciples of Buddha who visit Vimalakīrti to discuss nondualism: "tracing all the causes back / To nothing which is not the start" (70). Nothing is "not the start" because there is neither a single originary point of departure nor a linear trajectory. The notion of emptiness is a non-negative negation, an affirmation of our interrelatedness with all things.[8] The prologue ends with "(Now we love, but here we part) / And not a one can answer why / To the simple garden in my eye" (70). The use of parentheses here can be read as a framing device: right here, right now, this moment; it is in the void (the blank space) that "we part" with the dualistic notions of "you" and "I"—parting as two distinct entities, thus making the true here and now one of infinite interconnectedness. As mentioned above, the final couplet of *shih* generally ends with a run-on line, as does Snyder's. The "simple garden in my eye" brings us full-circle back to the Amra Gardens where Vimalakīrti and entourage return at the end of the *Vimalakīrti Sūtra* to continue their discussion with Buddha.

The *shih* prologue of "On Vulture Peak" is followed by the main body of the *sūtra,* which consists of nine numbered sections (Parts I–IX) in the form of a *Rinzai kōan* interview. In these "interviews," known as *sanzen,* Zen masters (*rōshis*) present their students with *kōans*—short narratives or poems that intentionally seem illogical, ambiguous, and paradoxical—that are designed to act as a medium through which understanding can be achieved intuitively rather than intellectually. They are not puzzles with single prescribed answers arrived at through logical analysis; rather, they are meant to provide insight through embodying key elements of Zen teachings. For example, in "Case 12" of *The Blue Cliff Records,* the oldest and one of the most complex texts in Zen literature, a monk asked Tōzan Shusho: "What is Buddha?" "Three pounds of Flax!" Tōzan replies, suggesting that enlightenment is not something distant and incomprehensible, but is embodied in the here and now of the unpremeditated and spontaneous (Sekida 179).[9] In a letter to Whalen written two months after sending him "On Vulture Peak," Snyder discusses his experience of the Zen interview: "Sanzen is terrifying, like going before a firing squad once a day & being told SPEAK & I just sit there 'speechless & intelligent & shaking with shame'----because no logic chopping or cleverness or suchlike will do. . . ."[10]

Parts I–IX are also based on conversations Snyder and Kerouac had earlier that summer, prior to Snyder's departure. As such, they aptly capture their energy and excitement in a way not dissimilar to Kerouac's depictions in *The Dharma Bums.* According to Snyder, "Our interchanges on Buddhism were on the playful and delightful level of exchanging the lore, exchanging what we knew about it, what he thought of Mahayana. . . . I introduced him to the texts that give the anecdotes of the dialogues and confrontations between T'ang dynasty masters and disciples, and of course he was delighted by that" (Gifford and Lee 203). The character of Kerouac actually begins Sndyer's nine-part *sanzen* session with a question which calls to mind both the dedicatee of *The Dharma Bums* (Han-shan, the T'ang dynasty poet-recluse Snyder translated in *Cold Mountain Poems* in 1958) and Kerouac's own reliance on alcohol: "Are bums and drunks truly Angels? / Hairy Immortals drinking poorboys in doorways?" (70). Buddhism stresses moderation, as seen in Japhy's comment to Ray concerning excess and enlightenment: "How do you expect to become a good bhikku or even a Bodhisattva Mahasattva always getting drunk like that?" (*DB* 144). However, rather than castigate Kerouac in "On Vulture Peak," Snyder offers him numerous *kōan*-like lessons on emptiness, compassion, desire, and buddha nature in the form of parables that act like fingers pointing at the moon.

The first of these abstractions is a seemingly out-of-place and out-of-time one-line parable of desire and subsequent suffering in the form of lust and castration: "Poor Abelard, thou'rt clipped!" (70).[11] Although this twelfth-century reference may seem like a completely irrelevant response, it is in fact a good example of the way in which *kōans* act as a medium through which understanding can be achieved intuitively rather than intellectually. For example, Snyder's "Abelard *kōan*" works similarly to "Jōshū's Oak Tree," a famous *kōan* found in *The Gateless Gate*, which is, like *The Blue Cliff Records*, a compilation of *kōans* accompanied by explanatory verses and notes. In the *kōan*, a monk asks Jōshū: "What is the meaning of Bodhidharma's coming to China?" Jōhshū responds: "The oak tree in the garden." Mumon's explanatory verse accompanying the *kōan* reads: "Words cannot express things; / Speech does not convey the spirit. / Swayed by words, one is lost; / Blocked by phrases, one is bewildered" ("Case 37," Sekida 110). As is the case with Kerouac's seemingly self-serving questions about "bums and drunks," Snyder's response "clips" Kerouac's conceptualizing short, pointing out that one should not grasp at definitions and concepts but instead stay in the present moment of pure cognition. The "oak tree in the garden" and the "three pounds of flax," then, are the "steaming mussels" of Kerouac's present, not the drunkenness in "doorways" of past, future, or another's present.

Part I also introduces the setting, the occasion, and the key players. One of the characteristics of Mahāyāna Buddhism is its inclusiveness of and respect for lay practitioners and the fact that its teachings and practices are not thought of as separate and distinct from people's daily lives. As such, both Snyder and Kerouac's *sūtras* involve lay practitioners – Snyder and Kerouac in the former, and, in the latter, men who use names akin to those of the loggers and hobos who people Snyder and Kerouac's work: "Montana Slim," "Big Daddy," and "Raggedy Dan." The body of "On Vulture Peak" opens, then, not with an assembly of Buddhist monks, but with an everyday event familiar to readers of *The Dharma Bums*;[12] Snyder says, "J.K. and me was squatting naked and sandy / At McClure Beach steaming mussels, eating / A pair of drunk Siwash starting a shellmound" (70). Kerouac recalled these outings in a 1957 letter to Snyder, saying, "I have never gotten over . . . those inexplicable moments of mutual irritation we shared, which were dissipated like at Stinson Beach jumping down cliffs, and those sad nights discussing death. . . ."[13] Snyder captures the sound of the wash of the waves during "those sad nights" by using alliteration with the repeated "s" sounds—"squatting," "sandy," "steaming," "mussels," etc. The stanza is casual, designating Jack as "J.K." rather than spelling out Kerouac's name as Snyder did a few months earlier in a poem titled "Migration of Birds." Also informal is the use of "&" in place of "and," the use of the objective case pronoun "me" rather than the more formal nominative "I," and "was" rather than "were." In contrast, the final two lines of this stanza are rather artfully rendered: "Neuri sleeping *off* a *hangover* face *down* / At the *foot* of a *cliff*; sea lions *off* shore"—producing a sense of suspension or hanging, as does the placement of the semicolon, dangling just off the cliff, ending without a period (my italics). The painter Neuri, or Psyche as she appears in *The Dharma Bums*, is also the "Hindu Deva-girl / Light legs dancing in the waves" whose vision "[k]ept [the poet] high for weeks" in "For a Far-Out Friend" (*R&CMP* 13–14).[14]

Part II, then, addresses what amounts to the crux of the first of the Four Noble Truths: life is suffering. The delusion of birth and death, which in turn leads to the delusion of separateness (I/you), is the hobgoblin of suffering. "All babies / Are unborn," this stanza tells us, an idea Snyder also addresses in the poem "Burning 14" in *Myths & Texts* (1960): "A skin-bound bundle of clutchings / unborn and with no place to go" (49). According to the *Lankāvatāra Sūtra*,[15] "[b]y emptiness of self-nature is meant that all things in their self-nature are un-born; therefore, it is said that things are empty of nature" (Goddard 295). In other words, when one views things with right knowledge, one recognizes that they have no self-nature, no individuality; thus they are un-born in the sense that they are not born of themselves or out of something other. Having "no place to go" is itself a key concept of Mahāyāna philosophy. Nirvana, which is right here right now, is not a metaphysical place to be arrived at; rather, it is a matter of waking up to one's always already present original nature. If one must "go" anywhere, it is to pass beyond discrimination to the realm of non-dualism. Or as Kerouac says in "113th Chorus" of *Mexico City Blues*, "—you just / numbly don't get there" (113).

In the final three lines of this stanza, Snyder exposes the delusion: that the mind that sees and grasps is merely a manifestation of its own ego-activity: "tracking the moon through / Flying fenceposts a carload of groceries, home – / What home, pull in park at, and be known?" (71). The moon, a traditional Buddhist symbol of enlightenment, is not something that can be chased after. "Tracking" it "through /

Flying fenceposts" is like watching it reflected on water: it appears to be in constant movement, broken up, wavy, which is analogous to "normal" consciousness. Herein lies Snyder's answer to Kerouac's opening question, as found in the final line of the stanza—a line set off by the previous one with a dash, as if saying "wait a minute": "What home . . . and be known?" The very notions of "home" and being "known" are themselves delusionary concepts like a self as separate from the moon. Another way to think about it, though, according to Snyder scholar Julia Martin, is that in "studying the self, we find it has no inherent essence, that home or our 'original nature' is Buddha-Nature" ("Seeing a Corner" 61). The "realm of quietude," to quote the *Lankāvatāra Sūtra*, exists only when we recognize everything is delusory, that we ourselves invest in our own self-existence, thus separating ourselves from the inextricable reality of interconnectedness (Goddard 298). Here, too, Snyder, rather than directly answering Kerouac's questions, presents him with examples of causality.

Part III continues the astrological trope which ends the previous section, drawing our attention away from the moon to "the little cloud" which opens this stanza. The "little cloud," a "nebula seen slantwise by the naked eye," is the Andromeda Galaxy, the only galaxy that can be seen from earth without the aid of a telescope. Once again, Snyder provides a "nebulous" *kōan*-like lesson that needs to be worked through, rather than one which is presented as self-evident. The Andromeda Galaxy, like the moon, is directly viewable by the naked eye; it needs no intermediary in much the same way that we need no intermediary to reach enlightenment—it is already there, all we have to do is recognize it. As Buddha says in the *Śūraṅgama Sūtra*, "It is like a man calling the attention of another man to the moon by pointing his finger toward it. The other man ought to look at the moon, but instead he looks at the finger and by so doing, not only misses the moon but misses the finger, also" (Goddard 136–137).

Part IV provides readers with the "firing squad" intensity Snyder describes above. Snyder says of his dharma talks with Kerouac that "[h]e made up names. He would follow on the Mahāyāna Sūtra invention of lists, and he would invent more lists. . . . He was great at that . . ." (Gifford and Lee 203). Snyder opens the stanza with another seemingly nonsensical statement: "Nearer than breathing / Closer than skin" (71). It is through meditation that one "arrives" at this state, allowing the ego "I," whom we normally think of as the one doing the breathing, to fall away. *Samādhi,* a state of deep concentration achieved during meditation, brings us "closer than skin" in the sense that the "I" dissipates and becomes one with the body and mind. Kerouac's somewhat belated response is physically set off on the page:

smack in the earballs

nosehalls, brainpans, tongueclucks

eyeholes, prickbones,

answer! answer! why! (71)

These phenomena, known as the Six Senses (eyes, ears, nose, tongue, body, and mind), are here connected with arbitrary conceptions in that they are being played with associationally: "earballs / nosehalls," etc. Kerouac is contemplating the senses as things (*dharmas*) in such a way that attaches meaning (sounds and shapes) to them, building an extra layer onto his thoughts rather than simply letting them rise and fall in the mindful practice of unfettered meditation-mind. In other words, he is projecting associations onto what should be passing thoughts, separating his senses from his mind by listing them as individual things and thus separate from one another and from his mind. Kerouac learned atop Desolation Peak that summer that "if it wasn't for [his] six senses, of seeing, hearing, smelling, touching, tasting and thinking, the self of that, which is non-existent, there would be no phenomena to perceive at all" ("Alone on a Mountaintop" 132). Indeed, as he read countless times in his beloved *Diamond Sūtra* that summer, part of the cessation of clinging to arbitrary conceptions is excluding "all thoughts connected with the phenomena of sight, sound, taste, smell, touch, and all discriminations based upon them" because in the dualistic world of causality, one thing (thought) leads to another ad infinitum until one recognizes that there is no distance between our minds, bodies, and what is "real," for they are one and the same (Goddard 90).

Kerouac here, before giving his Six Senses response time to air out, impatiently shouts: "answer! answer! why!" It is all Snyder can do, with patience, as his indented response indicates with white space on the page, to answer with the quote that closes the stanza:

"with lowered lids

i have entered

nibbana" (71)

There are several interesting things about this response. To begin with, *nibbāna* —which is Pāli for *nirvana*, and thus from the older Theravādan tradition—is usually not talked about in the first-person-singular. In the Pāli and Sanskrit canons, narrators such as Ananda generally open with the statement "Thus have I heard" as a way of not claiming personal enlightenment experience; they are, rather, merely the transmitters of the Buddha-dharma. Recall too that Theravāda's emphasis regarding enlightenment centers not on the *bodhisattva* ideal, but on the liberation of the individual "I." There is something jarring, then, about Snyder's response not only because it is in the ego-conscious first-person, but also because he answers with a quote that sounds as if it comes right out of Kerouac's *Mexico City Blues (MCB)*, written during the previous year. For example, the opening of the "111th Chorus" has a similar theme, tone, and layout:

I didnt attain nothin

When I attained Highest

Perfect

Wisdom (*MCB* 111)

Snyder's quote also calls to mind the scene at the beginning of *The Dharma Bums* when Ray, full of anxious questions ("answer! answer! why!"), asks the "old cook, with lidded eyes" the classic *kōan*: "Why did Bodhidharma come from the West?" His answer: "I don't care" (11). To enter *nirvana*, then, one must relinquish hold of the dualistic mind—that is, not "care."

This idea is further worked out in Part V, where we learn that even the "philosophers are horrified / because there is no cause." The "philosophers" are "horrified" because "everything exists / because the world is real and so are they / and so is nothing. . ." (72). Kerouac himself addresses this idea in "Poems of the Buddhas of Old": "Life is like a dream, / You only think it's real / Cause you're born a sucker / For that kind of deal; // But if the Truth was known / You ain't here nohow /And neither am I / Nor that cow or sow . . ." (123–124). Snyder helps explain this idea in a 1953 letter to Whalen that echoes the *Lankāvatāra Sūtra*: ". . . what irritates me constantly around these skolars is, they have no contact between their symbolic knowledge, i.e. all the buks they've read, & what happens to them every day, direct like."[17] And from the *Lankāvatāra Sūtra* itself: "As long as scholars remain on their philosophical ground their demonstration must conform to logic and their textbooks, and their memory-habit of erroneous intellection will ever cling to them" (Goddard 284). Recall Tōzan's "Three pounds of Flax!" above, suggesting that *nirvana* is found in the dependent co-origination of the here and now, not through renouncing the world for robes and books. As Engo's introduction to Tōzan's *kōan* suggests, "Scholars labor at their formulas like monkeys struggling to catch the moon reflected on the waves" (179).[18] Like "tracking the moon through / Flying fenceposts," the very concepts of *shūnyatā* and *nirvana* are ineffable and resist our capacity to describe them. The philosopher's horror stems, then, from the fact that "Relative-knowledge" or formula "rises from the mind itself," whereas the concept of nondualism according to the *Lankavatara Sutra* "is based upon the recognition that the objective world, like a vision, is the manifestation of the mind itself; it teaches the cessation of ignorance, desire, deed and causality. . ."(Goddard 283). Indeed, as Rexroth says in "Empty Mirror," "As long as we are lost / In the world of purpose / We are not free" (321). "Purpose" here refers to the dualistic self-acting in the world of "logic" and "erroneous intellection" as if it were unique, separate. To recognize that "everything . . . is real . . . and nothing is" is to understand that "form is emptiness," to "free" oneself from the "horror" of *samsāra*.

Part V of "On Vulture Peak" continues with distinct Kerouacesque phrasing:

> bony jungle spring
>
> Shakya in the boondocks.
>
> a broken start,
>
> sprout,
>
> is REALLY gone (72)

In fact, in response to reading "On Vulture Peak," Whalen wrote Snyder saying that "Kwack could not have written 'bony jungle spring / Sakya (sic) in the boondocks', but the rhyming is his, I agree."[19] Kerouac shared "Various Little Pomes"[20] in the form of *haiku*, *gatha*, and blues choruses with Whalen and Snyder while living in Berkeley and at Marin-an in 1955–1956. One such example, found in a six-page grouping called "[ENLIGHTENMENTS]," reads:

> Failure
>
> which is not really a failure
>
> really—
> Ripple of delusion is
>
> that it is (*Pomes All Sizes* 70)

Riffing on the concept of emptiness, both Kerouac—and Snyder's imitation of Kerouac—appear spontaneously laid out on the page in fits and starts, much like the improvisational saxophone playing of Kerouac's be-bop idol, Charlie Parker. Snyder's lines, which are some of the most obscure in the poem, describe Siddhartha Gautama's enlightenment. Siddhartha, himself emaciated ("bony") after practicing several years of fruitless asceticism, set off on his own to seek enlightenment. He chose a spot outside of the town of Bodhimanda (present day Bodh-gaya) to contemplate the causes of suffering. Chinese pilgrim-monk Fa-Hien (ca. 337–ca. 422) describes the city as desolate and empty ("the boondocks"), though "[a]ll around was forest" ("jungle spring") where Siddhartha sat nearby under the Bodhi-tree along the banks of the Falgu River (87).[21] "Shakya," the clan name from which Siddhartha gained the title Shakyamuni ("Sage of the Shakya clan"), sat for forty-nine days, finally achieving enlightenment at the age of thirty-five. The "broken start," a line itself nipped in the bud, refers to the fact that after becoming enlightened, Buddha continued meditating under the Bodhi-tree because he was unsure of how to transmit his new-found enlightenment to others. He soon encountered the five disciples who earlier abandoned him when he gave up asceticism for concentrated meditation (*samādhi*). Immediately recognizing that he had attained liberation, they asked Buddha for instruction, thus the "sprout" or beginning of the Buddha's teachings. The teachings are "REALLY gone," a phrase Whalen also uses for the Sanskrit word "Paragate" in "Sourdough Mountain Lookout" and which Goddard translates as "to that other shore" in the *Heart Sūtra* as seen below (86). The stanza concludes with the excited voice of Kerouac: "wow, he / always been standin there / sweatin' and explainin'?" (72). Has Buddha been preaching the *dharma* all along, Kerouac asks, almost Christianizing him into the figures of the African American street-side proselytizers Ray and Japhy encounter in *The Dharma Bums*.[22]

Like the cycle of existence itself (*samsāra*), Part VI picks up in mid-sentence where the previous section left off ("REALLY gone"), positing a question mark-less question: "gone where." Answer: "Nowhere, where he came from / thus that thing / thus that thing / where were you born from / born from, born from–" (72). Where are you going? and where are you from? are common questions posed in *Rinzai* interviews. Indeed, to say where one is from or where one is going implies both a point of departure and a point of arrival; for one on the path these two points are irrelevant. Thus Snyder's answer: "Nowhere, where he came from." "[T]hus that thing" means "thusness" or "suchness" (*tathatā*), and in Mahāyāna Buddhism indicates the true nature of things as they exist before humans subjectify them. *Tathatā* is formless, indefinable; it is nonphenomenal. In describing the *Tathagatā* (one of the ten names Buddha used to describe himself), Vimalakīrti refers to the "Thus Come One as not existing from past times, not departing in the future, nor abiding here at present" (the *Vimalakīrti Sūtra* 130). One's original or buddha nature is not contingent upon notions of conception, place, time, lineage—all connoting ego, individuality, birth. As Snyder told Joanne Kyger in a letter from Kyoto, "The Zen eye is looking at things before they are born, before there is man and women and the shapes of desire; the ground everything grows from neither 'is' nor 'is not' and it rejects nothing."[23] To attempt to define "the self" necessitates conceptualizations within the world of duality, which in turn separates the self from everything around it.

It is in Parts VI and VII that the "ghostly figures" of Noh drama Hunt mentions above come in to play. As he says of *Mountains and Rivers Without End*, these apparitions emanate from "the relatively recent political history of Native America or . . . [are] representative spirits of the Paleolithic way of life that the modern world has forgotten" (12). Often appearing as the "feminine 'Other'" in *Mountains and Rivers Without End* (Hunt 6), these "enlightening" spirits appear in "On Vulture Peak" in the form of "the reborn soul / of a bitter cheated chief" (72) and "Wobblies of the Six / Realms" (73). The "bitter cheated chief" here plays two roles. He can be read as Chief Seattle (1786–1866), situating him in Hunt's "recent political history of Native America," and when read in conjunction with the first-person narration of the stanza and the reference to a "salmonberry bough" can be interpreted as a Paleolithic "representative" as seen in the Sioux tale "The Story of Salmon" found in Lewis Spence's *The Myths of the North American Indians* (1914). In the tale, as with Part VI of "On Vulture Peak," we read of a hunter-hero, a badger, a ritual washing, a vision, and a close relative rescue figure.

The ghostly figures in Part VII are the "Hot wispy ghosts blown / down halls between births" in "hobo-jungles of the void." These spectral Industrial Workers of the World (commonly referred to as "Wobblies"), who are presumably "between" jobs, are "huddling by some campfire / in the stars" (73). As Hunt says of similar Noh characters, these ghosts appear in "settings that appear as magical as they are ordinary" (12). In Snyder's poetry, there is nothing more "ordinary" than Wobblies sitting around a campfire under the night sky. The Six Realms they inhabit, or the "territories of psychological passage" Snyder later describes in his note to "Three Worlds, Three Realms, Six Roads" in *Mountains and Rivers Without End*, are the psychological realms of existence which make up the *samsāra* "cycles" that open "On Vulture Peak."[24] We see similar apparitions described as "Bitter ghosts that kick their skulls like a ball" in "The Mountain Spirit," a poem towards the end of *Mountains and Rivers Without End*, that, like "On Vulture Peak," also addresses *samsāra* ("Ceaseless wheel of lives / ceaseless wheel of lives"). Likewise, his poem includes dialogue between the poet and a spirit figure and mentions Vimalakīrti's "one small room" (*MRWE* 142, 140, 146)—recall his "one-room shack" at the beginning of "On Vulture Peak." And, as with "On Vulture Peak," "The Mountain

Spirit" also "somewhat follows the Nō [sic] play . . . of a 'supernatural being' class
. . ." ("Notes," *MRWE* 163). With the "cheated chief" and "Wobblies" in the earlier
poem, and the poet's meeting with the female Mountain Spirit in the latter, Snyder
situates the "spirit[s] of the place" firmly within "the ancient, sacred Turtle Island
landscape" he remained "connected to" even while in Japan (*MRWE* 155).

Part VIII is of particular importance to "On Vulture Peak" in that all of
the parables addressed are presented by Buddha in two *sūtras* Snyder read in
Goddard—the *Śūraṅgama* and *Laṅkāvatāra sūtras*. As such, the penultimate
section, which deals exclusively with the concept of mind, contains some of the
most paradoxical-sounding lines of the poem. The stanza opens with a well-known
kōan question: "What can be said about a Rabbit / Solitary and without context /
Set before the mind. Was it born? / Has it horns?" (73). As in *Rinzai* interviews,
Snyder lays this conundrum out "without context . . . before the mind" to elicit an
unmediated, immediate response devoid of arbitrary phenomological conceptions
("answer! answer! why!"). An unenlightened mind deludes itself with transient
thoughts which are no more real than "hair on a tortoise, or like horns on a rabbit"
(the *Śūraṅgama Sūtra*, Goddard 121). Furthermore, "If things are not born of being
and non-being, but are simply manifestations of mind itself, they have no reality,
no self-nature: – they are like the horns of a hare, a horse, a donkey, a camel"
(*Laṅkāvatāra Sūtra*, Goddard 296). These fantastical animal images are often used
in Buddhism to distinguish between the deluded and awakened mind—the images
themselves falling on the side of delusion like birth and death.

The stanza continues to explore this concept with a line reminiscent of the
"1st Chorus" of Kerouac's "Desolation Blues": "we walk around clung / To earth /
Like beetles with big brains / Ignorant of where we are now" (*Book of Blues* 117).
In Snyder's version we see "Dream people walking around / In dream town" (73).
Indeed, we are "Dream people" "[i]gnorant of where we are now," according to
Mahāyāna philosophy, because all phenomena are empty; it has no "thingness" once
it is divested from the realm of the perceiving dualist mind. The next three lines
take this dream notion back to the imaginary city of the Gandharvas, a parable of
emptiness and delusion discussed in the *Laṅkāvatāra Sūtra*. Snyder first addressed
the imaginary city in "Burning 12" of *Myths & Texts*; here he quotes himself almost
verbatim:

> –the city of the Gandharvas–
>
> not a real city, only the
>
> –memory of a city– (47).

As Buddha tells Mahamati, "The city appears as in a vision owing to [people's] attachment to the memory of a city preserved in the mind as a seed. . . ." Likewise, people cling "to the memory of erroneous speculations and doctrines accumulated since beginningless time . . . such ideas as oneness and otherness [and] being and non-being. . ."(Goddard 280). Kerouac also addresses this imaginary city in a brief *gatha* in "Various Little Pomes," saying, "My dream of a / horrible city is / individual discrimination / – the actual / city is universal mind" (*Pomes All Sizes* 48). In this imaginary city, then, there are no questions of birth and death because there is no question about the city's reality, as in turn there is no question of our birth and death in Mahāyāna philosophy. The parable tells us when things are seen as they truly are, there is no discrimination, no individual self-nature.

The final three lines of the stanza, in the form of a quote which almost sounds like it comes from Shakespeare, is also from the *Lankāvatāra Sūtra*: "'The mind dances like the dancer / The intellect's the jester / The senses seem to think the world's a stage–'" (73). The paraphrase is conceptually off, though, and one is left wondering why Snyder includes it in quotation marks. In explaining the "Mind System" to his disciple Mahamati, Buddha says in the *Lankavatara Sutra*, "The discriminating-mind is a dancer and a magician with the objective world as his stage. Intuitive-mind is the wise jester who travels with the magician and reflects upon his emptiness and transiency. Universal Mind keeps the record and knows what must be and what may be" (Goddard 307). As laid out by Buddha, the intellect ("discriminating-mind") pirouettes to whatever tunes come its way; it is a "magician" in that it creates something out of nothing, such as imaginary cities and horns on a rabbit. Snyder, though, assigns the role of the intellect to the "jester" who, according to Buddha, should be the opposite, nondualistic "intuitive-mind." It is interesting that Snyder uses a simile here for the mind rather than a metaphor as in the original. Doing so calls attention to the functioning of the discriminating-mind in that the very act of thinking in terms of similes indicates discrimination, not intuition. That is, something is *like* something else; it is not what it is in and of itself. Snyder's version of the intellect (the jester) would lack the "wise" reflectivity of intuition; it would not be able to grasp "emptiness and transiency." Perhaps that is his point, though: the "skolars" cannot separate their "symbolic knowledge" (the intellectual discriminating-mind) "& what happens to them . . . direct like" (intuitive-mind),[25] thus hindering their path to "Universal Mind." Concluding the analogy, Buddha says, "Getting rid of the discriminating-mind removes the cause of all error" (307).

Neatly sewing his Mahāyāna *sutra* together in Part IX, Snyder ends it as it began, employing rhyme, meter, alliteration, and assonance, closing the poetic *sanzen* session with the noble silence of the tomb: "For forty years the Buddha begged his bread / And all those years said nothing, so he said, / & Vulture Peak is silent as a tomb" (73). This silence on the part of the Buddha refers to the fact that he is said to have claimed not to have preached a single word in the forty-nine years of his enlightened life, for even buddhas and patriarchs find it difficult to put the absolute in words. Towards the end of the *Vimalakīrti Sūtra*, for example, the aged host asks his guests how one enters into the "gate of nondualism." Thirty one *bodhisattvas* try intelligently and creatively to answer his question, but finally Mañjuśhrī, the last to answer, replies: "'To my way of thinking, all dharmas are without words, without explanations, without purport, without cognition, removed from all questions and answers. In this way one may enter the gate of nondualism." Mañjuśhrī then turns the question back to Vimalakīrti, who "remained silent and did not speak a word" (110). The silence of truth can only be found in absolute *samādhi* where there is no-thing, not even the *dharma*; where subject and object become one as habitual modes of thinking fall away "silent as a tomb."

As with the *Vimalakīrti Sūtra*, the lessons of "On Vulture Peak" are ambiguous, deliberately challenging, often humorous, and seemingly illogical; the poem leaves no conceptual traces, moving from one thought to the next unencumbered, while at the same time leaving ideas for deeper consideration. In it we see both Snyder's interest in the more performative forms he was experiencing in Japan, as well as the genesis for *Mountains and Rivers Without End*. The latter point is of particular import to Snyder studies because in "On Vulture Peak" we not only see Snyder's experimentation with non-Western artistic forms, but we also see a set of defining characteristics that can be concisely pointed to when trying to summarize the poem, a "privilege" seldom allowed readers of Snyder due to the difficulty of trying to pin down the heteroglossic riprap of Indian, East Asian, Amerindian, and backwoods cultural references, philosophies, and poetic styles prominent in most of his work. In reading the earlier poem as a trailhead leading down the path of *Mountains and Rivers Without End*, we are privy to Snyder's journeyman work with *shih* and *sūtra* forms, his early allusions to complex Buddhist concepts such as the Six Realms, *samsāra*, and *shūnyatā* that later show up in "The Mountain Spirit" and "Finding the Space in the Heart" (a poem also begun in 1956). We also see a certain playfulness and self-deprecation which was, perhaps, a conscientious humbling of self in the face of completing *Myths & Texts* and beginning the more complex and challenging *Mountains and Rivers Without End*, which would hold his attention for the next forty years. As Anthony Hunt asks at the beginning of *Genesis, Structure, and Meaning in Gary Snyder's* Mountains and Rivers Without End, "Where, among the events of the past, did diverse flows of energy come together to culminate in the making of a significant lifetime?" (1). If we indeed recognize that Snyder's mature "lifetime" work culminates with *Mountains and Rivers Without End*, a poem he calls a "sort of sūtra – an extended poetic, philosophic, and mythic narrative," then we must see the initial "flows of energy" of its "genesis" in "On Vulture Peak" (*MRWE*

158). Thus, in Snyder's own words, we can say that reading this early *sūtra* "will not only integrate and stabilize, it will break open ways out of the accustomed habits of perception and allow one to slip into different possibilities . . . [and] further new angles of insight" when reading his magnum opus ("What Poetry Did in China" 92–93).

I would like to thank Gary Snyder for permission to include selections from his unpublished correspondence with Philip Whalen and Joanne Kyger, as well as Norman Fischer of the Philip Whalen Estate. Thanks also to Gay Walker, Special Collections Librarian at Reed College; Tony Power, Curator, Contemporary Literature Collection, Simon Fraser University; and Daryl Morrison, Head of Special Collections, General Library, UC Davis. Bows of gratitude also extended to Joseph Harrington and Stanley Lombardo of the University of Kansas for their insightful suggestions and encouragement, and especially Nancy Grace and John Whalen-Bridge who helped this article find its form in emptiness.

Notes

[1] Gary Snyder, letter to Philip Whalen, March 8, 1957. Philip Glen Whalen Papers, Special Collections and Archives Manuscript Collections, Eric V. Hauser Memorial Library, Reed College. The following fall Allen Ginsberg referred to "On Vulture Peak" as a "drunk squiggling note from Vulture Peak" when Snyder sent him a copy in 1958. Ginsberg, who was unfamiliar with the setting of Snyder's poem ("By the way what's Vulture Peak a place, anyplace I know of?"), told him that he did not "dig [the] rhymed parts so much" (Morgan 25). What differentiates "On Vulture Peak" from Ginsberg's later "Vulture Peak: Gridhakuta Hill," and Whalen and Kerouac's poetry discussed here for that matter, is that rather than deal with the mind as individual perceiving object, Snyder's poetic *sūtra* deals with the larger concept of mind from a nondualistic perspective.

[2] Jann Garitty and Gary Snyder, e-mail to author, May 22, 2009.

[3] Gary Snyder, letter to Philip Whalen, March 8, 1957, Philip Whalen Papers, Reed College.

[4] As Snyder says in the poem following "On Vulture Peak," some *bodhisattvas* ". . . cheer and wave and levitate / And pass out lunch on Vulture Peak /

Enlightening gardens, parks, & pools" ("The Bodhisattvas," *Left Out in the Rain* 74).

[5]The historical Vulture Peak is near the ancient city of Rajgiriha and is where many of the most influential Mahāyāna discourses were delivered, such as the *Śūrangama, Heart,* and *Lotus sutras.*

[6]All quotes from "On Vulture Peak" come from *Left Out in the Rain: New Poems 1947–1985* (New York: North Point, 1997), 70–73.

[7]From "Hojoki": "The waterfall is muffled, / and my ten foot square hut lies / In the abysm of a sea / Of sibilant quiet"; from "Empty Mirror": "I sit / In my ten foot square hut. / The birds sing." (*The Complete Poems of Kenneth Rexroth* 285 and 321 respectively). Gary Snyder, letter to Philip Whalen, March 16, 1954, Philip Whalen Papers, Reed College.

[8]As Snyder said years later in "The Etiquette of Freedom," Vimalakīrti was "the legendary Buddhist layman . . . who taught that by directly intuiting our condition in the actually existing world we realize that we have had nothing from the beginning" (*The Practice of the Wild* 23).

[9]See Katsuki Sekida, *Two Zen Classics*: The Gateless Gate *and* The Blue Cliff Records.

[10]Gary Snyder, letter to Philip Whalen, May 17, 1957, Philip Whalen Papers, Reed College.

[11]Peter Abelard, a twelfth-century philosopher-theologian, sought a position as tutor in the house of Parisian canon Fulbert, whose niece, Heloise, was in his charge. Abelard seduced and impregnated Heloise, and against Heloise's wishes, the two wed in secret. When the union was announced, Heloise denied it and fled to a convent, prompting her uncle to think that Abelard wanted nothing more to do with her. Abelard was summarily castrated. Snyder probably became acquainted with Abelard while reading Kenneth Rexroth's 1944 long poem "The Phoenix and the Tortoise" ["Abelard crying for that girl"] (*Collected* 255).

[12]Kerouac's recollection of the event in *The Dharma Bums*: "[W]e borrowed Sean's jalopy and drove about a hundred miles up the seacoast to an isolated beach where we picked mussels right of the washed rocks of the sea and smoked them in a big woodfire covered with seaweed. We had wine and bread and cheese and Psyche spent the whole day lying on her stomach in her jeans and sweater, saying nothing. . . . There were natural caves on that beach where Japhy had once brought big parties of people and had organized naked bonfire dances" (137–138).

[13]Jack Kerouac to Gary Snyder, May 21, 1957 (*Selected Letters: 1957–1969*). Years later Whalen recalled that they "used to go down to Muir Beach years ago to gather mussels off the rocks. We'd build a bonfire, put seaweed on the

fire to steam the mussels. We'd eat them, then jump up and down in the waves and have fun." Philip Whalen, *Beneath a Single Moon: Buddhism in Contemporary American Poetry* (Boston: Shambhala, 1991. 331).

[14]Ray describes Neuri in *The Dharma Bums*: "[T]hey were all secretly jealous of Japhy's favorite doll Psyche, who came the following weekend real cute in jeans and a little white collar falling over her black turtleneck sweater and a tender little body and face. Japhy had told me he was a bit in love with her himself. But he had a hard time convincing her to make love, so he had to get her drunk, once she got drinking she couldn't stop" (137). According to Bill Morgan's *The Selected Letters of Allen Ginsberg and Gary Snyder*, "at one point Snyder hoped to have a relationship with [Neuri], but nothing ever came of it" (4 fn 2). Whalen set Snyder's mind at ease concerning his prospects with Neuri in a letter written one month after the latter's departure for Kyoto on May 6, 1956, by telling him that "Nobody, but nobody has got Neuri." As the letter further indicates, Neuri was there, along with Michael McClure, Whalen, and others, to see Snyder board ship for Kyoto. Philip Whalen, letter to Gary Snyder, March 23, 1957. Gary Snyder Papers, D-050, Department of Special Collections, General Library, University of California, Davis.

[15]The *Lankāvatāra Sūtra* is a "Mahāyāna *sūtra* that stresses the inner enlightenment that does away with all duality and is raised above all distinctions. . . . In the sūtra is also found the view that words are not necessary for the transmission of the teaching" (*SDBZ* 125).

[16]The *Lankāvatāra Sūtra* (Goddard 283).

[17]Gary Snyder, letter to Philip Whalen, November 20, 1953, Philip Whalen Papers, Reed College.

[18]Zen Master Engo (1063–1135) added introductory comments to each *kōan* in *The Blue Cliff Records* nearly a century after Setchō (980–1052), the original compiler, wrote his accompanying explanatory verses for each *kōan*.

[19]Philip Whalen, letter to Gary Snyder, March 23, 1957, Gary Snyder Papers, University of California, Davis.

[20]Title of Kerouac poem found in *Pomes All Sizes*, 48–50.

[21]For Snyder's visit to the site, see "X. Bodh Gaya" (*Passage Through India*, 47–53).

[22]"A big fat woman like Ma Rainey was standing there with her legs outspread howling out a tremendous sermon in a booming voice that kept breaking from speech to blues-singing music . . ." (*Dharma Bums* 86).

[23]Gary Snyder, letter to Joanne Kyger, November 9 1959, Gary Snyder fonds, Simon Fraser University.

[24]The Six Realms are divided into three upper (fortunate) and three lower (unfortunate) states. The former are made up of celestial beings, evil spirits,

and human beings; the latter consists of hell-beings, hungry ghosts, and animals. The six realms are not thought of as divided between the worldly and heavenly, but rather are considered concrete states of existence determined by one's karma.

[25]Gary Snyder, letter to Philip Whalen, November 20, 1953, Philip Whalen Papers, Reed College.

Works Cited

Conze, Edward. *Buddhist Thought in India: Three Phases of Buddhist Philosophy.* London: George Allen & Unwin, 1962. Print.

Fa-Hien. *A Record of Buddhistic Kingdoms, Being an Account by the Chinese Monk Fa-Hien of his Travels in India and Ceylon (A.D. 339–414) in Search of the Buddhist Books of Discipline.* Trans. and Ann. James Legge. Oxford: Clarendon, 1886. Print.

Gifford, Barry and Lawrence Lee. *Jack's Book: An Oral Biography of Jack Kerouac.* 1978. New York: Thunder Mouth's, 1994. Print.

Goddard, Dwight. *A Buddhist Bible.* 1932. Intro. Robert Aitken. Boston: Beacon, 1994. Print.

Gray, Timothy. *Gary Snyder and the Pacific Rim: Creating Countercultural Community.* U of Iowa P, 2006. Print.

Hunt, Anthony. *Genesis, Structure, and Meaning in Gary Snyder's* Mountains and Rivers Without End. Nevada: U of Nevada P, 2004. Print.

Kerouac, Jack. "Alone on a Mountaintop." 1958. *Lonesome Traveler: A Novel.* 1960. New York: Grove, 1989. 118–134. Print.

---. *Book of Blues.* 1956. New York: Penguin, 1995. Print.

---. *The Dharma Bums.* 1958. New York: Penguin, 2006. Print.

---. *Jack Kerouac: Selected Letters, 1957–1969.* Ed. Ann Charters. New York: Penguin, 1999. Print.

---. *Pomes All Sizes.* Pocket Poets No. 48. San Francisco: City Lights, 1992. Print.

---. *Mexico City Blues.* 1959. New York: Grove, 1990. Print.

Martin, Julia. "Coyote–Mind: An Interview with Gary Snyder." *Tri Quarterly* 79 (Fall 1990): 148–172. Print.

---. "Seeing a Corner of the Sky in Gary Snyder's *Mountains and Rivers Without End.*" *Western American Literature* 40.1 (April 2005): 55–87. Print.

Rexroth, Kenneth. *The Complete Collected Poems of Kenneth Rexroth.* Eds. Sam Hamill and Bradford Morrow. Port Townsend, Washington: Copper Canyon, 2004. Print.

Sekida, Katsuki, ed. *Two Zen Classics*: The Gateless Gate *and* The Blue Cliff
    Records. A. V. Grimstone Ed. and Intro. Boston: Shambhala, 2005. Print.
Snyder, Gary. "On Vulture Peak." *Left Out in the Rain: New Poems 1947 –1985*.
    New York: North Point, 1997. 70–73. Print.
---. *Mountains and Rivers Without End*. Washington, D.C.: Counterpoint,
    1996. Print.
---. *Myths & Texts*. 1960. New York: New Directions, 1978. Print.
---. *Passage Through India: An Expanded and Illustrated Edition*. 1983.
    Washington, DC: Shoemaker and Hoard, 2007. Print.
---. "What Poetry Did in China." *A Place in Space: Ethics, Aesthetics, and
    Watersheds*. Washington, D.C.: Counterpoint, 1995. 91–93. Print.
Spence, Lewis. *The Myths of the North American Indians*. 1914. Mineola, New
    York: Dover, 1989. 282–285. Print.
Watson, Burton. Trans. and Glossary. the *Vimalakīrti Sūtra*. New York: Columbia
    UP, 1997. Print.
Whalen, Philip. *Beneath a Single Moon: Buddhism in Contemporary American
    Poetry*. Eds. Kent Johnson and Craig Pauleninch. Intro. by Gary Snyder.
    Boston, Massachusetts: Shambhala, 1991, 331. Print.
---. "Zen Poet: Interview with Yves Le Pellec." *Off the Wall: Interviews with
    Philip Whalen*. Ed. Donald Allen. Bolinas, California: Four Seas Foundation,
    1978. 50–67. Print.

John Wieners in the Matrix of Massachusetts Institutions: A Psychopoeticgeography

Maria Damon

Guy Debord and the Situationists, writing and mayhemming around Paris at approximately the same time as John Wieners was emerging into poetic mayhem in Boston/North Carolina/San Francisco/Boston (1950s–1960s), made a poetics out of urban wanderings that valorized the underside and the unexpected as the wanderer contemplates her relationship between her own marginality and the staid institutions, underground rivulets of subversion, seams, crossovers, intersections, and minutiae of interactivity between the organic and the inorganic that comprise a cityscape. They deliberately sought to distort and alter such venerable mappings as the famous *Plan de Paris* that dictate and reinforce invisible and visible barriers between neighborhoods, placing instead the descriptive and experiential power of city life in the hands of the wanderer. Their contemporary online presence, Bureau of Public Secrets, offers this definition/how-to focused on the term *dérive* (drift):

> If one or more persons during a certain period drop their relations, their work and leisure activities, and all their other usual motives for movement and action, and let themselves be drawn by the attractions of the terrain and the encounters they find there. Chance is a less important factor in this activity than one might think: from a *dérive* point of view cities have psychogeographical contours, with constant currents, fixed points and vortexes that strongly discourage entry into or exit from certain zones.

> But the dérive includes both this letting-go and its necessary contradiction: the domination of psychogeographical variations by the knowledge and calculation of their possibilities. In this latter regard, ecological science, despite the narrow social space to which it limits itself, provides psychogeography with abundant data.[1]

Earlier than Bachelard's phenomenological *The Poetics of Space*, which appeared first in 1958 and thus coincides with both Beat and Situationist International eras, the French (Proust, Balzac) and the German (Jew)s (Simmel, Benjamin) had long been exploring the poetics of large cities, but other than a few rhapsodic passages from Walt Whitman, one could make a salient argument that, along with African American novelists such as Richard Wright, Ralph Ellison, and James Baldwin— and the proto-Beat Jack London—the Beats were among the first U.S. writers who took on the city as a serious site of ambiguous magic in which subjectivity could undertake its own experiments and undergo those imposed upon it. In the discussion that follows, I focus on John Wieners, although I don't want to reify the term *Beat* or to make broad claims for inclusion, exclusion, or tendency. Wieners is the center here, with *Beat* remaining an occasional reference point, sometimes appropriate and sometimes constraining.

The *dérive* beautifully describes how Wieners—part scholarship student/dropout, part junkie, part working-class boy on an upwardly mobile path who jumped the tracks—became a drifter of sorts, initially in San Francisco, as he describes in *707 Scott Street,* his journal from the late 1950s–early 1960s, with the trademark syntactical quirkiness that became a major principle in his writing:

> … the city is a fabled labyrinth, and sustenance there is subterranean. Life on the surface regiment, ordered mechanized the people move as robots, displaying neither love nor fear...At night when there is only one eye and the police prowl as roaches thru every layer. Searching like poets every face, gait, manner of dress. Under the streetlights only the eccentric stands out garbed in the costume of his game.…

> How long? Two years at it and I am worn out. My teeth half gone at 25. A racking cough all night. Little food and sour stomach in the morning unless drugs, not to deaden one, but open doors for the fantasy world. Sur-real is the only way to endure the real we find heaped up in our cities. (53–54)

For Wieners, anomie, anonymity, and alienation are constant themes, though unlike some Beat writers he does not sneer at mainstream commercial culture from a position of superior insight, nor does he rail with "Howl"'s indignation. Rather he seems to feel his frailty—his certainty of mortality and the unglamorous aspects of his abject conditions—in the face of that culture's ravaging of his body and mind, fearing, with good reason, for his safety and sanity. Later in Boston, where he did have fixed addresses, his compromised mental health put him in several places at once, drifting and oscillating among them without losing his lyric gifts. *707 Scott Street*'s poems and prose about scoring drugs, scoring (or not) sex, feeling abandoned, getting high, wandering the neighborhoods and the business districts, evoke an ethereal, disoriented, anguished sense of solitude, loneliness, and a peculiar kind of (un)belonging in relation to urban San Francisco and its demimondaine institutions (cheap ethnic restaurants, boarding houses, cafés, all-night diners, cruisy intersections) as well as business districts and bookstores, in which alienation and the longing to undo it become normative if never comfortable states. But however acute and poignant these passages are, Wieners' much longer sojourn in Boston, in his home state of Massachusetts, marks the period in which his relationship to and placement within civic institutions achieves expression in a prolonged *cri-de-coeur*; a sophisticated yet raw series of inscriptions on the body of his poetry that, in their fragility and lyricism, form a hymn to and bitter protest against this net of entanglements and subjections that effected his subjectification. In Boston, where he lived from 1960 (aside from brief sojourns in NYC and Buffalo) until his death in 2002, his relationship to the city became an integral part of his experience with mental illness and alcoholism (leading to brushes with medical institutions) and nocturnal cruising for love/sex under a repressive and punishing regime. The early period also coincides with the rise of the gay liberation movement and Wieners' participation therein as well as a certain affinity with the denizens of, if not outright incarceration in, penal institutions, the whole fabric of his interior and outer life shot through with loneliness, solitude, and yearning both fleshly and spiritual (see, for example, "To Sleep Alone")[2]. Indeed British poet Keston Sutherland makes the astonishing but entirely credible assertion that "[n]o poet in English was ever so destitute of a world as John Wieners." [3]

The Boston that Wieners inhabited was a rigidly bifurcated city. In 1973, the south and north slopes of Beacon Hill perfectly embodied the stark class divisions marking the city. On one side was the august, golden-domed Massachusetts State Capitol, designed and built in 1798 by Charles Bulfinch on land owned by the powerful John Hancock, famously a signer of the Declaration of Independence, president of the Second Continental Congress, governor of Massachusetts, and one of the primary economic sponsors of the American Revolutionary War. In other words, Hancock could be said to epitomize this side of the Hill as an historically important, moneyed and propertied figure, and indeed to exemplify the long history of what appears to be a contemporary phenomenon: the merger of personal or corporate wealth with public political influence. As one of the first thirteen colonies and the site of some of the oldest European settlements in what became the United States, the Commonwealth of Massachusetts has had ample time to exploit and accumulate the resources of the New World and traditionally has had close cultural ties with England through its quasi-aristocracy, the so-called Boston Brahmins, descendants of Mayflower passengers, and signers of the Declaration of Independence. These scions of New England aristocracy built their homes on the south slope and top of Beacon Hill, Louisburg Square, and Mt. Vernon Street. This side of the hill, specifically the front grounds of the State House, features statuary of many historic figures, including Mary Dyer, who was hanged for being a Quaker, and Anne Hutchinson, who, as every schoolchild raised in New England knows, was forced to leave Boston for her heretical views and her religious leadership, which threatened the orthodoxy in multiple ways. Does Boston contradict itself?

Very well, then. According to Jim Dunn, a close friend for the last few years of Wieners' life, Wieners rarely frequented this side of the hill.

On the backside, or north slope, of Beacon Hill, the demimondaines of drugs, art, the gay underworld, and petty crime made their homes. Joy Street, where Wieners lived for the last thirty years of his life, traverses Mt. Vernon and runs down this shadow side of Beacon Hill. The area "behind the state capitol," to cite one of his book titles, terminates at Cambridge Street, site of the side-by-side Charles Street (also known as Suffolk County) Jail and the Massachusetts General Hospital (also known as MGH), two institutions as iconic as, if far less glamorous than, the State House and the Boston Gardens and Commons (despite the latter's nighttime transformation into queer cruising grounds).[4] It would not be going too far to point out that if one side of the Hill has a history of great wealth and private ownership by the person whose name has become metonymic in the United States for "signature," authenticating and authoritative, then the north slope embraces anonymity, poverty, transience, non-ownership, and a tenancy aching with squalor and neglect. Boston, famous for its segregation as well as its status as the "cradle of liberty," is riven with such juxtapositions and dissymmetries.

This duality likewise marks John Wieners and his work. Working-class Irish Catholic, educated by Jesuits at Boston College High School and then Boston College itself, convolutedly erudite and streetwise (though never streetwise enough) by necessity, abjected through class origins, drug addictions and mental illness, patrician in his range of high literary and cultural allusions and sensitivities; and disgusted alternately by the philistinism of his parents and their milieu and by the rigidity and preciosity of highbrow institutions, Wieners inhabited—and performed—in particularly intensified form the purgatory of the in-between that marked upwardly mobile white male youth of the 1950s. On the one hand, he chafed at the trappings of upward mobility imposed on him at in high school and college ("I wasn't crazy about it," he averred to an interviewer in the 1990s, although this could be because he got "worked over a couple of times. . . coming down Commonwealth Avenue" rather than an objection to the uplift project imposed on him).[5] On the other hand, he submitted a biographical sketch for *The New American Poetry* (1960) that indicates his status as "the descendant of an old Irish family, the Laffans, prominent at the time of Elizabeth" (Brady 44). Which location or direction to choose: inside or out? Inside or outside of which worlds? Upward or downward movement? He always chose both, or they chose him, and it was a bumpy ride indeed, since they forced him to live out these contradictions stretched to breaking points again and again, and also forced him literally to inhabit this matrix of institutions and streets with only his *NERVES* (1971) to go on, a quivering, hypersensitive bundle of raw affect.[6] A poet of brokenhearted cruising and exquisite loneliness, he made Boston his backdrop, his imaginary and his actually existing ground of being. His texts, like his person, perform powerfully, in Lauren Berlant's words, a "falling apart without ceasing to exist."[7]

And of course, the duality I speak of somewhat simplistically—"raw and sophisticated"—undergirds Beat writing itself. The Marriage of Heaven and Hell—possibly the the archtypal trope of the Beats, borrowed from Blake—is not "marriage" in the culinary sense, that is, a smooth, transcendent blend of complements that creates a new thing altogether. Rather it is a marriage in the 1950s sense, an uneasy and oppressive yoking of two entities assumed to have nothing in common and to whom vastly different social power and roles are meted. Indeed, one could consider the Beat ethos to embody the "unequal binaries" so prevalent in pre-deconstructive thinking as to demonstrate just how much post-structuralist thought reacted against the conditions enabling the aesthetics it often praises. The Beat marriage of the street and the library, the needle and the pen, ornate Latinates and jive vernacular derives its jolting lyrical pathos from this yoking of dissimilars, but about each particularity there is much more to be said. Wieners' work, like that of most writers we can refer to by convention, chronology and disposition to be *Beat*, is much more.

"A Dérive With Psychogeographical Contours"

I choose 1973 as a central moment in the above discussion of Wieners in Boston because that year marks the moment at which my biography intersects, however tangentially, with his. His Boston touches mine at angular adjacency, and in the Beat spirit of hewing closely to the personal and its transpersonal potentials, I intertwine our histories, as the streets of Boston on which he lived have a particularly sharp place in my psychogeographic memory. Returning to this internal place helps to focus insight.

In July 1973, Wieners was living at 44 Joy Street, that street that runs down the back side of the Hill to the Charles Street Jail and Mass. General Hospital, two massive institutions that embody different aspects of human misery. In July 1973, freshly graduated from the exclusive and stultifying Miss Winsor's School in Boston, I walked down Joy Street every day in a state far from joy, from Mt. Vernon Street, where I was staying with some arch-patrician school friends whose French cousin was in town (their mother thought I'd like to work on my French, as I was headed to Paris for a scholarship year that September), to the MGH where my father, a first-generation Russian-Jewish Bostonian with Ivy League credentials (B.A., Ph.D., M.D.), was dying of lymphoma. Every day I traveled down the class continuum from eccentric, old-money wealth, toward the MGH and the jail, an overcrowded holding tank where mostly black men, deprived of their rights while awaiting trial, could be glimpsed on occasion from across the wall playing basketball in the jailhouse yard. Joy Street itself was studded with languid young men, white, black and brown, in undershirts, torn jeans and colorful bandanas, moving slowly in the crushing heat, sitting on stoops or hanging around doorways, waiting for their man. A very sheltered and un-streetwise eighteen-year-old, I scarcely dared raise my eyes from the sweltering sidewalk asphalt to take in these wondrous ambassadors from another reality, who nonetheless left a vivid impression: I intuited rather than wholly gazed upon them. I knew Joy Street was important although I didn't know that John Wieners made his home here, somewhat older than these youths burning into my peripheral vision but not too old for desire (though his way was mostly a "wished for love" even among the nearby heavy-cruising grounds of the Boston Public Gardens and the Commons [Wieners, 1986, 299]) nor, of course, did I have any idea that forty years later I'd be placing, in a scholarly essay, Wieners and his history along the social, emotional and psychological continuum whose extremes are marked by Mt. Vernon Street and the State Capitol, Charles Street Jail and the MGH, with a special detour to the Taunton State Hospital, a psychiatric hospital in which Wieners and his father both spent time as inmates.[8] I knew I was a writer, and that my interests tended toward people *like* John Wieners, but I didn't know about John Wieners. Some of the institutions he dealt with, though founded with reformist optimism and paternalistically benevolent intentions, became embodiments of historical and human wreckage, others (you know which ones) have continued to receive dollars that have allowed them to continually reinvent themselves in accordance with contemporary social needs. Indeed, the Winsor School (founded in 1885) was, as I experienced it in the 1960s and early 1970s, site of both extreme privilege and yet claustrophobic class disciplinarity, especially for those of us who were implicity or explicit part of an uplift project. Some of us "Winsor girls" were being trained for something that didn't come naturally to us.

In chronological order of their founding, then, what follows is a brief path through these institutions' histories, incorporating Wieners' history and bits of mine.

Massachusetts General Hospital

The Massachusetts General Hospital (known in its surroundings as "Mass General" or simply "MGH"), 55 Fruit Street, also, like the State House, a Bulfinch design, was built in 1811. Wieners died here in 2002. He had suffered a stroke a few days earlier in the MGH parking lot on Blossom Street, with what is believed to be an aneurism, after having attended a party with fellow gay activist and literary figure Charley Shively. "Because all those who had sufficient money were cared for at home, Massachusetts General Hospital, like most hospitals that were founded in the 19th century, was intended to care for the poor," notes the online history of Harvard University,[9] though by 1973, when I made my daily Oedipal trek down the slippery slope to the underworld of indefinite incarceration on the left hand and IV tubes, rampant tumors, and disinfectant on the right, it offered medical care to people like my father, who was, while hardly indigent, a chronically underpaid lecturer at Harvard, as well as Wieners, who could be said to be indigent, and though cared for by his family, carried no identification when he collapsed. His identity was tracked down by a persistent social worker who found a pharmacy receipt in Wieners's pocket that was traced to his cousin Walter, whose name appeared on the pharmacy account. And the MGH played a role in Wieners's daily life as well, for both social and health reasons. As his friend Jim Dunn writes in a reminiscence of a Wieners-centric Boston,

> Joy Street, originally called Belknap Lane, named after the Colonial Apothecary, Dr. John Joy, with its history of livery stables, was his home …. Once a week we would meet together to share the same routine. First, we would visit the lobby of Massachusetts General Hospital. Wieners' cousin Walter had set up a disbursement plan for a stipend of cash to be delivered by a male nurse, Brian, who was close friends with Walter. Wieners and I would wait patiently each week in the busy lobby of MGH amidst the flow of humanity, for Brian to arrive with an envelope. Often we'd have lunch in the hospital cafeteria. A few times we would walk up the steps of the original MGH building to visit the Ether Dome [Boston's surgical amphitheatre, site, in 1846, of the first public surgery with anesthesia].[10]

Charles Street Jail

In addition to the MGH, Wieners would have had, as a daily presence in his life, a view of the Charles Street Jail, or, as it is formally known, the Suffolk County Jail, built in 1851. This is a terrifying Quincy granite monolith thoroughly blackened by age and city pollution. Planning started in 1843, with a design for a 220-cell building by architect Gridley James Fox Bryant and input from prison reform advocate Reverend Louis Dwight that suggested that the so-called "Auburn plan"—that is, one prisoner per 8'x10' cell—be followed. However, by the 1970s, it was notoriously overcrowded and inhumane, with at least two prisoners sharing each cell. A judge who had apocryphally spent one night there in 1964 recommended that it be shut down—the shutdown was made law in 1973— though that closure was delayed, and inmates continued to be incarcerated there until the 1990s, because no alternative site could be found for them.[11] The jail housed, in wretched conditions, people who were as yet innocent before the law, that is, in a pre-trial status. This is not unusual; because a jail population is presumed to be transient—the assumption, often misplaced, is that trials will be held in a timely fashion—these liminal spaces are rarely if ever targeted for serious reform. Although he never spent time in jail or prison, John Wieners lived in close proximity to it in body and soul. For instance, in "A Poem for Vipers," he writes of a drug deal tinged with eroticism:

> I sit in Lees. At 11:40 PM with
> Jimmy the pusher. He teaches me
> Ju Ju. Hot on the table before us
> shrimp foo yong, rice and mushroom
> chow yuke. Up the street under the wheels
> of a strange car is his stash—The ritual.
> We make it. And have made it.
> For months now together after midnight.
> Soon I know the fuzz will
> interrupt, will arrest Jimmy and
> I shall be placed on probation. The poem
> does not lie to us. We lie under
> its law, alive in the glamour of this hour
> able to enter into the sacred places
> of his dark people, who carry secrets
> glassed in their eyes and hide words
> under the coats of their tongue.
>   (*SP* 28)

Acknowledging that the man of color faces harsher legal retribution than he, he is still, as a gay man and as a pot smoker (viper), vulnerable to punishment. And he writes later of his fears that impulse will "land me in the hospital, a total wreck, without / memory again; or worse still, behind bars" ("Acts of Youth," *SP* 62). "A Poem for Vipers" links homoerotic miscegenation, speaking, and the alterity of both race and altered consciousness through oral imagery (the word *viper* as a term for marijuana smoker came from the sound of inhalation similarity to a snake's hiss; the emphasis on lying and truth; the coated tongue's concealment of secret, initiatory words) with the constant danger of surveillance and inevitability of capture. Jimmy is serpentine, the offerer of illicit knowledge to Wieners the innocent, who then becomes complicit, though, as Adam and Eve are to Satan, fallen and in hope of redemption rather than outright Other and damned. The "oral transmission" of Jimmy's "dark people" and their "[coated/coded] tongue" meanwhile also contrasts with the hyper-literate Wieners, though the former is clearly coded as more potent both sexually and in terms of knowledge both worldly and otherworldly. The system of "ju ju" (West African charms, spells, and fetish objects) contrasts implicitly with Wieners's Irish Catholic schooling, but both intersect in the "ritual," the erotic transmission of illegal substances, illegal desire, and illegal language where the more marginal Other re-schools the relative naïf in magic. Where is "the poem" in this? Pun for pomme, the apple of wisdom and sin that's transmitted from Jimmy to John? More likely in the "glamour of that hour," in which glamour draws from its etymological past to signify both magic spells (identified with Jimmy, the dark person) and scholarship (identified with Wieners).

The two, binarized in true Beat fashion, meet in "the [truth-telling] poem," under which the lovers lie and lie, joining the whispered seductions of (magical) illusion with the rigidities and mysteries of the Church. In other words, "the poem" becomes a sort of God-term, in Kenneth Burke's taxonomy, that overarches and reconciles sacred and profane, intuitive mysticism and learned scholarship, and black and white lovers. "A Poem for Vipers" is thus, among other things, an exemplar of that problematic Negrophilia (or "romantic racism") that has been the target of critiques of Beat writing, especially, but by no means exclusively, in Kerouac's novels. However, rather than level a facile charge that Weiners is "slumming" with exploitive motives, it may be more relevant to note the ways in which, through a *car*nal and mystical encounter, he puts himself in proximity to in*car*ceration. As a subject with one foot in the straight world and one in the demi-monde, this proximity was a constant in Wieners' life, from the anxieties plaguing this poem to his own internments in psychiatric institutions to his geographic closeness to the Charles Street Jail. While Wieners can impute to the powers of "the poem" the ability to synthesize otherwise untenable contrasts, lived experience demonstrated no such resolution.

And as Boston area denizens are well aware, the most biting and corrosive irony of a neoliberal marriage of heaven and hell in a post-dialectical age is the following: the Charles Street Jail, after having been emptied of inmates and shut down in 1990, became the property of the Mass General Hospital, which sold it to developers, who in turn spent five years and $150 million turning it into the mega-luxurious and viciously named Liberty Hotel. Careful attention was paid to preserve the historic structure of the building while erasing the misery of its century-and-a-half's worth of occupants.

Taunton State Hospital

While never a prison inmate, Wieners, to repeat, was no stranger to other carceral institutions. Between 1960 and 1972, he spent time in the following state psychiatric hospitals, often for many months at a stretch: Medfield State Hospital (setting for a 2010 Martin Scorsese film, the psychological thriller *Shutter Island*) and Metropolitan State Hospital, both in Massachusetts; Central Islip Psychiatric Center on Long Island; and finally Taunton State Hospital, also in Massachusetts, where he composed his powerful accusation of a sadistic god, "Children of the Working Class." All of the aforementioned hospitals except Taunton have been shut down, mostly within the last two decades, and Taunton, while it is still in operation, has demolished the old Kirkbride structure that Thomas Kirkbride (1809–1883), a Philadelphia psychiatrist, designed and that gives the institution a creepy grandeur. These state psychiatric hospitals owed their mid-to-late twentieth-century decline to a series of causes: overcrowding, underfunding, changing philosophies about treatment of mental illness that led to de-institutionalization, and, most recently, privatization of medical practice, as well as the debunking of Kirkbride's architectural insights based on the belief in peace, serenity, and outside air in the form of elegant buildings structured on a system of staggered "wings" with long porches or "breezeways" flanking an administrative central point and surrounded by extensive grounds. A devout, reform-minded Quaker, Kirkbride considered elegant and restful features to be a starting point for psychiatric healing, and they became the predominant architectural model for psychiatric institutions in the United States from the 1850s to the 1990s.[12] Some of these institutions, like the jail, have been replaced by luxury condominiums, though the private McLean Hospital, affiliated with Mass General Hospital and Harvard Medical School, which has housed relatively privileged poets such as Robert Lowell, Sylvia Plath, and Anne Sexton, remains open and thriving.

Built just a few years after the Suffolk County Jail, the Taunton State Hospital (1854), originally known as the State Lunatic Hospital at Taunton, embodied some of the same principles of reformist architecture as the former, and came to share, in the twentieth-century, some of its haunted and torturous aura, an aura that seems peculiar to once-grand buildings in which one knows suffering and helplessness have been experienced. Indeed, many such hospitals (including Oregon State Hospital's use as a setting for Milos Forman's *One Flew Over the Cuckoo's Nest* based on the Ken Kesey novel), if their structures have not been completely razed, have served as sets for horror movies about haunted but still active psychiatric hospitals. Indeed it is not much of a stretch to add supernatural elements to an abandoned site already saturated with misery. Additionally, these enormous buildings are often featured in photographic essays or coffee table books about haunted sites, as an online search of "abandoned psychiatric hospitals" quickly reveals. Taunton's auratic creepiness, in particular, has been a photographer's dream.[13]

During Wieners' time in Boston, both Taunton State Hospital and the Charles Street Jail were worlds of their own, mini-hells for those too deviant for the normative socius to countenance; these persons literally could not be *faced* by their social superiors (as I could not "face" the denizens of Joy Street?) and were erased by heavy architectural sequestration in ornate-on-the-outside, sordid-on-the-inside structures tucked into (in the case of the jail) a busy downtown or (in the case of the mental institution) at the periphery. Taunton State Hospital stopped taking patients in 1975, three years after John Wieners' incarceration. However, the huge buildings stood for decades until the enormous cupola collapsed in 1999, and then in 2006 a fire demolished the remainder of the administrative building. The Kirkbride "wings" were the only remaining elements of the building, and these were dismantled in 2009. A curious undertow of controversy underlies this history: in early 2013, this terse sentence concluded the (always-a-bellwether-for-populist-sentiment-and-lore) Wikipedia entry on the institution: "The Commonwealth of Massachusetts has scheduled this hospital to shut down by 12/31/2012, and patients diverted to the new Worcester State Hospital," although the Hospital was saved and is still in operation, with forty-five beds for psychiatric patients. Significant for interest in Wieners is the observation that at the time of his incarceration conditions had deteriorated to the point that the institution was on the verge of being shut down, and that the state's treatment of the building itself, left to deteriorate for three decades, synechdochally mirrors its ambivalently negligent/fascinated regard for the inmates held there.

"Children of the Working Class," Wieners' 1972 poem written from inside Taunton, dramatizes this neglect; to some degree reflects a morbid fascination with the most abject of such poor, bare, forked animals (although he "is one of them"); and articulates the rage of the hidden-away. With auto-ethnographic dismay, Wieners protests his being surrounded by institutions in which humans are reduced to "bare life," in Giorgio Agamben's terms; that is, as if they had no human rights but only biological life. Though Agamben's primary referent is the World War II death camps and his current readers have been quick to invoke Guantanamo, equally relevant are state hospitals, holding tanks, and mental institutions in which inmates' own claims about their lives have no truth status, that is, those intended for non-[normative] subjects, the working- or underclass. In "Children of the Working Class," Wieners writes as a non-subject who is nonetheless quivering with undefended subjectivity. As a poet of bare life, the nonentity describes his condition:

> gaunt, ugly deformed
>
> broken from the womb, and horribly shriven
> at the labor of their forefathers, . . .
>
> their sordid brains don't work right,
> pinched men emaciated, piling up railroad ties and highway
> ditches

blanched women, swollen and crudely numb
ered before the dark of dawn

. . . .

 there are worse, whom you may never see, non-crucial around the
spoke, these you do, seldom
locked in Taunton State Hospital and other peon work farms
drudge from morning until night, abandoned within destitute
crevices odd clothes

. . . .

there is no hope, they locked-in key's; housed of course

 and there fed, poorly
off sooted, plastic dishes, soiled grimy silver knives and forks,
stamped Department of Mental Health spoons

. . . .

 Yes life was hard for them, much more hard than for any blo
ated millionaire, who still lives on
their hard-earned monies.

. . . .

I am one of them. I am witness
not to Whitman's vision, but instead the
poorhouses, the mad city asylums and re-
life worklines. Yes, I am witness not to
God's goodness, but his better or less scorn. (175)[14]

Perhaps most notable in this documentarian screed/scream, beyond its violent
tearing off of the veil of American democracy in which Whitman rejoiced and its
imagistic echoes of WWII forced-labor camp accounts ("pinched men emaciated,
piling up railroad ties and highway ditches"), are its formal eccentricities: staggered
and strange spellings, line breaks, and peculiar, non-idiomatic diction ("they locked-
in key's"). Andrea Brady has highlighted the significance that Wiener attributed to
errors: misspellings, typos, jammed typewriter keys, etc., in providing a clue to the

reality behind the cruel imperviousness of everyday normativity. The poet refused to amend and ameliorate these seeming mistakes, believing them to be revelatory of a truth that would otherwise be lost. This is his version of the oft-invoked Beat literary mantra "first thought best thought," though for Wieners it is more closely related to an interest in mystical/magical revelation—the errors are breaks in normative reality that allow insight into a transpersonal, metaphysical plane beyond even "unconscious" intention—than to a fetishizing of spontaneity that re-ratifies the importance of the author's personality. Just as the warped and broken souls of Taunton have subjectivities and subjecthood that must be attended to without being prettied up, a mistyped word is a spirit trying to have its fragile, ephemeral say. If we take Wieners' writing process and ethos as our guides for reading the civic architecture of Boston and its environs, the importance of such slippages as ruptures of reality in the façade of cruel normativity suggests that the rigidity of even the most well-meaning attempts to bring order to illness, addiction, insanity, and criminality are inevitably breached by the anarchic fire of the very deviations these liberal impulses seek to contain. The *dérivistes'* prizing of the underside and unexpected is emphatically in evidence in Wieners' attachment to his errata. The collision of hyper-articulate poetry and thorazined numbness disrupts the plan. Notable also is its emphasis on the spectacularly awful, the ocular affront that is oneself; the "witnessing" is also a form of internalized surveillance whereby the contemptuous God merges with the suffering inmate. A panopticon is at work, but no longer even necessary, as it has taken up residence inside the patient's psyche, structuring all of his perceptions and self-perceptions. This is true also, if less dramatically so, of the girls' school student, the medical school intern, the aspiring first-generation immigrant, the terminal cancer patient, and the drug-addicted Beat poet.

And it should be pointed out that Wieners was caught not only in a web of indifferent institutions: he hovered between also and in a matrix of self-created counter-institutions: the legendary Black Mountain College, which he attended in 1955–56, studying with Robert Duncan and Charles Olson; his own literary magazine *Measure*, which he began editing in Boston and continued for three issues into his sojourn in San Francisco; alternative Boston publications such as *Fag Rag* (founded 1971), a gay liberation journal published by a collective that made explicit links between homophobia, psychiatric abuse, racism, and other forms of institutional oppression; *Gay Community News* (founded 1973), a Boston-based national gay news journal spearheaded by Wieners' longtime friend Charley Shively; The Good Gay Poets publishing collective, also based in Boston, founded in 1972; the poet's main publisher Black Sparrow Press in Santa Barbara; the Stone Soup Gallery bookstore, tucked beneath the shadowy walls of the Charles Street Jail and next to the Mass. General Hospital, where owner Jack Powers instructed the staff to give John Wieners, a "squirrelly and impoverished Beat poet . . . , a gentle, timid soul and a veritable hermit at the time, who eschewed most human contact," whatever money he needed from the till as well as cigarettes on demand; and the informal network of family, friends and fellow poets who sustained him and whom he sustained with his generosity of spirit and intellect.[15]

A Final Dérive

Toward the end of 2013, I posted a link to the entirety of Wieners' "Children of the Working Class," from the Poetry Foundation's website, on my Facebook wall. It is a poem whose ethnographically-tinged loneliness I explored in a 2002 essay on ethnography, lyric, and divided subjectivity, before social media had completely restructured my own and many others' mode of knowledge production and distribution. Re-examining it in this new context and in this new era meant that I could contaminate my private enthusiasms almost immediately in a crucible of equally immediate response.[16] And indeed the poem was met with admiration from old Beat scholars but outrage and puzzlement from disability studies scholars, some of whom saw in it only hatred and scorn for the otherly, formed victims of poor health care policies and civic neglect. These scholars read Wieners as trying to distance himself from them in class and "ham-fisted[ly]" ableist terms. Out of this debate, a self-reflective paper by poetry and disability scholar Susan Schweik emerged, in which she examined her own ambivalences about the poem's repulsion—is its eugenicism a symptom of self-loathing, an unreflective reaction?[17] Or is the poem, notably written on May Day, a true howl of class anger that puts the revolution back in revulsion? If Wieners is really "one of them," why even say "them"? She carefully distinguishes the poem and Wieners' self-(dis)placement within it from other poems by his more canonically late-modernist (and more class-privileged) colleagues that also address either periods of internment in psychiatric hospitals (notably Lowell and Sexton) or visits to others there interned, such as the litany of "I-visited-Ezra-Pound-in-St.-Elizabeth's" poems that appear from the 1950s on. Schweik's counterpoint/supplementary concept to the *dérive* is the *ductus*, a term borrowed from medieval rhetoric to suggest the analogy between a journey through physical space and the mind's travel through a written passage, and the orderliness or disorderliness of that journey's outline/map by the writer and/or reader. Schweik, paraphrasing medievalist Mary Carrothers, writes that "ductus organizes meaning along a way or axis or sequence of spaces—for instance, through spatial or directional metaphors. Ductus is the instructions on way-finding through its space that a text gives us."[18] Schweik re-concretizes the term to turn to a reading of the space(s) of the institution, in particular the mental institution, especially when there's no way out, and reads "Children of the Working Class" in this context.

There is no way out of Wieners' text, but perhaps we don't want to escape the text any more than he ultimately wanted to escape the complexities of his beloved, familiar Boston in spite of its overdetermined class inequities and their corporeal and architectural manifestations. As noted earlier, escape comes in the form of unexpected textual malformations, if one is open to falling through their holes into other worlds rather than altered external conditions. This retreat into textual rather than social and political freedom is Wieners' version of the apolitical, post-HUAC nature of Beat resistance; the fatigue of the publicly vanquished left found new life in a spiritually charged bohemian underworld.

***

There is one area in which the stark dichotomies that Beat discourse addressed that not only remains but has become exacerbated—the area of economics, of class. As we can see from the fate of these monuments to modernity's optimism, these nineteenth-century institutions, built with reformist aspiration but like their inmates succumbing to social neglect and stigma, fade from the historical forefront or are obliterated to make room for today's very rich and are retrievable only through traces and intuitions—hauntings. And poems. The conditions that necessitated these attempts at uplift and reform come back into view exacerbated, with stark immediacy, and with them, so does the loneliness of thwarted lives. Arching over and subtending the foregoing stories of emotional isolation, the Boston immigrant (Irish, Jewish, fill in the blank) dream both gone awry and fulfilled are the institutions of Boston that held us captive and gave us some stability: the hospital, the jail, the reformist psychiatric asylum with its breezeways, elegant grounds and human wreckage, the girls' school, the Jesuit college … disciplining, punishing, protecting and destroying. Wieners transubstantiates these institutions not by portraying them as falsely redemptive or enabling, but by fracturing them through a broken psychogeographical poetry that "does not lie to us."

Appendix A

Children of the Working Class
By John Wieners

to Somes

from incarceration, Taunton State Hospital, 1972

gaunt, ugly deformed

broken from the womb, and horribly shriven
at the labor of their forefathers, if you check back
scout around grey before actual time
their sordid brains don't work right,
pinched men emaciated, piling up railroad ties and highway
ditches
blanched women, swollen and crudely numb
ered before the dark of dawn

scuttling by candlelight, one not to touch, that is, a signal panic
thick peasants after *the* attitude

at that time of their century, bleak and centrifugal
they carry about them, tough disciplines of copper Indianheads.

there are worse, whom you may never see, non-crucial around the
spoke, these you do, seldom
locked in Taunton State Hospital and other peon work farms
drudge from morning until night, abandoned within destitute
crevices odd clothes
intent on performing some particular task long has been far
removed
there is no hope, they locked-in key's; housed of course

and there fed, poorly
off sooted, plastic dishes, soiled grimy silver knives and forks,
stamped Department of Mental Health spoons
but the unshrinkable duties of any society
produces its ill-kempt, ignorant and sore idiosyncrasies.

There has never been a man yet, whom no matter how wise
can explain how a god, so beautiful he can create
the graces of formal gardens, the exquisite twilight sunsets
in splendor of elegant toolsmiths, still can yield the horror of

dwarfs, who cannot stand up straight with crushed skulls,
diseases on their legs and feet unshaven faces of men and women,
worn humped backs, deformed necks, hare lips, obese arms

distended rumps, there is not a flame shoots out could ex-
tinguish the torch of any liberty's state infection.

1907, My Mother was born, I am witness t-
o the exasperation of gallant human beings at g-
od, priestly fathers and Her Highness, Holy Mother the Church
persons who felt they were never given a chance, had n-
o luck and were flayed at suffering.

They produced children with phobias, manias and depression,
they cared little for their own metier, and kept watch upon
others, some chance to get ahead

Yes life was hard for them, much more hard than for any blo
ated millionaire, who still lives on
their hard-earned monies. I feel I shall
have to be punished for writing this,
that the omniscient god is the rich one,
cared little for looks, less for Art,
still kept weekly films close for the
free dishes and scandal hot. Some how
though got cheated in health and upon
hearth. I am one of them. I am witness
not to Whitman's vision, but instead the
poorhouses, the mad city asylums and re-
life worklines. Yes, I am witness not to
God's goodness, but his better or less scorn.

The First of May, The Commonwealth of State of Massachusetts,
1972

Charles Street Jail

Charles Street Jail

Charles Street Jail circa 1990

Massachusetts General façade

Taunton façade

Taunton after the 2006 fire

Taunton breezeway

Winsor

Notes

1. http://www.bopsecrets.org/SI/2.derive.htm.

2. Wieners, "To Sleep Alone," *Selected Poems*, Ed. Raymond Foye, Santa Barbara, California: Black Sparrow, 1986, 238: "To sleep alone / to wake alone // to walk alone / to wash alone // to write alone / to see alone // to think alone / to die alone // ," etc.

3. Keston Sutherland, "The World and John Wieners," *World Picture Journal* 7 (Autumn 2012) http://worldpicturejournal.com/WP_7/Sutherland.html.

4. John Wieners, *Behind the State Capitol: or Cincinnati Pike*. Boston. Good Gay Poets, 1975. Print.

5. "*Tenzone* Interviews John Wieners," *Tenzone 2*, reproduced in *Jacket2* https://jacket2.org/interviews/tenzone-interviews-john-wieners.

6. John Wieners, *NERVES*, London UK: TBS Book Service, 1971. Print.

7. Lauren Berlant, "Biopolitics and the Attachment to Life: No-World Aesthetics and the Ellipsis," panel on Mood Swings, MLA Convention, Boston Massachusetts, January 3, 2013.

8. Weiners alludes to "wished for love" in an interview with Charley Shively. In discussing his one long-term relationship (from 1952--1958), he avers that "it lasted long enough so that even now in wished for love, in solitude, I feel that I was gratified through some sort of interrelationship with a god or hero and that I was given the privilege of a passion returned. And that doesn't make me quite so needy toward satisfaction now in my late thirties and beginning my middle years."

9. http://www.hms.harvard.edu/about/history.html.

10. Jim Dunn, "The Old Brick City by the Atlantic: John Wieners's Boston Haunts," *Jacket2* http://jacket2.org/article/old-brick-city-atlantic.

11. See, for example, Michael Fieweger, "Consent Decrees in Prison and Jail Reform: Relaxed Standard of Review for Government Motions to Modify Consent Decrees," *Journal of Criminal Law and Criminality* 83:4 (Winter 1993): 1024–1054, 1035. And a bit of the 1978 argumentation over what was to be done with the inmates: http://openjurist.org/577/f2d/761/inmates-of-suffolk-county-jail-v-j-kearney.

12. Kirkbride, Thomas S. *On the Construction, Organization, and General Arrangements of Hospitals for the Insane*. Philadelphia: s.n., 1854. 40.

13. For one example, see Matthew Christopher, *Abandoned America*. http://www.abandonedamerica.us/taunton-state-hospital.

14. See Appendix A for the full poem. John Wieners, "Children of the Working Class," *Selected Poems 1958–1984*. Ed. Raymond Foye. Santa Barbara: Black Sparrow, 1986. 175.

15 For a memoir about *Gay Community News*, see Amy Hoffman's *An Army of Ex-Lovers*. Amherst, Massachusetts: U of Massachusetts P, 2007. For information on *Fag Rag*, see, for example, Patrick Moore, *Beyond Shame: Reclaiming the Abandoned History of Radical Gay Sexuality* (Boston Masschusetts: Beacon Press, 2004), 6–11. For Stone Soup reminiscences, see http://stonesouppoetry.blogspot.com/2010/11/memories-of-jack-i-lived-in-boston-for.html.

16 Maria Damon. "Some Discourses on/of the Divided Self: Lyric, Ethnography and Loneliness." *Xcp: Cross-cultural Poetics* 11 (Spring 2003): 31–60.

17 http://www.english.upenn.edu/Conferences/DisabilityAndModernism/Videos

18 Schweik, 12.

Works Cited

Brady, Andrea. "Making Use of This Pain: the John Wieners Archives," *Paideuma* 36. (July 2010). Print.

Christopher, Matthew. *Abandoned America*. 23 Apr. 2014. Web. April 24, 21014.

Damon, Maria. "Some Discourses on/of the Divided Self: Lyric, Ethnography and Loneliness." *Xcp: Cross-cultural Poetics* 11 (Spring 2003): 31–60. Print.

Debord, Guy. "Theory of the Dérive." *Internationale Situationniste* #2 (Paris, December 1958). Translation by Ken Knabb. *Situationist International Anthology*. Bureau of Public Secrets, 2006. No copyright. Print.

Fieweger, Michael. "Consent Decrees in Prison and Jail Reform: Relaxed Standard of Review for Government Motions to Modify Consent Decrees." *Journal of Criminal Law and Criminality* 83:4 (Winter 1993): 1024–1054. Print.

Hoffman, Amy. *An Army of Ex-Lovers*. Amherst, Massachusetts: U of Massachusetts P, 2007.

Kirkbride, Thomas S. *On the Construction, Organization, and General Arrangements of Hospitals for the Insane*. Philadelphia: s.n., 1854. 40. Print.

Moore, Patrick. *Beyond Shame: Reclaiming the Abandoned History of Radical Gay Sexuality*. Boston, Massachusetts: Beacon Press, 2004. Print.

"577 F. 2d 761: Inmates of Suffolk County Versus J. Kearney." *Open Jurist*. 16 July 2010. Web. 24 Apr. 2014.

Parmenteau, Chad. "Memories of Jack." *Stone Soup Poetry*. Web. 7 May 2014.

Schweik, Susan. "Modernist Eugenics and Post-Modern Poetics." University of Pennsylvania. Web. 24 Apr. 2014.

Wieners, John. *Behind the State Capitol: or Cincinnati Pike*. Boston, Massachusetts: Good Gay Poets, 1975. Print.

---. "Children of the Working Class." *Selected Poems 1958–1984*. Ed. Raymond Foye. Santa Barbara: Black Sparrow Press, 1986, 175. Print.

---. "A Poem for Vipers." *The Hotel Wentley Poems*. San Francisco: Auerhahn Press, 1958. N. p. Print.

---. *NERVES*. London UK: TBS Book Service, 1971. Print.

---. *Selected Poems 1958–1984*. Ed. Raymond Foye. Santa Barbara: Black Sparrow, 1986. Print.

The Enigmatic Relationship of Poets Isabella Gardner and Gregory Corso

Marian Janssen

Isabella Gardner glamorously photographed by her second husband Maurice Seymour, c. 1944. Courtesy Raoul van Kirk.

Hidden in *The Ohio Review* we find a letter by the poet James Wright written to his protégé, poet-friend and look-alike Roland Flint.

> One evening, a few years ago, I sat close enough to a certain Gregorius, a poet, to smell him.

> It is none of my business that this literary personage shook down one of my best friends for two grand by threatening to destroy her apartment. She is old enough to judge.

> It is none of my business that Gregorius laughed in the face of a schizophrenic young woman after she had meekly accepted his jeering challenge to go down on him in public.

> I do my best to mind my own business.

> But I had to sit close enough to smell him. . . .

> But Gregorius's age and mode of dress matter as little as his verses. Little does he realize, though very likely in his cruel vanity he would care, that his poetry and his bodily stink are alike timeless. (Wright, "Epistle to Roland Flint: On Ancient and Modern Modes")

A copy of this letter-poem is in the Isabella Gardner Papers in Washington University, St. Louis, inscribed "To Belle, with the only love I care about, for Roland's sake, and John's, and mine, Jim." The friend who was "shaken down" for two grand was the poet Isabella Gardner, known as "Belle," and the cousin of Robert Lowell as well as the great-niece of art collector Isabella Stewart Gardner, for whom she was named. The girl said to be schizophrenic who "went down on" Gregorius was probably Gardner's daughter Rose Van Kirk, and "stinky" Gregorius was, of course, Gregory Corso. The "John" of Wright's dedication is lyrical poet John Logan, a loving friend to both Wright and Gardner.[1] In his "Verse Testament for Isabella Gardner," Logan also mentions this instance of Corso's extortionate violence that took place in the 1970s at the Chelsea Hotel: "Gregory Corso, that hood, conned her. / He'd left two bags in her workroom / and they were stolen. He solemnly claimed their value / at two thousand bucks and threatened / to smash to bits her apartment / if she did not produce the cash" (1981). Corso, for his part, denied guilt, blaming Gardner in a 1982 interview with Gavin Selerie for his having published so little since the mid–1960s.

> GC: [. . .] See, there are two books missing in all this. They were lost. One was stolen and that book was called *Who am I—Who I am.*
> GS: How did that get stolen?
> GC: They knew it was a good fucking book—in 1974. It was in two suitcases and I had all my letters from Kerouac and everything and I was living in this fucking Chelsea Hotel in New York City. A supposed friend, a woman, who's a very rich lady and all this shit, a poet named Isabella Gardner, got hold of it; once it was in her hands, it was lost.
>
> . . .
>
> GS: Do you know what happened to those other poems?
> GC: Destroyed or stolen or hidden.
> GS: Do you think someone's sitting on them?
> GC: Sure. She doesn't need money so she ain't selling. (32-33)

Based largely on unpublished letters and interviews, this biographical essay will sketch a measured picture of the relations between the Beats and the more or less traditionalist literary establishment. It will concentrate primarily on Gregory Corso and Paul Carroll, respectively the most vociferous of the Beat writers and a poet who moved in and out of Beat territory, and the poet Boston Brahmin Isabella Gardner.[2] In her assumptions and poetic practice, if not her personal life, Gardner represents the traditionalists. Additional discussion involving William S. Burroughs, Allen Ginsberg and Allen Tate further supports my notion that at mid-century the lives of the Beat poets touched those of the established poets rather more intimately and diversely than is usually assumed. Believing in the "necessary nakedness involved in the act of writing," Gardner bared her soul in her letters, evoking a similar and often unexpected openness in young poets like Corso and Carroll ("The Fellowship with Essence: An Afterword" 161).

The relationship between Gardner (1915–1981) and Corso (1930–2001) had started out auspiciously in 1954 when Corso wrote one of his earliest letters about literature to Belle Gardner. At the time, she was living in Chicago, and, as associate editor of *Poetry Magazine*, editor Karl Shapiro's right hand. In fact, Gardner spent much more time working for the magazine, unpaid, than did its editor, for Shapiro, in order to provide for his family, often held down three jobs simultaneously. He called her his "angel stuck in [a] broom closet" (Letter to Nicholas Joost and Sue Neil, March 5, 1960). Indeed, Gardner proved such an industrious and independent reader that Shapiro, in "his big carpeted office," was soon "staring out of the window into Lake Michigan and feeling foolish and in a sense out of work" (Shapiro, *Reports of My Death* 37).[3]

Though almost forgotten now as an editor and poet, Gardner was at the height of her short-lived fame in the mid-to-late 1950s. When she started writing in the late 1940s, poetry was still very much a man's preserve. Most women poets were regarded as merely "romantic," and the few, like Marianne Moore, who were admitted to the contemporary canon fitted the tradition of intellectual, academy-trained male poets. Gardner's first book, *Birthdays from the Ocean* (1955), about death, sex, and children, was the surprising runner-up for the National Book Award (W.H. Auden won) and was a critical and popular success; during her apprenticeship Sylvia Plath saw Gardner as a rival to the title of "The Poetess of America" (Plath 211). Though her second book, *The Looking Glass* (1961), was also nominated for the National Book Award, by that time openly confessional poetry was setting the tone, and Gardner's formalized vulnerability was no longer explicitly personal enough.

Gardner's poetry is traditional: she was a master of poetic forms from villanelle to triolet, making them fitting vials for autobiographical content, always concentrating on their musicality. She wrote detailed animal poems, but whereas Moore armed her poems, her animals, and herself, Gardner stressed the susceptibility she felt involved in the act of writing, as expressed in "The Sloth": "Arm over hairy arm you travel having no heels / to take to on your unsoled feet, no hole to hide in, and no way to fight" (*Birthdays from the Ocean* 8). Flinching at such sensitivity, Moore disapproved of Gardner's poetry.[4] But other moderns as dissimilar as T.S. Eliot—"There is some very good stuff there"— and William Carlos Williams—"I have been much moved by them and surprised that I have not long since been acquainted with this writer . . . . I wish her all success and shall back her henceforth in whatever she undertakes"—praised *Birthdays*, extolling its sensibility, freshness, and rhyme (Gardner 133, 134). Quite a few of the poems in *Birthdays* are colloquies and point the direction in which Gardner's poetry would develop. As her verse became more explicitly autobiographical, her idiom became more conversational, but she continued to experiment within formal boundaries and, consequently, *The Looking Glass* was out of step with poetic fashion, receiving less than one-third of the reviews of *Birthdays*. However, the comments it elicited were almost without exception laudatory. James Wright, for one, bracketed her with Denise Levertov (early on associated with Beat writers) as "two of the best living poets in America." He praised Gardner's "power of incantation," called her poetry "sensitive and civilized," but cautioned against its explosive power: "you are not advised to hold a lighted match near it" ("Gravity and Incantation," 424,426). And in his article in *The New York Times Book Review*, Shapiro recollected the encomia *Birthdays* had gathered on both sides of the ocean because Gardner's poetry was "paint raw from the tube—without being amateurish or offensive. It had the quality this reviewer admires most, of being primitive, the direct opposite of the modern, extremely fashionable baroque. . . . The present volume, though small, is even better than the first. . . . It is an outstanding book. If I had anything to do with it I would nominate it for the Pulitzer Prize" ("Voices that Speak to the Critic in Very Different Rhythms" 4–5). But their voices were not heeded. Meanwhile, Gardner's later work continued to communicate raw emotions in highly formalized structures at a time when rigorously formal verse was considered dated in the wake of the breakthroughs of Allen Ginsberg's innovative, rhythmic "Howl" (1956) with its anaphoric, long-breath repetitive lines, and Lowell's unflinchingly autobiographical *Life Studies* (1959), with its loosened adherence to meter and form. An early example of Gardner's commitment to traditional form is her sestina about her privileged but loveless childhood:

The Music Room
You must never unlock the cedar closet,
Nor open the white doors to the music room
To be stared at by the french windows and drained
Flabby by the sucking mouths of pastel plants
Unseasonably bred, denatured, deformed.
There in the corner crouches the piano

That vibrates pianissimo piano
And crescendoes con amore in the closet
Of your mind, there by agons of time deformed
And dimmed, but resonating, leaving no room
For any theme but dread. Behind the white doors plants
Alone were smiled at, but with joyless pride that drained

Odor and pollen. It was indifference drained
The marrow from the bones of the piano,
Gutted the child, but watered the tuneless plants.
Only camphored clothing hangs in the closet
No souvenir, no clue to another room
Paper sealed the clothes are tidily deformed.

Go away, do you think you can be deformed
Only once in the same way, that once drained
You cannot be drier? Play the piano
Louder than the echoes of pain but the room

With the staring windows will again closet
You with the chords of terror and the deaf plants.

O multiply impotent is he who plants
His target heel on these thresholds so deformed
By strangled battles that the air is drained
Of sustenance as a sealed up closet,
As the tense unplucked strings of a piano.
Step back. There has been blood in the music room.

Totem's whistle skirled and dwindled in this room
Of slaughter. Rosily embalmed the corpse plants
Frill the bald windows behind the piano.
The keyboard grimaces at the most deformed
Of all, at him who snail-wise wears his closet
On his back: the leech by which his veins are drained.

Drained child, child still, you are buried in this room.
Embalmed like the plants, hanging in the closet.
Mute in hate as the piano, and deformed. (*The Collected Poems* 107–108)[5]

Later titled "Sestina," "The Music Room" was an early poem that appeared in *The Kenyon Review* (Vol. 14, 1953: 613–614). Because she did not want to hurt her father, Gardner did not publish "The Music Room" in book form until after his death in 1976, when she included it in *That Was Then* (1979).

In 1953, when Gardner wrote this very controlled poem, Corso had already met Ginsberg and other members of the Beat Generation in New York City, and had been introduced by them to more experimental verse, with cadences of spoken English, which was the direction his own poetry was taking. When he first wrote Gardner, in 1954, Corso was living in Cambridge. He had been sent there by Violet "Bunny" Lang, Boston-born poet and dramatist, and taken under the patronage of Archibald MacLeish, modernist poet, professor and friend of Gardner's father. But, then, the Gardners knew everyone in genteel Boston, Brookline, and Cambridge.

The first Gardner had set foot on American soil in the early seventeenth century, and his descendants, intermarrying with Endicotts, Peabodys, and of course Lowells, were prominent Bostonians, owning most of AT&T, United Fruit, General Electric, and a bank or two. Robert Gardner, Belle's youngest brother, then a budding filmmaker, was attracted to lyric otherness and, like so many others, enamored of the young, handsome, talented corsair Corso, his coeval.[6] He gave him funds and food and helped him find shelter in the house of unconventional landscape architect Paul Frost on 12 Ash Street Place. Corso's "12 Ash St. Place" appeared in his first collection, *The Vestal Lady on Brattle and Other Poems* (1955).

Indeed, culturally-aware Cambridge initially warmly embraced Corso. He was active in the famous Poet's Theatre, founded by Lang and Irish-Bostonian playwright Mary Manning Howe, who was a close friend of the Gardner family, too, and had chaperoned Belle Gardner on one of her first voyages to Europe.[7] Robert Gardner suggested that Corso send a poem to his beloved sister at *Poetry Magazine*—then and now a grail for poets. She was impressed and wrote her brother: "I quite like Corso's poem—wd like him to send 3 or 4 others before I pass this one on to Karl" (Letter to Robert Gardner, September, 29 [1954]). Shapiro, however, vetoed Corso's poems, and he didn't make it into *Poetry*'s pages under Shapiro's editorship. But Gardner salved Corso's poetic pride with a supportive letter, and Corso was pleased: "Dear Mrs. Gardner—Thank you for a beautiful helpful letter. 'Mental muscle'--yes, how right you are" (Letter to Isabella Gardner, November 18, 1954). Clearly, Corso did not suffer from immoderate modesty, as is also apparent from another early letter, written in 1956. He thought himself "if not the best, at least the closest thing to what a poet should be." He continued:

> The more I read these Cambridge poets, the more I'm convinced of this. These New England poets, apocalyptic crocodilians, the whole horde of them. They do not realize that poems are nothing without the poet. Why are Shelley, Chatterton, Byron, Rimbaud, to name but a few, so beautiful? I'll tell you why, they and their works are one the same, the poet and his poems are a whole. These New England poets aren't hip enough to realize that. They stand away from their poetry, as though it was something they were ashamed to be associated with. That's why they write for the New Yorker. Not only can they be poets, but sophisticates, too. How can anyone truly be a poet who goes to the john with a clothespin on his nose? Fops, that's what they are, not poets. (*An Accidental Autobiography: The Selected Letters of Gregory Corso* 4)

Gregory Corso was one of the youngest among the Beat Generation writers, which included William S. Burroughs, Allen Ginsberg, and Jack Kerouac. He was the third writer to be published: his *The Vestal Lady on Brattle Street* appeared in 1955 (Kerouac published *The Town and the City* in 1950 and John Clellon Holmes published *Go* in 1952.) Poet-critics as different as Hayden Carruth and Kenneth Rexroth thought him extremely talented. Between the late 1950s and early 1960s, Corso published several of the books for which he is still most famous: *Gasoline* (1958), *The Happy Birthday of Death* (1960), and *Long Live Man* (1962). His two most anthologized poems, the controversial "Bomb," in which he mixes humor and politics, and "Marriage," a witty and critical meditation on that institution, were published in *The Happy Birthday of Death*. Consider, for instance, the following excerpt from "Marriage:

> Should I get married? Should I be good?
> Astound the girl next door with my velvet suit and faustus hood?
> Don't take her to movies but to cemeteries
> tell all about werewolf bathtubs and forked clarinets
> then desire her and kiss her and all the preliminaries
> and she going just so far and I understanding why
> not getting angry saying You must feel! It's beautiful to feel!
> Instead take her in my arms lean against an old crooked tombstone
> and woo her the entire night the constellations in the sky—
> When she introduces me to her parents
> back straightened, hair finally combed, strangled by a tie,
> should I sit knees together on their 3rd degree sofa
> and not ask Where's the bathroom? (*The Happy Birthday of Death* 29)

"Marriage," with its long flowing lines, shows his vivid imagery and vitality. But after *Long Live Man*, Corso's poetic production slowed. *Elegiac Feelings American* appeared in 1970, *Herald of the Autochthonic Spirit* in 1981, and his final collection of new and selected poems, *Mindfield*, in 1989.

Where Gardner's youth was privileged, Corso's early days were extremely disadvantaged and traumatic. He was born in Greenwich Village, New York City, son of sixteen-year-old Michelina Colonni and Samuel Corso, who was seventeen. His parents separated shortly after his birth, and Corso was put into a foster home. His mother abandoned him from the start, but after Corso had spent more than ten years in foster care, he was taken out by his father, who had remarried and tried to avoid the military draft. Samuel Corso was drafted nevertheless, and Corso became a street child, ending up in prison several times for minor offenses. When he was seventeen, he was sent to one of New York's toughest prisons, Clinton State, where he, paradoxically, found the freedom to read literature, philosophy, and history, and started writing poetry. Once out of prison, Corso became part of the bohemian world of Greenwich Village, where he met Allen Ginsberg, who welcomed him into his circle of friends. In 1952, Bunny Lang sent him to Cambridge, and this is when the Corso–Gardner connection started.

Gregory Corso in Paris, 1958, photographed by Graham Seidman.

In anger at what he saw as its foppish, fastidious, over-refined literati, separated from both society and self, Corso left the Boston-Cambridge area in 1956 for San Francisco, looking for Ginsberg. He went on to live in Mexico City, Washington D.C., and New York City, ending up in a small run-down hotel at 9 Rue Git-le-Coeur—now known as the "Beat Hotel"— in Paris, France, in 1957. From there he sent Gardner a mad fan letter about *Birthdays*. To compliments by poets as non-Beat as Archibald MacLeish—"It's a very exciting performance. . . . The real thing is rare but all the easier to recognize for that and this is the beginning of the real thing" (Letter to George Peabody Gardner, September 19, [1955])— and Wallace Stevens—"I thought the book the freshest, truest book of poetry that I had read for a long time"—(Letter to A. Ford, March 14, 1955), Corso added his:

> [H]ow happy and wonderful your book of lovely spring-wild poems made
> me, I read all your poems the entire noon on the side steps of the Louvre;
> I fell in love with your poetry, it is marvelous wondrous beautiful
> poetry . . . . Cockatrice! Chanticleer! What lovely words, eyesounds! I
> felt so elated reading your poems, really; Of Flesh and Bone, I never read
> anything more brilliant and mad about Death. . . .I really have nothing but
> mature praise for you, and that's something I'm awkward to be.

Corso goes on in this vein, ending with "Ah your poetry, I used to think Robert Lowell was the only and final energy of Albion's stifled child. My love, Gregory" (September 1958).[8] That Corso was not just praising Gardner to her face—using inimitable word combinations such as "spring-wild" and synesthetic tropes like "eyesounds"—is apparent from a letter he wrote to Peter Orlovsky, Ginsberg's lover, that October: "I am corresponding with Isabella Gardner who, Allen, you should pickup on, she being a female Lowell almost, and, without malice, much more DREAM and WILDNESS OF THOUGHT in her than Levertov female poets" (*An Accidental Autobiography: The Selected Letters of Gregory Corso* 162).

Corso's extraordinary letter amazed Gardner and she answered him politely, aloofly; but by return, from Paris, he poured his heart and poetics out to her in a letter full of flair and energy. He raved about the Beat poets and hipsters as new souls who would "defy the system of academic poetry that has been the death to American poetry"; he was sure that they would permanently change America's literary landscape. But a few paragraphs further on, he complained that they had already become "a generation of social-declaimer decriers"—with a couple of exceptions, of course: Allen Ginsberg and Corso "were great poets" and "both of us, somewhat romantically yes, but not cornily, will die for our poetry." Corso mentions another exception: "Nor have I anything against tradition; if there is one poet I love writing today it's Robert Lowell; but the world goes and its cattiness of who to love and who not to love, will make impossible, let's say, a meeting and a love between he and Ginsberg, whereas they both have that SOUL. But in my little stay at Harvard I saw much that made academic poets guilty; not their going to conformity; but their selfdestruction [sic] that might have been poetry in them" (October 1958). Somewhere near the end of this long letter, he explained that he had gone on for pages about poets and poetics because he wanted to awe Gardner with his learning.

Gardner was not impressed. At the time, Gardner was in the first throes of maudlin, adulterous love for Southern conservative poet-critic Allen Tate. Tate's nine books of poetry and his three biographies of Southern luminaries had appealed to an admiring but select audience since 1923. As one of the high priests of the New Criticism, he was a force to be reckoned with in the highbrow literary world.

She sent Corso's outpouring to Tate: "[I enclose] a fan letter to me which might amuse my love, from Gregory Corso. <u>Why</u>, he wrote me, I do not know. I . . . got <u>pages</u> to-day about his prison experiences as a boy--he's in his twenties now—his friendship with Ginsberg + Kerouac etc.—I know I shall not like his poems" (October 17, 1958). What, indeed, did Corso think to gain by this extraordinary letter to an older poet by whom he was truly moved, but had never met, a letter that was simultaneously confessional and much more schooled and polite than the letters he sent off to the poet-friends of his generation? Perhaps he wanted to stay in touch with rich Boston Brahmin Belle Gardner, cousin of Robert Lowell, hoping that she would be his poet patroness and send some of her considerable money his way? He did mention a financial disagreement with Gardner's brother Robert:

> Once, when the man, a sociologist, who collect[ed] rent for Frost's house, asked me for rent, I went raging to Bob Gardner crying that I am writing beautiful poetry, I have no money, for the first time in my life I am living in a lovely place, all is good and peace, why cant I stay and write!—I felt I deserved that; I wasnt begging, I was arrogant about it; I was deserved, I went [through] enough of horror. . . . I thought perhaps Bob would have understood when I cried there, but he didn't; well, I cant blame him because he knew nothing about me; but I was doing good work there; I wrote that good careless Vestal Lady On Brattle there. (October 1958)

Some years ago I asked Bob Gardner about Corso's fury at having to pay rent for Frost's house, because it seemed very out of character for Gardner to be so coldhearted towards a struggling, gifted poet like Corso, whom he liked, but Gardner was, even after all this time, still so angry with the way Corso had treated him and his friends that he, usually very frank, refused to clarify the incident. I also questioned candid, acerbic-tongued Mary Manning Howe a number of times, but even she declined, dismissing him maliciously as "that criminal Corso" (1989 interview with the author).

Already in his October 1958 letter from Paris, Corso had overplayed his hand in writing that "poetry that sounds like poetry is bad poetry," because to Gardner, as to John Logan, poetry had to be musical, "a ballet for the ear."[9] And his attacks on the "academic" poets, foremost among them Allen Tate, did not endear him to her either. Soon after, at the beginning of 1959, Gardner met up with Corso, Ginsberg and Paul Carroll, the editor of the new magazine *Big Table*.[10] She was confirmed in her judgment and wrote that "I spent 2 hours yesterday with Allen Ginsberg + Gregory Corso. The latter was quite drunk + bleated + baahed about his 'love' for me whom he doesn't know! He wants a mother, poor little boy. He + Ginsberg read a poem or two a piece + they just <u>aren't</u> any good really" (Letter to Edward Dahlberg, January/February, 1959).

Gardner was more positive about the poetry of Paul Carroll, whom she had gotten to know as an aspiring poet in Chicago in 1953. As a poet Carroll is impossible to categorize. Many of his poems of the 1950s and early 1960s were carefully crafted and closed and do not chime in with the Beat tradition. He was a disciple of Morton Dauwen Zabel, who had been an associate editor at *Poetry Magazine* from 1928 to 1936 and, subsequently, for one year its editor. Thanks to Gardner's intervention, Carroll appeared in *Poetry Magazine*'s March 1955 issue with his classicist tribute to Charles Baudelaire, "Un Voyage à Cythère," where "Pan naps at noon on the hill. / Never merely desirable, / Music is indispensable, / The air we breathe in Arcady" (319). But Carroll's best known poem, the thirteen-page-long foldout "Ode to Severn Darden About Angels, the Common Cold, Nuclear Disarmament, and Popcorn" was clearly fueled by his editing of the Beat poets and is campy, corny, sensory, oral, and playful. It starts:

> The weather, today, Severn, is as blue as the cerulean blue of the
>
> lovely artificial blue of the plastic tulips in the windows of the
>
> Woolworth 5 & 10C
>
> It is like the mackerel which you bought at Burhop's and swaddled
>
> in a newspaper and forgot beneath a couch of sorrows in
>
> the office of your psychoanalyst
>
> Or like the odor of a 1937 Shirley Temple doll
>
> Or like a Goodyear tire about to have a flat
>
> Or like the fact that everybody is a poem (*Odes* 34)

Apart from a permanent predilection for alliteration and repetition, Carroll changed his style drastically every few years. His *Odes* (1969) consists of poems written over nearly two decades, ranging from religious to autobiographically Freudian to Beat. Indeed, Carroll put into practice his own credo that "Every good poem is like a person: it has its own skin" (*The Poem in Its Skin* v). Versatile to an extreme degree, to his detractors he was a poet without a voice of his own.

His eclecticism, his eye for what was extraordinary in each unique poem, made Carroll a discerning critic, as is apparent from both his *The Poem in Its Skin* (1968) and his anthology *The Young American Poets* (1968), rather than, to his dismay, a powerful poet. As the trailblazing editor of *Big Table*, Carroll published the Beats extensively, and although he kept his distance from them personally[11], he is best remembered for helping Burroughs, Ginsberg, and other Beat writers to prominence. But there, too, he was catholic, excellence of the poem on the page being his only criterion. In his introduction to *The Poem in Its Skin*, he wrote:

> What has the poet *written?* is of course the only valuable challenge. To help in trying to meet this challenge by experiencing any poem in its own skin, as it were, the reader today is able much like a warlock to summon from the world of criticism such a bewildering and intimidating rout of 'lemans, demons, fallen angels / and Familiars' (as Isabella Gardner writes in her elegy for Dylan Thomas 'When a Warlock Dies') that at times he must long as I have for the orthodoxy of such critical positions as: Every decent poem owns at least one of seven ambiguities. (vi)

His second wife, Maryrose Carroll, remembered in 2004 that Beat writers "were always telling Paul how he should write his poetry. Or what he should put in his magazine. But, in the end, he was a very resilient and independent man, like his father. He said, more than once: 'I would publish Richard M. Nixon if he wrote a good poem'" (M. Carroll). In contrast to what Corso believed, to Carroll the poet and the poem, the writer and the writing, were totally separate; for *Big Table 6*, which in the end never appeared because Carroll had run out of finances, he had planned a symposium on "Post-Christian Man," with conservatives Russell Kirk (who was in favor of Nixon during the 1960 presidential election) and Allen Tate.

There were many reasons why Paul Carroll, like Corso, came under Gardner's spell, but, in contrast to Corso, Carroll remained devoted to her, not only because of her associate editorship at *Poetry Magazine* but also because of her own poetry, which Carroll, from the first, admired greatly. In *The Poem in Its Skin*, Carroll included Gardner as the only woman among ten very different poets—John Ashbery, Robert Creeley, James Dickey, Allen Ginsberg, John Logan, W. S. Merwin, Frank O'Hara, W. D. Snodgrass, and James Wright. He called them "barbarians . . . inside the gate" and admired them for their bravery in writing poems that were either alien or hostile to the Eliotic tradition. He argued that the anti-Eliot revolt was not synonymous with Ginsberg's "Howl": "Equally important and radical innovations were being explored at the same time by poets as alien to the San Francisco poets as well as to one another as John Ashbery in Paris, Robert Creeley in Majorca. . . . Isabella Gardner in Elmhurst . . . and James Wright in Minneapolis" (207). Of Gardner he said that among his ten chosen poets, she was

> best at exploring the mystery, ugliness, pain and sexuality of human relationships. What distinguishes her poems of relationships such as "The Widow's Yard" or "Mea Culpa" or "Zei Gesund" or "To Thoreau on Rereading Walden" in *West of Childhood: Poems 1950–1965* is how the relationship is experienced in its own existential terms: she refuses to gloss over either the twisted or the graceful or the erotic by letting the relationship stand for this or that 'significant' message or moral. (213)

Cover of the first issue of Big Table *with the complete contents of the suppressed Winter 1959 Chicago Review, including work by William S. Burroughs, Edward Dahlberg, Gregory Corso, and Jack Kerouac.*

His favorite Gardner poems "bear witness to the exhilarating reality of things-as-they-are," such as "That 'Craning of the Neck'" and "Part of the Darkness," which delineate relationships between people and animals (213). Carroll never wavered in his admiration for her poetry, as is apparent from Carroll's widow Maryrose naming Gardner, John Logan, Kathleen Norris, and Denise Levertov as his most beloved poets. Gardner was not as admiring of Carroll's poetry as he was of hers. She published his "Un Voyage à Cythère" only at the very end of her editorial stint at *Poetry Magazine*.

Isabella Gardner with her fourth husband, Allen Tate, c.1960. Gift to the author from Evalyn Shapiro, Karl Shapiro's first wife .

When in August 1959 Gardner became the adoring wife of Allen Tate, who was viscerally anti-Beat, she followed his literary lead. But ad hominem comments Tate made about William S. Burroughs were so far beyond the bounds of acceptability that even his brand-new bride balked. Carroll had asked Tate to support his case against the U. S. Post Office Department for the impending suppression of *Big Table 2*. But Tate refused, for he found literary merit only in the parts from Edward Dahlberg's autobiography *Because I Was Flesh* (1963). *The Yage Letters* "by a certain Mr. Burroughs" were "offensive not only for their obscenity, but for their ludicrous pretensions to serious treatment of a serious experience." Tate thought they were poorly written and was "at a loss to understand how an editor can permit such a writer to be praised as the centre of a literary group whose purpose is to 'recapture American poetry for the complete personality.' The personality of these letters is, by internal evidence, warped and sick, and the irresistible inference is that the homosexuality and drug-addiction of their author explain the sickness." On the subject of censorship, Tate wrote: "I do not believe in the suppression of books by government agency; yet it must be remembered that all societies practice censorship, direct or indirect; and in a secular, democratic society such as ours, the government will intervene, in spite of its dubious claims to moral authority, unless there is a prior principle of selectivity at work in the democratic community. So far as the publication of books and magazines is concerned, this principle must be operative in the mind of the editor, as representative of his culture at its highest level" (Letter to Paul Carroll, August 17, 1959).

Carroll was civilly livid as is apparent from his respectful but trenchant answer: "To forbid publication to a serious and committed writer because he happened to offend my notions of what is good and evil would be I think an act of barbarism. William S. Burroughs, for example, strikes me as one of the damned. But even the damned deserve a voice" (Letter to Allen Tate, August 31, 1959). Tate grudgingly admitted that an editor should not simply exercise moral censorship, but then fudged the issue by stating that the editor "should mediate between the subject matter, considered apart from matters of 'form,' and the total intention of the work." Judge Woolsey's ruling on Joyce's *Ulysses* he thought exemplary of such a decision.[12] Whereas Carroll had called Burroughs "one of the damned," but did not mind as he considered his contribution to *Big Table* great literature, Tate now suddenly could not care less about Burroughs' "sickness," arguing that his writings were "third-rate" (Letter to Paul Carroll, September 9, 1959). He ended by saying that he knew that Carroll was a very good friend of his wife's and expressed the hope of seeing him that winter in Chicago.

Gardner herself had to placate another of her friends, Edward Dahlberg, who was offended that Tate had not taken his stand against the Post Office Department's suppression of *Big Table 2*. Gardner had to explain to Dahlberg that "Allen's attitude to Big Table should not be construed as any criticism of you for appearing there" (Letter to Edward Dahlberg, September 30, 1959). The longer she remained married to Tate, the more Gardner's acute literary sensibility became influenced by his, and in 1960 she blew up—not only at the Beats, but, referring to Donald Allen's just published anthology, dismissing recent American poetry in general:

> I can't see what is so <u>new</u> about "The New American Poets"? Olson is far
> from new. Harold Norse is no better than he was eight years ago when his
> outpourings inundated Poetry Magazine + drove Karl + me to distraction.
> Frank O' Hara I like much better but he's been around in magazines for

> years, so has Koch. And there is nothing really <u>new</u> about the <u>poetry</u> itself.
> It is old-fashioned and dates back into the early twenties. . . . most of the
> poems strike me as nose-thumbing scribbles on a latrine wall--+ far less
> poetic than "Kilroy was here." They seem designed to epater" (Letter to
> Paul Carroll, October 12, 1960).

These angry quotes are part of a letter in which Gardner apologizes for yet another epistle written by Tate to Carroll about Big Table. Carroll had forgiven his earlier outburst, but this time Tate had questioned Carroll's editorial honesty and honor as well as implied that the Beats controlled policy at Big Table. Carroll was crushed. Gardner thought Carroll justifiably angered by her husband's gratuitous and cruel remarks about his editorial integrity. Nevertheless, she leapt to his defense. Gardner clearly did not yet know the depths of Tate's devious, charlatanic, yet charismatic personality: playing literary games and playing around were what he loved most. Carroll was mollified: "Your letter, so warm, considerate, yet firm in your opinions & feelings, was so you: I thank you for it. . . . Let's not devote another letter—at least for the time being—to quarrelling over the merits and/or demerits of Allen Ginsberg. Suffice it to say that I do not feel—emphatically do not—that Ginsberg calls the shots on Big Table. He never has. He never shall" (October 18, 1960). Carroll was not impressed by some of the work by Beat writers that Ginsberg was promoting. Gardner herself had earlier described the Beat poets as "little black sheep who have lost their Maw" as "publicity hungry little boys of early Middle Age" (Letter to Paul Carroll, November 1959). But then, she confessed, "as you know, I am hopelessly square" (Letter to Paul Carroll, September 21, 1960).

Hopelessly square? Absolutely not in the eyes of her upper-class Boston family, who had expected her to follow the proper path from finishing school to society hostess. But a drunk driving accident during her debutante days had effectually removed her from the *haut monde* marriage market and she was sent off to Europe to shield her from disgrace. After her affair with Erskine Childers there, and some meddling in Irish politics, she was called home by her irate father, became an actress and, in her early twenties, married a divorced drama-director twice her age who was after her money. In Chicago, on a successful tour as a comic actress, she met and soon married photographer Maurice Seymour, who had close connections to the Mob. She divorced him and married a well-to-do Chicagoan, Robert Hall McCormick, only to leave him for Allen Tate. Gardner could perhaps be called square in that she had at least *married* most of the men she had had affairs with, but four times was unorthodox by anybody's standards at mid-century, and, as a member of a socially prominent Boston family dating back to early colonial days, to have chosen divorced men, twice from questionable backgrounds, had made her very much a pariah among her own.

Gardner became unsettled when in 1965 Tate threw her over for a young nun, whom he, as the disgusting joke went in Minneapolis, "had gotten out of the habit." He made it intolerable for Gardner to stay on in their hometown, where he now lived with his new love. She had no intention of slinking back to stiff-upper-lip Boston and chose to live in New York at the bohemian Hotel Chelsea. At the artistic shabby-chic Chelsea it was impossible not to run into Beat writers, among them Corso, who lived there off and on. Corso was no longer the youthful, adoring admirer of Gardner's poetry, no longer the handsome gifted young Beat poet of the late 1950s, but had become a blocked writer, a seedy junkie constantly on the lookout for drink and drugs, who accused her of having stolen his manuscripts. While his obstreperous behavior worsened, loyal friends such as Allen Ginsberg and Patti Smith stood by him. Corso tried to convince himself as well as his publishers that he was writing as he sank deeper into silence. Gardner's and Corso's lives became intimately intertwined when Corso moved in with Gardner's unstable daughter Rose, who, when in New York City, also stayed at the Chelsea. It was easy for Corso to dominate Rose, but Corso also would deliberately taunt Gardner, describing the sex he had had with her daughter or making sure that she would come upon them copulating in the Chelsea's elevators or hall.

Paul Carroll and Allen Ginsberg at the benefit reading for Big Table at the Sherman Hotel, Chicago, on January 29, 1959. Courtesy University of Chicago Library

When she wanted to introduce her young artist friend Jay Bolotin to Allen Ginsberg, who by that time had become a truly influential established poet, she warned her protégé that Ginsberg was "very much aware of . . . my own and my daughter's difficulties with Gregory Corso who when I first met him seemed gifted (to some degree) and although we were never friends in any real sense, there was something rather disarming, not charming, in his infantilism. That was 20 years ago and now he is corrupt. . . . and I cannot like him. Allen [Ginsberg] . . is a <u>good</u> human being, generous and compassionate to the . . . Corsos of this world" (Letter to Jay Bolotin, January 25, 1976). Her sharp criticism of Corso here indicates the depth of the damage she felt he had done to her daughter and herself.

Although taken for true by some Beat aficionados—and still turning up in references to Corso on the internet—the stolen manuscript story clearly is fictitious.[13] By threatening to destroy her apartment if she did not pay him for his supposedly stolen manuscripts, Corso had both an excuse for his nonproductivity and a possibility to extort a considerable amount of money. Even his interviewer Gavin Selerie was doubtful: "You tend to have long intervals between publishing books. GC: I told you—the losses they're stolen. GS: That explains all? GC: Yes" (33). While the mature Corso was a hustler, Gardner, too, had deteriorated. Some two decades since their first meeting, Gardner spent most of her days at the Chelsea in an alcoholic haze. Her white patrician parents gave up on her when she took the hotel's black bell-hop for her live-in lover and sold the family silver. Filled with fear when she had to attend family gatherings, Gardner heavily fortified herself with vodka and wine, which only made her family disapprove of her the more. She was tortured, too, by her failing poetic powers, but, unlike Corso, Gardner did not torture others because of this. She blamed herself for the major tragedies in the last decade of her life: the disappearance and death of her drug-addicted talented son Daniel Seymour and the beating that brain-damaged her daughter Rose forever.[14]

Eventually, Gardner herself was consigned to oblivion; her multi-faceted musical poetry had become unfashionable and her recent output meager. Since her involvement with Tate, she had written very little. At the end of her life, she published a small collection of poems, *That Was Then* (1979), to acclaim. *That Was Then* was nominated for the American Book Award and won her the first New York State Walt Whitman Citation of Merit Award, in effect New York State's poet laureateship. The prize went to her posthumously: Gardner died alone in 1981.

As a tribute to Gardner, Michael André published one of her death-haunted poems, "Knowing," in the third Corso issue of his magazine *Unmuzzled Ox*. In the end, Corso's and Gardner's literary lives touched there, as they had in the beginning. The last of the best-known Beat writers, Corso struggled on, with his love for poetry as his saving grace, for almost two decades, passing away in 2001. "Knowing" is quoted here in its entirety as a tribute to both Belle and the Beats.

"Mon Moi! Ils m'arrachent mon moi"
—Michelet

I will be lonely at half past dead
Weep none or many beside my bed

At dead center of all alone
I must unwillingly work at dying
While silently and incredulously
I shall be crying crying crying:
Not I, Not I, Not my flesh
Not my bone, and not my only I
*Unamuno says ". . . in my supreme anguish I cry with Michelet, *mon moi, ils m'arrachent mon moi*." (41)

Notes

---

[1] John Logan (1923–1987) described his melodic poetry to *Contemporary Authors* as "a kind of anonymous loving." He wrote fourteen books of poetry; his *Only the Dreamer Can Change the Dream* (1981) won the 1982 Lenore Marshall Poetry Prize. He was poetry editor of *Critic* and the *Nation*, and founded and edited *Choice*. See for more information my entries on Logan in *Post-war Literatures in English*, June 1993 and *The Greenwood Encyclopedia of American Poets and Poetry*.

[2] A Boston Brahmin is a member of Boston's traditional upper class; the most representative Boston Brahmins are descendants of the earliest British colonists. The term was coined in 1861 by Oliver Wendell Holmes and refers to the highest ranked group of people in the traditional Indian system of castes. From Paul Carroll's description of their first meeting, it is clear Gardner could be quite the Boston Belle: "Isabella was working at *Poetry Magazine* and had accepted John Logan's 'Cycle for Mother Cabrini' and John and Isabella became friends. . . . John and I came to hear her read at an extension kind of school. Isabella appeared in a green velvety dress. She made a spectacular appearance: she had her hair up as if she was going to a debutante cotillion. . . . Everybody was stunned by her appearance, because this was an adult, middle-lower class audience" (Telephone interview with the author).

[3] She left in 1955 when Shapiro left. Both Paul Carroll and John Logan had hoped Gardner would succeed Shapiro—not quite altruistically, because they saw Gardner as a champion of their poetry. But the only successors Shapiro had in mind were male, from Michael McClure to, in the end, fellow Chicagoan Henry Rago. When I asked Shapiro in an interview why he had not suggested Gardner as his successor, he replied with surprise: "Why, I never thought of that" (Interview with the author, 1990).

[4] See for more information about Isabella Gardner's poetry, her tumultuous life, and her relationship with Beat writers my *Not at All What One Is Used To:*

The Life and Times of Isabella Gardner. Columbia: U of Missouri P, 2010. Elizabeth Bishop had written Gardner in 1955: "If I were you I wouldn't feel at all concerned that Marianne Moore doesn't like your poetry—if you are sure you are right about that—I'm sure you've seen for yourself that the greatest poets are often extremely poor judges of other people's poetry, and I think Miss Moore, particularly, is often apt to make moral judgments or fasten on something really unimportant and go by that." Elizabeth Bishop to Isabella Gardner, October 21, 1955. Isabella Gardner Papers, Washington University Libraries, St. Louis.

[5] See also my entry on Paul Carroll in *The Greenwood Encyclopedia of American Poets and Poetry*.

[6] Robert Gardner is a renowned filmmaker and author. Some of his most prominent films include *Dead Birds* (1963), a lyric account of the Dani, a Stone Age society living an isolated existence in the Highlands of former Netherlands New Guinea; *Rivers of Sand* (1974), a commentary on the Hamar people of southwestern Ethiopia; and *Forest of Bliss* (1985), a cinematic essay on the city of Benares, India, which explores ceremonies and rituals associated with death and regeneration. Gardner founded the Film Study Center at Harvard.

[7] In Europe, Mary Manning Howe became involved with Samuel Beckett, leaving Gardner, who began an affair with the married Erskine Childers, future President of Ireland.

[8] In *An Accidental Autobiography: the Selected Letters of Gregory Corso*, editor Bill Morgan dates this letter 1957, but it is apparent from a letter by Isabella Gardner to her brother Robert (in Robert Gardner's Private Papers) that it was written around September 1958.

[9] See John Logan and A. Poulin Jr., Eds., *A Ballet for the Ear: Interviews, Essays and Reviews*. Ann Arbor: U of Michigan P, 1983.

[10] Paul Carroll was poetry editor, under Irving Rosenthal, of the University of Chicago's *Chicago Review*, publishing work by Allen Ginsberg, William S. Burroughs and Jack Kerouac. Attacked for obscenity, its Winter 1959 issue was suppressed, and Rosenthal and Carroll published its content in their quickly founded journal *Big Table*. When Rosenthal left, Carroll went on to publish four more issues. See also Jaap van der Bent, "Beats on the Table: Beat Writing in the *Chicago Review* and *Big Table*," *Tijdschrift voor tijdschriftstudies*, juni 2012, 5–19.

[11] As *Big Table*'s editor, Carroll was extremely influential in furthering the careers of Burroughs, Ginsberg, and Kerouac, but personally he kept his distance from them, as is apparent from a letter he wrote in 1964: "During the heyday of *Big Table* I happened to be in New York City to give a reading with Jim Dickey at

the Poetry Center—it was due to your kind recommendation, Isabella, remember?—and I accepted an invitation to read at one of the Beat coffee houses. Due to the fact that a few weeks before I had rejected a long, wretched poem by Ginsberg, I was made to feel under a cloud of bad feeling by various Beat poets and camp followers whom I met at parties and saloons. Well, I arrived at the coffee house, dressed in a Brooks Brothers suit and vest . . . and I proceeded to read for two hours from various translations I had made over the years of the Odes and Songs of Quintus Horatius Flaccus, whom I identified carefully as the Roman poet Horace. You can imagine the sullen response such a performance received from the audience of Beats sulking behind dark glasses and whiskers. I recommended, as editor of *Big Table*, that any aspiring young poet in the audience make a careful, loving study of Horace instead of the various hip perversions of poetry howling about the scene at that time. I almost got lynched" (Letter to Isabella Gardner and Allen Tate, September 10, 1964).

[12] In 1933, in the famous "United States Versus One Book Called *Ulysses*," the issue was whether James Joyce's *Ulysses* (1922) was obscene. Judge John Woolsey decided *Ulysses* was a serious novel, not written with pornographic intent, and not an aphrodisiac. It was therefore not objectively obscene within the meaning of the law and could therefore be admitted into the United States.

[13] See, for instance, the Corso entries in poetryfoundation.org and poets.org.

[14] Daniel Seymour followed in his father's footsteps and became a photographer and filmmaker. His *A Loud Song*, published by Lustrum Press in New York City in 1971, is one of the first stream-of-consciousness photographic diaries and a poignant visual account of both the author and his times. It has reached cult status over the years and is a testimony to his talent. It is not clear who assaulted Rose.

Works Citied

André, Michael. "An Interview with Gregory Corso." *Unmuzzled Ox* 1981: 123–158. Print.

Carroll, Maryrose. *Oral History Interview*. Tonya Hassel. 2004. Web. 17 Nov. 2013

Carroll, Paul. "Letter to Allen Tate." August 31, 1959. T.l. (carbon). Paul Carroll Papers, University of Chicago Library.

---. "Letter to Isabella Gardner." October 10, 1960. T.l.s. Isabella Gardner Papers, Washington University Libraries, St. Louis.

---. "Letter to Isabella Gardner." October 18, 1960. T.l.s. Isabella Gardner Papers, Washington University Libraries, St. Louis.

---. "Letter to Isabella Gardner and Allen Tate." 10 September 1964. T.l.s. Isabella Gardner Papers, Washington University Libraries, St. Louis.

---. "Ode to Severn Darden." *Odes*. Chicago: Big Table, 1969. 34-37. Print.

---. *Odes*. Chicago: Big Table, 1969. Print.

---. Telephone interview with the author. January 9, 1990.

---. *The Poem in Its Skin*. Chicago: Follett, 1968. Print.

---. *The Young American Poets*. Chicago: Follett, 1968. Print.

---. "Un Voyage à Cythère." *Poetry Magazine* (1955): 319–321. Print.

Corso, Gregory. *An Accidental Biography: The Selected Letters of Gregory Corso*. Ed. Bill Morgan. New York: New Directions, 2003. Print.

---. *Elegiac Feelings American*. New York: New Directions, 1970. Print.

---. *Gasoline*. San Francisco: City Lights, 1958. Print.

---. *Herald of the Autochthonic Spirit*. New York: New Directions, 1981. Print.

---. "Letter to Isabella Gardner." [October 1958]. T.l.s. Isabella Gardner Papers,Washington University Libraries, St. Louis.

---. "Letter to Isabella Gardner." November 18, 1954. A.l.s. Isabella Gardner Papers, Washington University Libraries, St. Louis.

---. "Letter to Isabella Gardner." [September 1958]. T.l.s. Isabella Gardner Papers, Washington University Libraries, St. Louis.

---. *Long Live Man*. New York: New Directions, 1962. Print.

---. "Marriage." *The Happy Birthday of Death*. New York: New Directions, 1960. 29–32. Print.

---. *Mindfield*. New York: Thunder's Mouth P, 1989. Print.

---. *The Vestal Lady on Brattle Street*. Cambridge, Massachusetts.: R. Brukenfeld, 1955. Print.

Dahlberg, Edward. *Because I Was Flesh*. New York: New Directions, 1963. Print.

Gardner, Isabella. *Birthdays from the Ocean*. Boston: Houghton Mifflin, 1955. Print.

---. "Knowing." *Unmuzzled Ox* 1981: 41. Print.

---. "Letter to Robert Gardner." September 29,[1954]. A.l.s. Robert Gardner Private Papers.

---. "Letter to Allen Tate." October 17,[1958]. A.l.s. Isabella Gardner Papers, Washington University Libraries, St. Louis.

---. "Letter to Edward Dahlberg." September 30, 1959. A.l.s. Edward Dahlberg Papers, Harry Ransom Humanities Reserach Center, University of Texas.

---. "Letter to Edward Dahlberg." [January / February 1959]. A.l.s. Edward Dahlberg Papers, Harry Ransom Humanities Research Center, University of Texas.

---. "Letter to Jay Bolotin." January 25, 1976. A.l.s. Jay Bolotin Private Papers.

---. "Letter to Paul Carroll." (Late November 1959). A.l.s. Paul Carroll Papers,
     University of Chicago Library.
---. "Letter to Paul Carroll." October 17, 1960. A.l.s. Paul Carroll Papers,
     University of Chicago Library.
---. "Letter to Paul Carroll." September, 21 1960. A.l.s. Paul Carroll Papers,
     University of Chicago Library.
---. *That Was Then: New and Selected Poems*. Brockport New York: BOA Editions,
     1979. Print.
---. *The Collected Poems*. Brockport, New York: BOA Editions, 1990. Print.
---. "The Fellowship with Essence: An Afterword." *The Collected Poems*.
     Brockport, N.Y.: BOA Editions, 1990. 161–162. Print.
---. *The Looking Glass*. Chicago: U of Chicago P, 1961. Print.
---. *Un' Altra Infanzia*. Trans. Alfredo Rizzardi. Bologna: Libraria Antiquaria
     Palmaverde, 1959. Print.
---. *West of Childhood: Poems 1950–1965*. Boston: Houghton Mifflin, 1965.
     Print.
Ginsberg, Allen. *Howl and Other Poems*. San Francisco: City Lights, 1956. Print.
Hamilton, Ian. *Robert Lowell: A Biography*. New York: Random House, 1982. Print.
Howe, Mary Manning. *Interview with the author*. September 20,1989.
Janssen, Marian. "John Logan." *Post-War Literatures in English*. Eds. Johannes
     Willem Bertens, et.al. Houten: Bohn, Stafleu, Van Loghum a.o., 1988. June
     1993. Print.
---. "John Logan." *The Greenwood Encyclopedia of American Poets and Poetry*.
     Ed. Jeffrey Gray, James McCorkle and Mary McAleer Balkun. Westport,
     Conn.: Greenwood Press, 2006. Print.
---. *Not at All What One Is Used To: The Life and Times of Isabella Gardner*.
     Columbia, Missouri.: U of Missouri P, 2010. Print.
---. "Paul Carroll." *The Greenwood Encyclopedia of American Poets and Poetry*.
     Eds. Jeffrey Gray, James McCorkle and Mary McAleer Balkun. Westport,
     Conn.: Greenwood P, 2006. Print.
Kizer, Carolyn. Interview with the author. August 21, 1990.
Logan, John. "Verse Testament for Isabella Gardner." July 12, 1981. Typescript
     (carbon). Isabella Gardner Papers, Washington University Libraries, St. Louis.
Logan, John and A. Poulin Jr., *A Ballet for the Ear: Interviews, Essays and Reviews*.
     Ann Arbor: U of Michigan P, 1983. Print.
---. *Only the Dreamer Can Change the Dream*. New York: Ecco, 1981. Print.
Lowell, Robert. *Life Studies*. New York City: Farrar, Straus and Cudahy, 1959. Print.

MacLeish, Archibald. "Letter to George Peabody Gardner [father]." September 19, [1955]. T.l.s.(carbon) Isabella Gardner Papers, Washington University Libraries, St. Louis.

McNees, Matthew. "Suffering and Liberation: The Personal Poetics of Robert Lowell and Allen Ginsberg." Greensboro, N.C.: University of North Carolina at Greensboro, 2011. Dissertation.

Plath, Sylvia. *The Journals of Sylvia Plath*. Eds. Ted Hughes and Frances McCullough. Ballantine, paperback edition 1983. New York: Random House, 1982. Print.

Selerie, Gavin. *The Riverside Interviews: 3. Gregory Corso*. London: Pinnacle, 1982. Print.

Seymour, Daniel. *A Loud Song*. New York: Lustrum, 1971. Print.

Shapiro, Karl. Interview with the author. August 18, 1990.

---. "Letter to Nicholas Joost and Sue Neil." March 5,1954. T.l.s. Poetry Papers, University of Chicago Library.

---. *Reports of My Death*. Chapel Hill: Algonquin, 1990. Print.

---. "Voices that Speak to the Critic in Very Different Rhythms." *The New York Times Book Review*. December 24,1961: 4–5. Print.

Stevens, Wallace. "Letter to A. Ford at Houghton Mifflin." March 14, 1955. T.l.s. (carbon) Isabella Gardner Papers, Washington University Libraries, St. Louis.

Tate, Allen. "Letter to Paul Carroll." August 17, 1959. T.l.s. Paul Carroll Papers, The University of Chicago Library.

---. "Letter to Paul Carroll." September, 9 1959. A.l.s. Paul Carroll Papers, University of Chicago Library.

Van der Bent, Jaap. "Beats on the Table: Beat Writing in the *Chicago Review* and *Big Table*." *Tijdschrift voor tijdschriftstudies* (2012): 5–19. Print.

Wright, James. "Epistle to Roland Flint: On Ancient and Modern Modes." N.d. Copy, with handwritten addition. Isabella Gardner Papers, Washington University Libraries, St. Louis.

---. "Gravity and Incantation." *Minnesota Review* 1962: 424–426. Print.

REVIEWS

Pilgrims to Elsewhere: Reflections on Writings by Jack Kerouac,
Allen Ginsberg, Gregory Corso, Bob Kaufman and Others.
Gregory Stephenson
Afterward by Bent Sørensen.
(Roskilde: EyeCorner Press, 2013).

Well known in the area of Beat studies, Gregory Stephenson, author of *The Daybreak Boys: Essays on the Literature of the Beat Generation* (1990), has compiled another collection of essays ranging from some of the core Beat writers he addressed in his earlier collection, such as Ginsberg, Kerouac, and Corso, to late nineteenth- and early twentieth-century writers James S. Lee and Fitz Hugh Ludlow, who Stephenson suggests we consider Beat predecessors. At sixty-seven years of age, Stephenson has assembled his recent writings on the Beats in *Pilgrims to Elsewhere*, a slim 111-page volume made up of fourteen chapters and an afterward by Bent Sørensen (publisher of EyeCorner Press). *Pilgrims* contains five close readings, a set of explanatory notes for readers of *The Dharma Bums*, three book reviews, a substantial essay on the work of Bob Kaufman, three brief cultural studies essays on Kerouac and Corso, as well notes on Ken Nordine and James S. Lee. What ties these disparate essays together, according to Stephenson, is a certain "disposition of spirit" shared by these writers; a sense of "being in exile on the earth . . . even as they share a desire to discover . . . a spiritual home" ("Preface" n.p.). Stephenson echoes here the concluding paragraph of his introduction to *The Daybreak Boys*: "The enduring value of these works lies in their particular pertinence to the central issues of human existence, their probing of human identity, and their quest for sacred vision" (15).

The content of *Pilgrims to Elsewhere* is anchored by the first three essays—a close reading of Ginsberg's "Supermarket in California," the Kaufman overview, and a close reading of Kerouac's *Old Angel Midnight*, the latter of which is one of six chapters on Kerouac in the volume, including two brief close readings of *On the Road*, a review of Isaac Gewirtz's *Kerouac at Bat: Fantasy Sports and the King of the Beats*, the above-mentioned explanatory notes, and a short cultural studies look at Kerouac and Harpo Marx. The first of these close readings explores the motif of rivers in *On the Road*. Stephenson sees the "river image as a potent, central symbol enriching and uniting [Kerouac's] narrative" (48), one which suggests "a larger, deeper scheme of things within which the lives of the novel's characters take place" (49); rivers "evoke a mystic or metaphysical sense of our place in history and eternity and thus act to underpin one of the novel's deepest truths, the sense of life's wonder and mystery, the sense of the infinite" (49). The second brief essay, which is partly a close reading and partly a cultural studies analysis, centers on Sal's night in Cheyenne, Wyoming, a place where, Stephenson suggests, the novel's "thematic strands . . . of anticipation and disappointment, ideals and realities, purpose and weakness, and knowledge of human duality and of the sorrow inherent in existence" first intersect (50). It is in Cheyenne that Sal experiences an emotion that will reoccur throughout the novel: "watching figures recede into the vastness behind him or away from him, feeling as they vanish from view an implacable sense of loneliness and loss"; here he learns the "inevitable forlornness of the human condition" (52–53). The latter half of this essay provides explanatory notes gleaned from the Cheyenne Genealogical and Historical Society for "the deeply devoted reader of *On the Road*"—facts and figures from radio station call letters and street names, to a brief history of chili con carne, a dish Sal indulges in during his night in Cheyenne.

The most fully realized of the Kerouac essays is "Earwitness Testimony: Sound and Sense, Word and Void in Jack Kerouac's *Old Angel Midnight*," which, interestingly, is the only essay in the collection that cites previous Beat scholarship. In fewer than thirty words, Stephenson quotes Dennis McNally, Gerald Nicosia, and James Jones as a jumping off point for his own reading of *Old Angel Midnight*. The book's lack of engagement with other Beat scholars is acceptable, though, considering that the subtitle informs us that these are "Reflections," not necessarily all-encompassing cutting-edge scholarship. The three "sympathetic readers," Stephenson argues, find *Old Angel Midnight* "'devoid of meaning in the common sense'" (quoting McNally), whereas he suggests that "the poem as a whole is not incomprehensible, and that (whatever other motifs may be present) *Old Angel Midnight* is essentially an expression of the most fundamental theme in Kerouac's writing—the search for reality" (36). Although McNally does refer to the poem as "devoid of meaning in the common sense" in *Desolate Angel: Jack Kerouac, the Beat Generation and America* (1979), he does not argue that it is the "Deathblow Putdown" Stephenson links his reading to; rather, McNally suggests *Old Angel Midnight* attempts to catch the "infinite sound of the universe . . . [in a] . . . high argument between Jack and God . . ." (216), a reading which seems to coincide with Stephenson's own argument. Likewise, Nicosia claims the poem is "animated by the tension between the knowledge that reality is deceptive and the hope that art can be truer . . ." (518). These points aside, Stephenson's subtle reading of the poem is substantial in content and length; indeed, it is twice as long as the combined number of pages all three critics he cites dedicate to the poem themselves. Stephenson sees *Old Angel Midnight* as a "kind of Buddhist cartoon, a vignette of infinity" in which "the teeming, babbling, multitudinous, mad world in all its mystery, comedy and horror" can be seen in "miniature, . . symbolizing the serene eternal emptiness of the Void or Divine Mind" (44). As such, he situates the poem alongside other Buddhist-themed texts such as *Tristessa, Visions of Gerard,* and *Mexico City Blues.*

As is the case with several of the chapters in *The Daybreak Boys*, "'The Beginning of the End': The Poetry of Bob Kaufman" provides readers new to the poet's work with a broad overview and discussion of the trajectory of his aesthetics from his earliest to most recent work. Indeed, this appears to be Stephenson's preferred mode of writing, which is understandable considering he was, according to Sørensen, the "one and only serious Beat scholar and specialist in Denmark" before the recent establishment of the European Beat Studies Network, which just "launched *Pilgrims to Elsewhere* at their second conference in Aalborg, Denmark" ("Afterward" 110). In other words, these essays tend to address themselves more toward new readers of the Beats than to seasoned American and other Beat scholars. However, as I discuss later, this focus gives the book an intriguing place in the Beat studies classroom.

Stephenson situates Kaufman's poems within three categories: "the personalist lyric, the poem as social protest, and the visionary poem," providing close readings of representative examples from each of Kaufman's books (21). Stephenson sees Kaufman primarily as a surrealist poet who employs "disjunction, ellipsis and fragmentation, inconsequence and juxtaposition" (21), and while he does acknowledge that Kaufman's improvisation comes from both jazz and surrealism, he does not discuss the former at any length.[1] The "personalist" theme, according to Stephenson's brief close readings, are "expressed in terms of surrealist metaphors" (22) in poems such as "I Have Folded My Sorrows," "Dolorous Echo," and "The Poet." Kaufman moves from "a calm control of the speaker's sadness and anguish" in the former (*Solitudes Crowded with Loneliness* 1965), to accepting his fate as a poet "despite the suffering inevitably to be endured" in taking on that role in the latter (*The Ancient Rain* 1981). His protest poems, such as "Benediction" and "The Ancient Rain," see "post-war American society as one compounded of interlocking, overlapping, mutually reinforcing systems or structures of power . . . [which] promote . . . homogeneity, complacency and passivity . . . ." (28). Kaufman's weapons, according to Stephenson, are humor and horror, calling to mind Corso's "Bomb," which Stephenson discusses later in the book. In his last collection, *The Ancient Rain*, Kaufman, while still openly critical of the United States, "remains resolutely optimistic as to the future glory of the nation" (29), a stance that was not fashionable among the literary left of the 1970s. What is needed, akin to Walt Whitman and Langston Hughes' visions of American equality, is the acceptance from the "waves of immigrants who fled . . . tyranny and hunger and injustice" ("The Ancient Rain" 77) of African Americans into the "great Sun of the Center" of democratic practices and ideals (81). Finally, Stephenson addresses what he refers to as Kaufman's "visionary and revelatory" poems. By "visionary," he does not suggest oracular meaning; rather, he argues that the "visionary quality of his poetry derives from his recurrent concern with supernatural experience," which often produced "startling, extravagant and magical images" through the poet's spontaneous composition of poems such as "Sun" and "Slight Alterations" (30). Though "uneven in quality," Stephenson closes by saying that Kaufman's most successful poems "manifest a powerful visual imagination and a daring intelligence" rife with "urgency and vividness of expression" (34).

In his earlier essay on Corso in *The Daybreak Boys*, "'The Arcadian Map': Notes on the Poetry of Gregory Corso," Stephenson argued that Corso's poetics of the imagination is founded on "a rejection of the tyranny of the real" (75). As he does in his Kaufman essay above, Stephenson posits an overarching thesis on the poet's aesthetic and follows its development throughout the poet's oeuvre. In the current volume, Stephenson includes two short three-to-four page close readings of two of Corso's poems: one well-known ("Bomb"), the other ("On Seeing Shelly's Paintings") a poem about painter Patrick Shelly who was "rediscovered" by Stephenson in *Scene* magazine. The latter essay, "A Few Notes on a Fugitive Poem by Gregory Corso," is as much an intriguing cultural studies discussion of period "men's magazines" such as *Nugget*, *Swank*, and *Mayfair*, which once published "serious literature, including poetry [that] cohabitated unapologetically with provocative photographs of nude women," as it is about this uncollected poem (81). "On Seeing Shelly's Paintings" is important to Corso scholarship in that it extols, like his other poems on artists such as Uccello, Bosch, and Kandisky, "Shelley's bold, potent 'Sensualism,' with its visual evocations of heightened experience, and scorns those artists . . . who fail to arouse humanity from its sensual slumber and self-satisfaction" (83).

One of the things this reader likes about the brief essays in *Pilgrims* is that what they lack in length and depth they more often than not make up for in sparks of interest; that is, they prompt one to rummage through one's own shelves, to take notes in the margins of the books/poems under discussion while reading the essays. Stephenson's discussion of this "fugitive poem" prompted me to likewise pick up "a magazine from the early 1960s" that "I had the good fortune to acquire" (81) a few years ago, thus enabling me to explore firsthand the "alliance . . . between men's magazines and the writers of the Beat Generation [as they] both sought to challenge traditional sanctions on the expression of sexuality . . ." (84). Like Stephenson's 1962 copy of *Scene*, my March 1961 issue of *Swank* is itself an interesting historical document in that Kerouac published selections from his just-released *Book of Dreams* (City Lights, December 1961) in a special nineteen-page section titled "The Swinging Modern Scene." Also included are "two of the freshest poet-prose writers on the downtown scene—Diane Di [sic] Prima . . . and Joel Oppenheimer" (51). Of more importance to Beat studies, though, is the inclusion of an essay by then twenty-two year old John Fles, former managing editor of the *Chicago Review*, titled "The Great Chicago Poetry Reading." Fles details the reading given by Ginsberg and Corso on the heels of the *Chicago Review* debacle which famously led to the founding of *Big Table* by Paul Carroll and other ex-*Chicago Review* editors. As one of the editors of *Swank* informs readers, "The true story [Fles] tells here rises into drama by its felt life and lack of phoniness. It also gives you some straight inside dope on the new literary movement that has shaken up the academies" (65). Indeed, as Stephenson tells readers in the closing of his Corso essay, "magazines such as *Scene* and its ilk helped in their time both to disseminate Beat writing and to make reading serious literature seem not an elitist or coterie activity, but an ordinary, pleasurable pursuit" (84–85).

    Pilgrims is rounded out with two review essays on books by Beat predecessors and fellow-travelers Fitz Hugh Ludlow and James S. Lee. The first of these is a review of the 2011 reprint of *The Hasheesh Eater: Being Passages from the Life of a Pythagorean* (1857) by twenty-two-year-old New Yorker Ludlow, whose method of composition was seemingly similar to Kerouac's spontaneous bop prosody in that *The Hasheesh Eater* was "composed . . . in urgent haste and without revision" while Ludlow was "enduring the after-effects" of the drug (91). Though Stephenson doesn't mention Williams S. Burroughs in the review, one can't help but see similarities to *The Yage Letters* as a "record of visions . . . interspersed with passages of reflection and analysis" (90) in Ludlow's own drug experiments "as a vehicle of exploration, a tool of discovery, in that it can provide glimpses of 'hitherto unconceived modes and uncharted fields of spiritual being . . .'" (93). Hints of the Burroughs to come also emerge in Stephenson's review of James S. Lee's *The Underworld of the East: Being Eighteen Years' Actual Experiences of the Underworlds, Drug Haunts and Jungles of India, China and the Malay Archipelago* (1937). While working as a miner in India in 1894, just twenty years before Burroughs' birth, Lee developed a morphine habit while suffering from malaria. Like the fictional William Lee "[i]ntrigued by drug-induced visions" in one of Burroughs' novels, James Lee "explores the narrow streets [of Calcutta and Benares] thronged with humans of every sort and condition—beggars, lepers, merchants, magicians [—] with keen interest in the strange and rich visual world of images deriving from the subliminal mind" (97). As with Burroughs in *The Yage Letters*, Lee, "[f]aced in the Sumatran jungle with Herculean endeavours . . . sustains himself with his drugs and continues his experiments, gathering local plants and roots said by the natives to be psycho-active" (98). It is not until the brief essay following the review of *The Underworld of the East* ("A Note on James S. Lee") that Stephenson explicitly makes the Lee-Burroughs connections: "Lee's long-term use of drugs of various kinds, his travels in jungles in search of unknown psychoactive plants, his explorations of the lower strata of cities, his opposition to the regimentation of industrial civilization, his interest in paranormal phenomena, his independent mind, all seem to prefigure William S. Burroughs" (103).However, the real connection between Lee and the Beats, Stephenson tells us, rests in his "cosmic optimism" that has more in common with the Buddhism of Snyder, Kerouac, and Ginsberg than with Burroughs.

In the conclusion to *The Daybreak Boys*, Stephenson argues that the Beats engage in "primitive ritual and archaic thought and with archetypal patterns of consciousness" (172), aligning them with the shamanistic tradition which "counter[s] the negative energies of the age with positive energies . . ." (185). The "Beat hero," he suggests, undergoes an initiation of "psychic transformation" to reach a "beatific state" of awareness and "universal liberation" (178–79). These are not new interpretations of Beat writers. But unlike in his earlier volume, Stephenson does not frame the essays in *Pilgrims* with a critical introduction and conclusion other than to briefly reiterate his earlier findings by suggesting the writers herein explored are "Pilgrims to Elsewhere" longing to "discover somewhere a haven, a heaven, a spiritual home" ("Preface" Pilgrims n.p.). If read as a companion volume to the earlier, more developed book, one does not so much need the conceptual framing; however, it would have been interesting and useful to read more about how Stephenson's overall understanding of the Beats has developed over the last twenty-five years—a twenty-five years of scholarship no doubt influenced by *The Daybreak Boys*, one of the first books to move away from Beat biography towards cultural contextualization and serious readings of the actual literature.

While *Pilgrims to Elsewhere* does not purport to break new scholarly ground, nor offer yet another historical retelling of the Beats, Stephenson's reflections add insight to the field of Beat studies, though as mentioned above, they are geared toward the general reader rather than to the specialist. In this regard, the real value of Stephenson's latest book lies in its potential for classroom application. Assigning the essays on "Supermarket in California," Kaufman's poetics, and the explanatory notes on *The Dharma Bums*, for example, can provide students new to the Beats with adequate background information, solid models for writing their own close readings, and useful examples of cultural studies approaches to help unpack the historical and cultural milieu in which the Beats were writing.

--- Todd Giles, Midwestern State University.

Notes

---

[1] For Kaufman's jazz aesthetic, see Lorenzo Thomas's "'Communicating by Horns': Jazz and Redemption in the Poetry of the Beats and the Black Arts

Movement" in the *African American Review* 26.2 (Summer 1992): 291–298; and Amor Kohli's "Saxophones and Smothered Rage: Bob Kaufman, Jazz, and the Quest for Redemption" in *Callaloo* 25.1 (Winter 2002): 165–182.

Works Cited

Jones, James T. *Jack Kerouac's Duluoz Legend: The Mythic Form of an Autobiographical Fiction*. Carbondale: Southern Illinois UP, 1999. Print.
McNally, Dennis. *Desolate Angel: Jack Kerouac, the Beat Generation and America*. 1979. New York: Random House, 2003. Print.
Nicosia, Gerald. *Memory Babe: A Critical Biography of Jack Kerouac*. 1983. Berkeley: U of California P, 1994. Print.
Stephenson, Gregory. *The Daybreak Boys: Essays on the Literature of the Beat Generation*. Carbondale: Southern Illinois UP, 1990. Print.
"The Swinging Modern Scene." *Swank* 8.1 (March 1961): 51–70. Print.

Scientologist! William S. Burroughs and the "Weird Cult"
David S. Wills
(Beatdom Books, 2013).

In 1984, I asked William Burroughs, "What is the connection between Dianetics and the cut-ups?" and I have been waiting a long time for someone to explain his answer. I had arrived in Lawrence straight from the archives at Columbia University where, among many unpublished letters, I discovered the startling sequence from October 1959 in which Burroughs announced his simultaneous discoveries of cut-up methods and Dianetics. I had transcripts of these revelatory letters with me when Burroughs replied briskly and precisely with just two words to my question about the connection: "None whatever." Thirty years ago, it was well known that Burroughs had become involved with the Church of Scientology in the late 1960s and early 1970s and that he had engaged in a series of public battles with L. Ron Hubbard in the pages of such magazines as *Mayfair* and *Rolling Stone*, culminating in Burroughs' *Ali's Smile/ Naked Scientology* (1978). At least I thought I knew that history well. David Wills reveals there is a good deal more to it, and although his book has too many flaws and limitations to be the one I have waited three decades for, it does go some way to explaining the baffling answer Burroughs gave in 1984.

For Burroughs, the rewriting of history was both a creative strategy and a biographical temptation—"Few things in my own past I'd just as soon forget," as his narrator puts it in *The Ticket That Exploded*—and his attempt to erase Scientology from the origins of his cut-up project is a reminder that for many years he infamously dismissed as "absurd" the true circumstances in which he shot and killed his wife, Joan Vollmer, in 1951. In fact, you might say that these denials are themselves connected and that Burroughs embraced Scientology and tried to turn *Dianetics: The Modern Science of Mental Health* into a creative method precisely in order to cut up the past. Certainly, his denial of Dianetics is significant since it has a material bearing on understanding his most important experimental work. *Scientologist! William S. Burroughs and the "Weird Cult"* focuses more on the psychology of the man than the creativity of the artist, which is one of its major flaws, but it has the great merits of being the first book to take the subject seriously and the first to dig into the archives—this time the vast and rich resources in the Berg Collection of the New York Public Library—to build on the truth that cut-ups did indeed go together with Scientology from the very start.

Burroughs' letters in October 1959—which climax with his insisting to Allen Ginsberg that "I tell you: 'Find a Scientology Auditor and have yourself run'"—were published twenty years ago, and the fact that they have attracted little attention since is one of David Wills' starting points. He sees it as a failure of imagination to realize that, back then, it was possible to take Scientology entirely seriously as a therapeutic science and an even greater failure of nerve to recognise that Burroughs' interest could have been both deeply serious and long lasting. More than that, he challenges the biographers and critics for effectively airbrushing out the unwelcome truth that the great iconoclast and skeptic could possibly have been such a credulous dupe. In effect, and quite rightly, Wills insists that it's time to give up the defensiveness inherited from an earlier period in Beat studies history, when sympathetic critics who championed Burroughs were battling academic marginalisation and mockery. Although Wills indulges in his own mocking of Burroughs—"he never did learn to stop believing incredible claims and bizarre promises"—it is this refusal of hagiography that allows him to rewrite the central narrative line of Burroughs' life and make visible the place of Scientology in it.

Scientologist! presents Hubbard's ideas about language, trauma, and control as logical and seductive for a man both acutely aware of how psychologically damaged he was and desperate to do something about it. The first chapter accordingly summarizes Burroughs up until 1959 as "a deeply disturbed man, loaded down with dark memories, insecurities, and traumas," and although the tone is breezy and reductive, it is also refreshingly provocative: maybe the Burroughs who tramped through the jungles of Central America in 1953 looking for a vine that could endow him with telepathic powers was indeed "excitable and gullible."

The bulk of *Scientologist!* documents Burroughs' ambivalent but enduring engagement with Scientology, from his taking up auditing techniques in Paris in 1959 to his enrollment at the church's British head office, Saint Hill, in 1968. The standard account of Burroughs' life is at times dramatically rewritten: in all the biographies, for example, Edinburgh is important for the August 1962 International Writers' Conference, at which Burroughs was publicly acclaimed for the first time; but in Wills' book, it is his success as a student at the Advanced Org Scientology Center there in 1968 which matters. (The Center's magazine graded his work highly, and highly amusingly: "Burroughs has made immense gains in his ability as a top professional writer, to start and finish major literary work."). Unearthing some fascinating evidence of Burroughs' Scientology studies, Wills proves his point that, without Hubbard, the story of Burroughs' life and of the whole decade-long cut-up project "is missing something." However, missing from Wills' own book is convincing textual evidence to show the significance of Scientology for the writer we think we know. Although he declares that Burroughs "learned from it and used it in the creation of his finest literary works," when he comes to those works the cupboard is disappointingly bare.

To begin with, Wills doesn't explore the potential impact of Scientology on the non-literary work Burroughs produced throughout the 1960s and early 1970s, his extensive experiments with photomontage, scrapbooks, and tape recordings. There has been some very good critical analysis of Burroughs' work with tapes, and it would have been interesting to reconsider those sonic experiments from the point of view of the early and direct crossover between cut-up methods and Scientology auditing techniques. Wills also limits the category of "literary works" by excluding the mass of short texts Burroughs wrote at this time. And yet these limits are not set pragmatically in order to focus more fully on the major books of the Cut-Up Trilogy. If "*The Soft Machine*, one of his best known novels, is utterly inspired by Scientology," it would take more than a single page of commentary to show it. Quoting only one passage, Wills concludes, vaguely, "This all takes off from the notion of the reactive mind." The rest of the trilogy fares little better: two pages on *The Ticket That Exploded*, focused on the most obvious passage explicitly about Scientology, and a slightly longer discussion of *Nova Express* that includes a quotation from the text with more than half a dozen transcription errors. Although you wouldn't expect polished writing and perfect proofreading from a self-published book, such visible sloppiness is a distraction that also undermines confidence where it is most needed: in the original archival research, which is the major claim to value of Wills' book.

Anyone who has worked in the Berg Collection in the New York Public Library, or just scanned the nearly 200-page Burroughs Papers catalogue, will sympathise; it is overwhelming in size and exceedingly difficult to navigate. The frustratingly skimpy Notes section in *Scientologist!* suggests its research was based on raiding the archive as if making a Google search, which is to look where the light is shining. To give just two examples: Wills speculates that Burroughs picked up ideas about "waking suggestion" at Saint Hill in 1968, unaware of explicit archival evidence dating from 1960; and the irony of discovering that Burroughs accused Hubbard of anti-Semitism and invoked the Protocols of Zion is lost without knowing that, elsewhere in the Berg archive, there's ample, alarming evidence of Burroughs' own earlier subscription to identical views. More substantially, work on the archival manuscripts might have shown which literary material bearing the stamp of Scientology *did not* make the final cut for the Cut-Up Trilogy or *The Wild Boys*. Such work could also reveal what, if anything, lay behind the direct appearance of Hubbard in *Minutes to Go* (1960), where he is named and quoted after Burroughs, Gysin, Beiles, and Corso as if he were the fifth author of the launching manifesto of cut-up methods. Such shortcomings in the research, together with the book's failure to demonstrate Scientology's creative importance in the oeuvre, do not, however, lessen its value in making us rethink Burroughs' biography and in serving as a wake-up call to those who take the skeptic on his own terms and treat the iconoclast as an icon—which in the end counts for more than whether Burroughs was a good Scientologist.

---Oliver Harris

Works Cited

Burroughs, William S. *Ali's Smile/Naked Scientology*. Bonn: Expanded Media Editions, 1978. Print.

---. *Nova Express: the Restored Text*. New York: Grove, 2014. Print.

---. *The Ticket That Exploded: the Restored Text*. New York: Grove, 2014. Print.

---. *Wild Boys*. New York: Grove, 2014. Print.

Burroughs, William S., Gysin; Brion, Beiles; Sinclair; and Corso, Gregory. *Minutes to Go*. Paris: Two Cities Edition, 1960. Print.

L. Ron Hubbard. *Dianetics: The Modern Science of Mental Health*. New Edition. Commerce, California: Bridge, 2007. Print.

Text and Drugs and Rock 'n' Roll: The Beats and Rock Culture
Simon Warner
(London: Bloomsbury, 2013)

A comprehensive account of the many connections between the Beat Generation and rock music is long overdue, and the expansive nature of the topic is clear from the very fact that Simon Warner's new book spins out more than five-hundred pages without exhausting its possibilities. True, the volume acquires some of its heft from multiple iterations of various facts, descriptions, references, and citations that come around on the guitar again and again, to paraphrase the immortal "Alice's Restaurant" by Arlo Guthrie. Generally speaking, though, *Text and Drugs and Rock 'n' Roll: The Beats and Rock Culture* gallops through the territory at a lively clip, drawing on a large, if incomplete, storehouse of existing books, articles, broadcasts, interviews, and e-mails. It isn't exhaustive or exhausting, but in both departments it comes close.

Warner's fundamental idea is that the original Beat writers, first prominent in the 1950s, and the musicians of the British invasion and acid rock, most prominent in the 1960s, were connected in ways that both symbolized and facilitated the breakdown of constraining boundaries between "high" and "low" culture, which had needlessly divided audiences, critics, and academics into divergent camps of mutually uncomprehending partisans. The key year in this development was 1965, the key location was San Francisco, and the key event was the so-called "Last Gathering of the Beats" at the City Lights Bookstore, which brought Lawrence Ferlinghetti, Allen Ginsberg, Peter Orlovsky, Michael McClure, and a few other literati together with Bob Dylan, then making his transition from progressive folk musician to dynamic rocker. Those present were famously photographed by Larry Keenan, although as Warner notes in one of the book's many historical ironies, the image later seen most widely—of sundry Beats and fellow travelers hobnobbing outside the bookstore—does not include Dylan.

In his opening pages, Warner posits the importance of that occasion through a string of questions that the rest of the book addresses in a semi-organized series of essays, interviews, reviews, and obituaries. The following provides a good example of Warner's questions and style:

> What could an older generation of writers, all close to, or well past, that
> age that baby-boomer rock 'n' rollers appeared to fear most – the onset of
> the dreaded 30 – impart to this open-minded, loose-limbed, long-haired
> superstar who had caught the attention of a billion disciples. What could the
> crusty, curling leaves of a book of verse, the thumb-eased, dog-eared pages

> of a well-turned novel, teach this freewheeling, folk-strumming general
> at the head of much younger battalions raised on the television's magic
> eye, the arrival of the space age and the mesmerizing cacophony of a new
> music that promised dreams of love, of life, of liberty. How could the grey
> 1950s, broadcast in monochrome and cowering in the Cold War shadows,
> lend any energising spark to the glowing 1960s, shot in Technicolor and
> screened in Cinemascope?[1] (3)

The breathless, near-logorrheic prose is typical of Warner's writing, as is the casual way with punctuation, question marks included. Matters of orthography are details, but details are the heart and soul of this book, which makes up in teeming minutiae what it lacks in big-picture analysis.

Like many historians of the Beats and their context, Warner opens with an overview of the American sociocultural landscape in the years after World War II, pointing out its strengths—a booming economy, a flood of new technologies and conveniences—along with its weaknesses, from racism and materialism to conformity, consumerism, and cold-war paranoia. Bebop, abstract-expressionist painting, William Carlos Williams's revolutionary verse, and J.D. Salinger's 1951 novel *The Catcher in the Rye* are among the touchstones in Warner's account. But the events that best crystallize the era for him are the arrival of "Howl," which Ginsberg unveiled as a work in progress at the legendary 6 Gallery reading in San Francisco in 1955, and the ascent of Bill Haley and His Comets to the top of the singles charts with "(We're Gonna) Rock Around the Clock," a 1954 hit that achieved pop-culture ubiquity when it rang out in Richard Brooks's movie *Blackboard Jungle* the following year.

Tying the epic poem and the pop single together is a tricky business. Warner makes more than one stab at the task in a chapter called "Sifting the Shifting Sands," eventually pulling it off with a double maneuver. For his first move, he identifies "Howl" and "Rock Around the Clock" as early clues to the new direction of the American ethos, foreshadowing the radical shifts of the middle 1960s, when "the jump and jive innocence of rock 'n' roll" would mature into "the earnest exhorting of a new rock" that was sophisticated enough for Beat writers to "feed into and bounce off" in fresh, productive ways (67–68). For his second and more substantial move, Warner places the Ginsberg poem and the Haley recording under the rubric of postmodernism, which stems (according to cultural critic Fredric Jameson, whom Warner cites) from a hypothetical break with the century-old modernist movement that happened sometime around 1960. The convergence of styles and traditions in pop music—black and white, blues and country—was not so very different from the heterogeneity of Beat writing, which intermingled anecdote, autobiography, performance, and an array of other resources while to some degree rejecting academic formalism and steering clear of establishment publishers. All of this started, Warner suggests, with the advent of a poem and a song in the middle 1950s.

My admiration for "Howl" and affection for Bill Haley and His Comets notwithstanding, I am skeptical about Warner's quest for a quasi-originating moment in the marriage of Beat literature and rock music. For one thing, "Rock Around the Clock" wasn't the first of its kind or even unique among Haley's early records with the Comets, as those of us who dug their 1954 recordings of "Shake, Rattle and Roll" and "Thirteen Women (and Only One Man in Town)" can attest. More broadly, the glories of pre-1960 rock 'n' roll were far too varied and ingenious—not in lyrics or harmonies, of course, but in texture, mood, economy, and passion—to be written off as throwaway commodities, reductively described by Warner as "merely concerned with…boy-meets-girl . . . adolescent-oriented obsessions" (68). Most importantly, the paradigm-changing breakthroughs in songwriting made by Dylan and the Beatles were extensions, not revocations, of earlier pop traditions. The Beatles produced many brilliant covers of rock 'n' roll classics and embodied the spirit of their predecessors to the end of their joint career, and Dylan was influenced by the Everly Brothers and Elvis Presley as well as Woody Guthrie and Ramblin' Jack Elliot. Then too, Warner treats Dylan's move from acoustic, folk-oriented music to electric, rock-oriented music as a singular seismic event, whereas it was actually one of many self-reinventions that Dylan has accomplished, some before 1965 and others since.

Again these are details, but I dwell on them because this chapter lays the groundwork for all the pages to come, and Warner's methodology—subordinating synthesis and analysis to the accretion of facts, conjectures, opinions, and endless "name-checking," a term he uses way too often—yields scattershot results. It's also regrettable that Ginsberg and Burroughs get far more attention than other Beats. It would have been difficult to bring Kerouac in more frequently, given his obstreperous aversion to progressive politics, but Gregory Corso and Gary Snyder deserve more space. On the bright side, there's a marvelous interview with the marvelous poet David Meltzer, and Warner conducts worthwhile talks with photographer Keenan (it's too bad the book includes no illustrations) and composer David Amram, whose credits include the music for Robert Frank and Alfred Leslie's 1959 film *Pull My Daisy*, still the Beat Generation movie par excellence. For variety, there's also an interview with McClure in which the poet proves surly, defensive, and self-important.

My complaints aside, *Text and Drugs and Rock 'n' Roll* is a goldmine for anyone fascinated with the particulars of Beat and rock in the all-important postwar era, which exerts an uncanny sway over pop culture even now. Few essential names of the period are left unchecked. Substantial chapters home in on Dylan's relationships with Beats and beatniks; Ginsberg's illuminating trip to Liverpool in 1965; the heyday of hippies, flower power, and S*gt. Pepper's Lonely Hearts Club Band*; the exploits of Patti Smith, Jim Carroll, Genesis P-Orridge, and Steven Taylor; and welcome treatment of Beat women in a section called "Muse, Moll, Maid, Mistress?", plus wild rides through the British counterculture. While Kerouac makes fewer appearances than Ginsberg and Burroughs, there's ample coverage of Tom Waits' romance with his writing and the ways Kerouac has been commemorated in his hometown since his death.

The present time is highly interesting for people who care about the Beat Generation's legacy. New books on the subject continue to appear, and an unexpected spate of feature films—Walter Salles's *On the Road,* John Krokidas's *Kill Your Darlings,* Rob Epstein and Jeffrey Friedman's *Howl,* and Michael Polish's *Big Sur,* the best of the bunch—have brought Beat stories, personalities, and aesthetics to the big screen. *Text and Drugs and Rock 'n' Roll* may ride this wave to high visibility and a broad readership, or it may sink under the weight of its prolixity. Either way, it's a unique contribution to the field.

---David Sterritt

Notes

¹ CinemaScope is the proper spelling of that quintessentially 1950s screen format.

Works Cited

Ginsberg, Allen. "Howl." *Howl and Other Poems*. San Francisco: City Lights, 1956. Print.
Jameson, Fredric. *Postmodernism, or, The Cultural Logic of Late Capitalism.* Durham, NC: Duke U P, 1991. Print.
Salinger, J.D. *The Catcher in the Rye*. Boston: Little, Brown, 1951. Print.

The Beats: A Very Short Introduction
by David Sterritt

The Beat Generation: A Beginner's Guide
by Christopher Gair

Short cut guides clamor for our attention: "10 Easy Ways To Lose Weight," "Five Investments the IRS Doesn't Want You To Know," "Lower Your Credit Scores With This One Weird Trick." Problems arise when we over-rely on quick hits for academic purposes. Teachers complain that students depend on Wikipedia for research rather than on vetted academic sources, but students vow that for quick, basic information, Wikipedia can be, in the words of its founder Jimmy Wales, "good enough information." In addition, the information appears in seconds on their smart phones. Several months ago, I learned all that I needed to know about AC power plugs and sockets from Wikipedia's entry on the topic. But that does not qualify me to do electrical work, and likewise these brief guides to financial gain or weight loss do not qualify us to invest our money wisely or give dietary counseling, either. David Sterritt and Christopher Gair have written academic, reliable, limited guides that draw from their academic backgrounds. Just as a ten-step guide to AC power plugs and sockets will not qualify someone to, say, wire my neighbor's house, neither will these books set someone up to be an authority on the Beat Generation—and that is not their aim.

David Sterritt's *The Beats: A Very Short Introduction* is referred to by Regina Weinreich as a "primer," and with dimensions of about seven inches by four and-a-half inches, and but a half-inch thick, it is praised by Lisa Jardine for its "snappy, small format." Its subtitle announces the book's value as well as its limitations. The Very Short Introductions series, according to Oxford University Press's webpage, provides "the perfect introduction to subjects you previously knew nothing about," and there are literally hundreds of titles in the series, from Advertising, Ancient Warfare, and Continental Philosophy to Folk Music, Quantum Theory, and Viruses. A first impression can lead one to imagine certain people reading these guides by the dozens and growing insufferable at dinner parties. Only closer analysis reveals the value of specific guides. Sterritt, for example, is a Beat scholar and film critic: his Beat-related studies include *Mad to Be Saved: The Beats, the '50s, and Film* (1998) and *Screening the Beats: Media Culture and the Beat Sensibility* (2004). His introduction to the Beats is compellingly well written, culturally comprehensive, and generally free of both the patronizing putdowns and the glazed idolatry of many introductory items written about the Beats.

When introducing a topic such as the Beats with its nebulous origins and serpentine ongoing influences, one might consider literature, biography, politics, cultural issues, commercialization, and religion among the topics to be sorted through, a task that seems beyond the range of a "very short introduction." Sterritt plots a sensible course that allows him to touch on these while foregrounding the Beat Generation as an artistic movement that responded to the pressing cultural issues of its time, concluding with a treatment of the Beats' legacy. Sterritt presents the Lost Generation for contrast before providing readers a condensed version of the "less-than-fabulous" 1950s, succinctly describing the pervasiveness of the six Cs—Conformity, Conservatism, Consumerism, Consensus, Common Sense, and Cold-War Paranoia—deftly working in references to *The Man in the Grey Flannel Suit*, "planned obsolescence," and "Leave It to Beaver." He also leaves the specific and frequently problematic definition of the Beat Generation to sufficiently vague generalities: "The Beats were an informal group, to the extent that they were a group at all" (35). As for the literary impact of the entire "Beatnik" movement, Sterritt points out that "fewer than ten percent of them (one-hundred and fifty or so) ever published any writing at all" (92). Sterritt does not indicate how he arrived at this fascinating figure, or how he determined which published writers had "beatnik" backgrounds, but if we accept his general point, then we can situate the writers he focuses on at the productive center of a movement that was then spun by Beatsploitation books, movies, and televisions shows as well as picked up by bohemian-sympathetic types across the country and ultimately around the globe.

In between outlining the Beats' origins and describing their impact on popular culture, Sterritt focuses on the Beat novel (the works of Jack Kerouac and William S. Burroughs), on Beat poetry (the works of Allen Ginsberg and Gregory Corso), and on "more" (works of Lawrence Ferlinghetti, Neal Cassady, John Clellon Holmes, Kenneth Rexroth, Gary Snyder, Leroi Jones, Ken Kesey, and Bob Kaufman). Despite the proliferation of critical works that position women in central roles within the Beat movement, Sterritt considers only Anne Waldman and Diane di Prima among them. A few other caveats need to be mentioned as well: on the first page, Sterritt describes the Beat impulse as an "angry assault" that "took aim" with its "provocative works." These terms sound more like those used by the Beats' contemporary media than those associated with the objectives of Beats themselves or with more recent critical discourse about them. Since Introductions leave lasting impressions, readers might be better served with a different cast of terms.

As is typical of Beat starter books geared for the general reading audience, Sterritt treats Kerouac to more ink than any of the other Beat figures, which may be helpful for teachers assigning a Kerouac novel who wish to include a helpful sense of the Beat background. *The Beats: A Very Short Introduction* may also be a useful *supplement* for courses beyond ones that focus on Kerouac: those that treat the Beats generally, that deal with sociological/historical issues, that deal with mid-century U.S. history, and so on. In a recent upper-level undergrad course on Literary Modernism, I assigned *Modernism: A Very Short Guide* (2010) by Christopher Butler. After the first month of our course I asked my students to read it over a weekend, and they struggled to get through it. I learned that such introductions might be short but do not necessarily serve easily as do-it-yourself guides for undergrads who do not have sufficient contextual background in the arts.

Christopher Gair's *The Beat Generation: A Beginner's Guide* (2008) is a volume in Oneworld Publications' Beginners Guides, a counterpart to Oxford Universtiy Press' Very Short Introductions. The book is structured similarly to Sterritt's: the Beats' cultural and historical background, the origins of the movement, significant devotion to Kerouac, a treatment of "other voices," and, finally, the "Legacy of the Beat Generation." Gair contrasts his study with other Beat introductions by enlarging the focus to include more writers while at the same time avoiding the dilution he believes is problematic in other (unidentified) studies. At the same time, Gair distinguishes his book by limiting the scope of his study to "texts written during or directly about the Beat world of the 1940s and 1950s" (5). Such limitation means that he does not provide analysis of, say, *Naked Lunch* or *The Soft Machine*. On the other hand, Gair does provide an assessment of the arts of the 1940s as prototypes of the developing Beat writers, a grounding not frequently undertaken in basic Beat introductions. Gair also strategically insets text boxes in his chapters that deal with associated issues and writers. For example, readers make connected side trips into Transcendentalism, Thomas Wolfe, and William Blake. Gair also traces core themes in Kerouac's work, as opposed to Sterritt's novel-by-novel treatment, a strategy that then incorporates these themes into his overall book.

In addition to a few pesky errors (he states, for example, that thirty-five-year-old Jack Kerouac appeared on *The Tonight Show* with Steve Allen; in fact, Kerouac's famous television appearance was on *The Steve Allen Show* in November 1959, when Kerouac was thirty-seven), Gair typically cites secondary sources in his notes instead of the original sources. He might be doing this because secondary sources are often easier for general readers to locate, but digital research makes it much easier than it used to be for readers to locate primary sources.

This basic format for Beat introductions employed by Sterritt and Gair seems to be universally applied. Edward Halsey Foster's *Understanding the Beats* (1992) is the same: a chapter introducing hipsters and Beats; one each on Kerouac, Ginsberg, Corso, and Burroughs; and then a chapter on the legacy. In fact, Foster's book, probably the most critically insightful among these various introductory books, and his individual chapters suffice as stand-alone critical treatments more or less independently of his overall book. Gair's book, by contrast, is more thoroughly integrated thematically, so that readers benefit most by considering it as a whole as he aims to outline the history, reception, and legacy of the Beats.

The first book-length analysis of the Beats is Bruce Cook's entertaining *The Beat Generation: The Tumultuous '50s Movement and Its Impact on Today* (1971). Cook was a journalist who covered cultural issues, and he portrays the personalities of the Beat writers whom he interviewed and attempts to convey the feeling of the 1950s in which they wrote. Cook's overview was followed in 1976 by John Tytell's masterful *Naked Angels: Lives and Literature of the Beat Generation*. Since then, readers have an onslaught of guides, not just anthologies or collections of critical essays, and their relative merits very greatly. *The Birth of the Beat Generation: Visionaries, Rebels, and Hispsters 1944–1960* by Steve Watson (1998) provides provocative and useful photgraphs of a range of Beat male writers, as well as important timelines of Beat events. *This Is the Beat Generation* by James Campbell (2001) focuses on Kerouac, Ginsberg, and Burroughs, erroneously calling them "Beats" as if no other existed; the text is pitched somewhat too high for most fans and newcomers to the Beats but also provides little that is new for the informed Beat Studies scholar. *The Beats: A Graphic History* by Harvey Pekar, Paul Buhle, and Ed Piskor (2010) is not intended for scholars, with many of the drawings conveying misleading portraits of history, especially in the first half. Later portraits of Diane di Prima and LeRoi Jones effectively expand the Beat circle. However, there are no scholarly apparatuses, and overall no newcomer to Beat history should rely upon this graphic version. That same year, 2010, also saw the publication of *The Typewriter Is Holy: The Complete, Uncensored History of the Beat Generation* by Bill Morgan. The title itself warns off any seasoned reader, since no "complete" history exists, and those familiar with the basic figures, texts, and themes of this complex coterie will not profit much from the reading. But it is an accessible, reliable portrait for those new to the Beats, in no small part because it clearly outlines a kind of time-map that positions key Beat figures; readers can readily understand where various Beat figures were in relation to one another at a given time. For these and other reasons, one might consider it for classroom use and general reference. Morgan's *Beat Atlas: A State by State Guide to the Beat Generation in America,* published in 2012, is a very different sort of introductory text, blending the tourist's walking guide with a historical/cultural study. The result is somewhat mixed: travelers may find it difficult to follow it geographically from location to location, and Morgan's cultural metaphor of the process of aesthetic mapping does not push scholarship into the transitional arenas now opening up. But, as Jimmy Fazzino wrote in his review of the book for the *Beat Review*, "Morgan's Beat map of America is open, decentered and non-hierarchical, shot through with the radical immanence of proliferating sites of contact and community," which a sholar might well find captivating and enlightening, especially since Morgan's title relies upon the expansive "America" rather than "United States." Finally, as of March 2013, we have *Mania: The Story of the Outraged and Outrageous Lives That Launched a Cultural Revolution* by Ronald Collins and David Skover, which begins with the highly sensationalized killing of David Kammerer by Lucien Carr. The text is by no means a comprehensive introduction to Beat history and literature, since both started long before that tragic event, but it does provide solid material on legal histories related to key Beat writers, such as Allen Ginsberg and the *Howl* trial in San Fransico. The text, however, is written as a third-person dramatic monologue, so readers view this history and culutural analyses through the vision of an unknown and unreliable narrator. The narrative is engaging but conscientious readers should rely on the comprehensively listed sources that Collins and Skover provide. Despite the authors' efforts at exhaustive research, the book would be stronger had they availed themselves of more recently available archival materials. All in all, *caveat emptor* to any reader seeking reliable introductions to Beat writers and Beat studies.

David Sterritt and Christopher Gair's books ably assist their readers; they impart information and background to construct suitable introductions for students and general readers. Since no doubt the genre(s) of Beat writers and their social impacts will be packaged for new readers, certainly the volumes we have seen set the pattern, and subsequent books will build on their predecessors. Yet introductions are limited by nature. The traits that will not be included and excluded in upcoming years will vary depending on the perspectives of the literary and social scholars who produce them; selection is never free from bias. Readers would be helpfully challenged by introductions that maintain historical context while offering insights relevent to their contemporary audience. In any case, the role of women needs to be more fully integrated into any comprehensive introduction. Gender roles were far more delineated in the middle of the century than they are today, and any young readers would benefit from understanding how the frank Beat impulses resonated so powerfully with women who made their own solid contributions to social and spiritual liberations.

Basic print formats for introductions will change as well. Academcis might not go to Wikipedia for a quick dose of information, but everyone else does. Some literary topics on Wikipedia are thoroughly and credibly developed; the Beats would be well served if Beat studies scholars would take the time to correct Beat-related errors or misinterpretations on Wikipedia when they see them and to back the information with authoritative sources. Wikipedia will not be the only one digitally accessed source for readers interested in the Beats. The Beat writers are enmeshed in such sites as poets.org and more thoroughly at poetryfoundation. org. In addition, interested fans and scholars have put together web sites devoted to the Beats and inidividual writers (one thinks of Levi Asher's litkicks.com and allenginsberg.org among them), and Google corrals these effectively. It is likely that as access to digital information continues to grow and the perspectives on the Beats proliferate, individual users will assemble their own collations to serve as introductions, stored on their own devices, effectively decentralizing the role of the authoritative guide. The Internet is not the only medium that alters readers' receptions of the Beats; many new readers discover the Beats because of the explosion of movies in recent years that deal with them. Readers may accept that these often-overdramatized movies provide all the introduction they require. Carolyn Cassady fought an exasperating battle during the last half of her life to undo what she claimed were damaging misrepresentations of the people she knew in the 1940s and '50s. Such distortions are likely to grow more pronounced as time passess. On the other hand, the passing of time also provides perspective. What will happen when people ask their smartphones, "What is the Beat Generation?" Until those answers grow to be more satisfying, we should recommend books such as those by Sterritt and Gair that are intended as footholds for initiates. Then we should recommend futher guides that more fully develop the complexity of the topic in a way that brief introductions are not designed to do.

---Matt Theado,
Kobe City University of Foreign Studies. Kobe, Japan

Works Cited

Campbell, James. *This Is the Beat Generation*. Berkeley: U of California P, 2001. Print.

Collins. Ronald and David Skover. *Mania*. Chicago: Top Five, 2013. Print.

Cook. Bruce. *The Beat Generation: The Tumultuous '50s Movement and Its Impact on Today*. New York: Scribner, 1971. Print.

Fazzino, James. Rev. of *Beat Atlas: A State by State Guide to the Beat Generation in America*. (San Francisco: City Lights, 2012. Print.) in *The Beat Review* 5:3 (2012). N. pag. Web. Jan. 3, 2012.

Morgan, Bill. *Beat Atlas: A State by State Guide to the Beat Generation in America*. San Francisco: City Lights, 2012. Print.

---. *The Typewriter Is Holy: The Complete, Uncensored History of the Beat Generation*. New York: Free, 2010. Print.

Pekar, Harvey, Paul Buhle, and Ed Piskor. *The Beats: A Graphic History*. New York: Hill and Wang, 2010. Print.

Tytell, John. *Naked Angels: Lives and Literature of the Beat Generation*, New York: McGraw Hill, 1976. Ivan Dee edition, 2006. Print.

Watson, Steve. *The Birth of the Beat Generation: Visionaries, Rebels, and Hipsters 1944–1960*. New York: Pantheon, 1998. Print.

The Beat Index 2013

To continue to keep our readers abreast of current scholarship, we will publish an annual index of books, articles, and dissertations on the Beat Generation and writers associated with the Beat movement.

If you wish to have your scholarship included in the annual index, send bibliographic information and a summary abstract to Nancy Grace (Ngrace@wooster.edu).

Abstracts are from the publisher's website, from the journal in which the article appeared, or prepared by the *Journal of Beat Studies* editorial staff.

Beat Generation (general)

Ashton, Jennifer. *The Cambridge Companion to American Poetry since 1945.* New York City, New York: Cambridge UP, 2013. Print.

> The extent to which American poetry reinvented itself after World War II is a testament to the changing social, political, and economic landscape of twentieth-century American life. Registering an important shift in the way scholars contextualize modern and contemporary American literature, this *Companion* explores how American poetry has documented and, at times, helped propel the literary and cultural revolutions of the past sixty-five years. Offering authoritative and accessible essays from fourteen distinguished scholars, the *Companion* sheds new light on the Beat, Black Arts, and other movements while examining institutions that govern poetic practice in the United States today. The text also introduces seminal figures like Sylvia Plath, John Ashbery, and Gwendolyn Brooks while situating them alongside phenomena such as the "academic poet" and popular forms such as spoken word and rap, revealing the breadth of their shared history. Students, scholars, and readers will find this *Companion* an indispensable guide to post-war and late twentieth-century American poetry. (Cambridge University)

Feldman, Gene and Max Gartenberg. *The Beat Generation & The Angry Young Men.* Eureka, California: Stark House, 2013. Digital.

> A celebration of the anti-establishment literature of the 1950s including excerpts from the works of those who led the movements in the U.S. and England. Originally published by Citadel Press in 1958, this new edition

offers the best of the anti-establishment authors like Jack Kerouac, William S. Burroughs, Allen Ginsburg, Kingsley Amis, Norman Mailer, Colin Wilson and many more, with a new introduction by the editors' daughters. The Beat Generation and the Angry Young Men voiced a cry, and it is still being heard today. (General abstract)

Grace, Nancy M. "The Crisis of Beat Studies Scholarship." *Resources for American Literary Studies*." 36.1 (2013): 311–319. Print.

The review-essay considers *Capturing the Beat Moment: Cultural Politics and the Poetics of Presence*, by Erik Mortenson, as a vehicle not only to assess Mortenson's text but also to explore the current state of the field of Beat studies. Specifically, this review-essay addresses the roles of graduate programs, the early reputation of Beat writers as nonacademic no-nothings, the quality of seminal studies of Beat literature, and the popular and academic publishing worlds—all of which have contributed to an erosion of scholarly standards in the field. (General abstract)

Johnson, Ronna C. "Three Generations of Beat Poetics." *The Cambridge Companion to American Poetry 1945*. Ed. Jennifer Ashton. New York City, New York: Cambridge UP, 2013. 80–93.

The Beat generation emerged after World War II in New York City and San Francisco, concurrently with abstract expressionism in painting and bebop jazz. Characterized by Allen Ginsberg as "a group of friends who had worked together on poetry, prose and cultural conscience from the mid-forties until the term became popular nationally in the late fifties," the Beat movement carried its diverse poetics and composition techniques through three generations into the mid-1960s, forming a coherent and mature identity. Beat's eclecticism absorbed the aesthetics of abstract expressionist painting and bebop jazz, Buddhist ethics and practices, nineteenth-century American Romanticism, and twentieth-century modernism. While Beat poetry drew from Ezra Pound and William Carlos Williams and the modernist imperative to "make it new," it transcended these forms to construct a new poetics suited to the Atomic Age. And while it owed a debt to Charles Olson's "Projective Verse," it translated Olson's privileging of the breath into the collective space of the performance, anticipating slam and other recent modes of open improvisation. (Cambridge)

Johnston, P.J. "Dharma Bums: The Beat Generation and the Making of Countercultural Pilgrimage." *Buddhist-Christian Studie*s. 33.1 (2013): 165–179. Print.

The article offers the author's insights regarding the spirituality of the Beat generation and the formation of countercultural pilgrimage. The author mentions that the scholarly neglect of Beat spirituality continues because religious studies retain problematic theoretical components such as the Eliadean fetishization and the Durkheimian assumption that religion is genuine. The author adds that the best countercultural pilgrimage account is the first-person description of the traveler. (General abstract)

Martin, Michelle. "The Burden of Legend: Beat Studies in the Twenty-First Century." *Journal of Modern Literatur*e. 36.4 (2013): 161–172. Print.

This review considers five new books related to the Beat Movement. *Jack Kerouac and Alien Ginsberg: The Letters*, edited by Bill Morgan and David Stanford, compiles a vast wealth of exchanges between the two Beat icons, spanning several decades of their friendship. Bill Morgan's new history, *The Typewriter is Holy*, presents an extensive overview of the movement, encompassing key figures and events in an accessible narrative. Todd F. Tietchen's book, *The Cubalogues: Beat Writers in Revolutionary Havana*, focuses on the experiences of Beat authors in Cuba and provides an in-depth analysis of how Cuban-American interchanges influenced the political orientations of these Beat writers, claiming that Cuba's early revolutionary era inspired radical Beat politics while later serving as a cautionary example. In *Capturing the Beat Moment: Cultural Politics and the Poetics of Presence*, Erik Mortenson argues that Beat artistic p r a c t i c e s should be understood as a "poetics of presence" and re-periodicizes Beat literature as early postmodern. For the 25th anniversary of the publication of William S. Burroughs's *Queer*, Oliver Harris has edited a new, substantially changed edition of the novel. In his introduction, Harris provides his rationale guiding the changes and examines the scope of the novel's politics. (General abstract)

Mortensen, Erik. "The 'Underground' Reception of the Beats in Turkey." *Comparative American Studies*. 11.3 (2013): 327–341. Print.

This article examines how Beat texts are received in Turkey as underground literature and what that reception reveals not only about the possibilities for cultural dissent in Turkey, but also about the extent to which the

Beats are still capable of promoting social change in general. While translations of Beat Generation texts are a fairly recent phenomenon in Turkey, the internet has provided them with additional exposure, with the result that Beat texts play a role in discussions of the growing genre of underground literature in Turkey. This study analyzes that role in order to discuss questions of commodification, transgression, censorship, and cultural difference that have had an impact on Beat texts in Turkey. Beat writers offer a form of resistance that allows Turkish readers to challenge mainstream values and mount legal challenges through the classic figure of the Beat rebel. This unique situation provides insight not only into the possibilities of culturally translating an imported counterculture, but also provides a refracted view of the assumptions operating in that countercultural model as it is redeployed in a different nation at a different moment of history. (General abstract)

Mackay, Polina and Chad Weidner. "Introduction: The Beat Generation and Europe." *Comparative American Studies*. 11.3 (2013): 221–226. Print.

The article introduces the September 2013 issue of the journal, highlighting its central theme of the Beat generation's transnational influences in Europe, citing contributions by Luke Walker, Véronique Lane, and Maria Jackson. (General abstract)

Petrich, Tatum L. *The Girl Gang: Women Writers of the New York City Beat Community*. Diss. Temple University, 2012. Philadelphia: Temple U, 2013.

The Girl Gang: Women Writers of the New York City Beat Community seeks to revise our understanding of the Beat community and literary tradition by critically engaging the lives and work of five women Beat writers: Diane di Prima, Joyce Johnson, Hettie Jones, Carol Bergé, and Mimi Albert. This dissertation argues that, from a position of marginality, these women developed as protofeminist writers, interrogating the traditional female gender role and constructing radical critiques of normative ideas in fiction and poetry in ways that resisted the male Beats' general subordination of women and that anticipated the feminist movement of the late 1960s and 1970s. A project of recovery and criticism, *The Girl Gang* provides literary biographies that explore how each writer's experience as a marginalized female writer within an otherwise countercultural community affected the development of her work; it also analyzes a range of works (published and unpublished texts from various genres, written from the early 1950s through the turn of the twenty-first century) in order to illustrate how each writer distinctively employs and revises mainstream and Beat literary and cultural conventions. The dissertation's critical analyses examine each writer's engagement in various literary, cultural, and social discourses, drawing attention to their incisive and provocative treatment of thematic issues that are central to the postwar countercultural critique of hegemonic norms—including fundamental Beat questions of identity, authenticity, and subjectivity—and that are developed through experimentation with literary conventions. Ultimately, *The Girl Gang* argues that the literary achievements of the New York City women Beats collectively reconceptualize the prevailing notion of the Beat community and canon. (General abstract)

Shaffer, Andrew. *Literary Rogues: A Scandalous History of Wayward Authors.* New York City, New York: HarperCollins. 2013. Print.

Rock stars, rappers, and actors haven't always had a monopoly on misbehaving. There was a time when authors fought with both words and fists, a time when poets were the ones living fast and dying young. This witty, insightful, and wildly entertaining narrative profiles the literary greats who wrote generation-defining classics such as *The Great Gatsby* and *On the Road* while living and loving like hedonistic rock icons, who were as likely to go on epic benders as they were to hit the bestseller lists. *Literary Rogues* turns back the clock to consider these historical (and, in some cases, living) legends, including Edgar Allan Poe, Oscar Wilde, Zelda and F. Scott Fitzgerald, Ernest Hemingway, Dorothy Parker, Hunter S. Thompson, and Bret Easton Ellis. Brimming with fascinating research, *Literary Rogues* is part nostalgia, part literary analysis, and a wholly raucous celebration of brilliant writers and their occasionally troubled legacies. (HarperCollins)

Sterritt, David. *The Beats: A Very Short Introduction.* Oxford: Oxford UP, 2013. Print.

In this Very Short Introduction, David Sterritt offers a concise overview of the social, cultural, and aesthetic sensibilities of the Beats, bringing out the similarities that connected them and also the many differences that made them a loosely knit collective rather than an organized movement. (Amazon, abridged)

Strausbaugh, John. *The Village: 400 Years of Beats and Bohemians, Radicals and Rogues: A History of Greenwich Village.* New York City, New York: Ecco. 2013. Print.

Illustrated with historic black-and-white photographs, *The Village* features lively, well-researched profiles of many of the people who made Greenwich Village famous, including Thomas Paine, Walt Whitman, Edna St. Vincent Millay, Mark Twain, Margaret Sanger, Eugene O'Neill, Marcel Duchamp, Upton Sinclair, Willa Cather, Jack Kerouac, Allen Ginsberg, Jackson Pollock, Anais Nin, Edward Albee, Charlie Parker, W. H. Auden, Woody Guthrie, James Baldwin, Maurice Sendak, E. E. Cummings, and Bob Dylan. (HarperCollins, abridged)

Tytell, John. "Beat Mexico." *Studies in Latin American Popular Culture*. 31. (2013): 50–68. Print.

William Burroughs, Jack Kerouac, and Allen Ginsberg felt that they needed to leave their own culture in order to see it more clearly, and they were almost magnetically drawn to Mexico. Each of these writers spent formative years in the early 1950s living in Mexico, and each was startled by the perspectives afforded by what Burroughs characterized as an "oriental culture." Mexico was still quite impoverished in the 1950s Gulf oil development created a middle class in Mexico only in the 1960s. What these writers saw in Mexico and the circumstances of their lives there (e.g., Kerouac's destitution and vagrancy, Burroughs' awareness that drugs would become his subject and his fatal shooting of his common-law wife) would find reflections in Burroughs's novels like *Junky*, *Queer*, and *Naked Lunch*; Kerouac's *On the Road* and *Tristessa*; and such poems by Ginsberg as the early "Siesta in Xbalba" and "Howl." Crucial letters, journals, and other writings on the Mexican experience have helped the author to chart the evolution of respective views—Kerouac at first sees Mexico as a pastoral idyll; Burroughs as an opportune occasion for libertarianism; Ginsberg experiences a place "beyond Darwin's chain." Such evolving views affected the development of each of their own literary voices. (General abstract)

Warner, Simon. *Text and Drugs and Rock 'n' Roll: The Beats and Rock Culture*. London: Bloomsbury, 2013. Print.

Text and Drugs and Rock 'n' Roll considers the myriad ways in which two different artistic worlds found common ground in the final third of the 20th century. The rock musicians who came to the fore at the heart of the 1960s and a radical community of writers who had originally made their mark in the 1950s forged friendships and alliances that would challenge the traditional divide between popular music and the realm of the literary. (Bloomsbury, abridged)

Jack Kerouac

Abbott, Philip. "The State of Nature on 66: Jack Kerouac's *On The Road* and the Social Contract Tradition." *Philosophy & Literature*. 37.1 (2013): 210-227. Print.

Jack Kerouac's *On the Road* occupies an unusual status in American letters. It is an American classic but also a contested text. An early reviewer's assessment of *On the Road* as an American masterpiece has been consistently reiterated, but so have initial dismissals that the work is an incoherent, naïve, and narcissistic travel narrative. This ambivalence is heightened by Kerouac's own idiosyncratic political and social views. These conflicting assessments can be reconciled, however, if *On the Road* is evaluated as a work of political thought, especially as an iteration of the social contract tradition exploring relationships in a "state of nature." (General abstract)

Dunagan, Patrick J. "The Poet Rolls On." *American Book Review*. 34.4 (2013): 26. Print.

While Jack Kerouac's novels such as *On the Road* (1957), *Dharma Bums* (1958), and *Big Sur* (1962) continue to generate much of the predominate buzz surrounding his significant body of work, his poetry deserves no less dedicated attention. As a few scholars—along with his notable pal Allen Ginsberg—have argued over the years Kerouac is a poet, through and through. (Excerpt)

Genter, Robert. "Mad to Talk, Mad to Be Saved: Jack Kerouac, Soviet Psychology, and the Cold War Confessional." *Studies in American Fiction*. 40.1 (2013): 27–52. Print.

This article explores Kerouac's fictive representations of the confessional voice in the context of his anti-communistic statements, Pavlovian psychology, and his journey as a life-long Catholic. (JBS Editorial Staff)

Hampton, Timothy. "Tangled Generation: Dylan, Kerouac, Pertrarch, and the Poetics of Escape." *Critical Inquiry*. 39.1 (2013): 703–731. Print.

In this essay, Hampton explores the ways in which Dylan deploys earlier traditions of writing about "generational experience, from Dante and Petrarch to Rimbaud and Jack Kerouac," as a way of marking a break with his earlier work. (JBS Editorial Staff)

Jackson, M. E. "French Friends, American Allies: Ethnic Dynamics in the Writing of Jack Kerouac." *Comparative American Studies*. 11.3 (2013): 280-328. Print.

The way the scroll text of Kerouac's *On the Road* creatively manifests the writer's unconscious concerns about his dichotomous hybrid French-Canadian-American heritage is analysed. The characters of Gabrielle Kerouac, Henri Cru, and Neal Cassady are shown to operate metaphorically to symbolize Kerouac's tumultuous relationship with the various elements of his genealogy. How the writer's depiction of and the protagonist's allegiances with these characters, who, respectively, represent French-Canadian maternity, European respectability and American unreliability, betray Kerouac's covert attempts to reconcile his autobiographical feelings about the dualities implicit in his identity and mirror his efforts to navigate disparate cultural ideologies is examined. (General abstract)

Johnson, Joyce. *The Voice Is All: The Lonely Victory of Jack Kerouac*. New York, New York: Penguin. 2013. Print.

Tracking Kerouac's development from his boyhood in Lowell, Massachusetts, through his fateful encounters with Allen Ginsberg, William S. Burroughs, Neal Cassady, and John Clellon Holmes to his periods of solitude and the phenomenal breakthroughs of 1951 that resulted in *On the Road* and *Visions of Cody*, Johnson shows how his French Canadian background drove him to forge a voice that could contain his dualities and inform his unique outsider's vision of America. This revelatory portrait deepens our understanding of a man whose life and work hold an enduring place in both popular culture and literary history. (Amazon, abridged)

Kerouac, Jack. *The Sea is My Brother* (*The Lost Novel*). Cambridge, Massachusetts: Da Capo, 2013. Print.

In the spring of 1943, twenty-one-year-old Jack Kerouac set out to write his first novel. Working diligently day and night to complete it by hand, he titled it *The Sea Is My Brother.* Nearly seventy years later, its long-awaited publication provides fascinating details and insight into the early life and development of an American literary icon. (Da Capo, abridged)

Kupetz, Joshua. "Jack Kerouac." *The Cambridge Companion to American Novelists.*
     Ed. Timothy Parrish. Cambridge, England: Cambridge UP. 2013.
     219–229. Print.

> This *Companion* examines the full range and vigor of the American
> novel. From the American exceptionalism of James Fenimore Cooper
> to the apocalyptic post-Americanism of Cormac McCarthy, these newly
> commissioned essays from leading scholars and critics chronicle the
> major aesthetic innovations that have shaped the American novel over
> the past two centuries. The essays evaluate the work, life, and legacy of
> influential American novelists including Melville, Twain, James, Wharton,
> Cather, Faulkner, Ellison, Pynchon, and Morrison, while situating them
> within the context of their literary predecessors and successors. The
> volume also highlights less familiar, though equally significant, writers
> such as Theodore Dreiser and Djuna Barnes, providing a balanced and
> wide-ranging survey of use to students, teachers, and general readers of
> American literature. (Cambridge)

Lane, Véronique. "The Parting of Burroughs and Kerouac: The French Backstory
     to the First Beat Novel, from Rimbaud to Poetic Realist Cinema."
     Comparative American Studies. 11.3 (2013): 265–279. Print.

> The first so-called beat novel, *And The Hippos Were Boiled in Their Tanks,*
> was co-written by Burroughs and Kerouac in 1945 but only published in
> 2008, and dismissed as little more than a biographical curiosity. However,
> a comparative analysis of the text with its unpublished second version—
> the archival typescript of "I Wish I Were You" composed by Kerouac alone
> —invites us to reread it from entirely new perspectives. An examination
> of the crucial role played by allusions to French culture from one version
> of the text to the other shows how Kerouac emerged from Burroughs'
> shadow. In "I Wish I Were You," Kerouac refocuses the story through self-
> reflexive references to visual works of art, specifically the French poetic
> realist cinema of the 1930s, and by doing so asserts for the first time his
> ethic and aesthetic as a writer of "bookmovies." (General abstract)

Pacini, Peggy. "Satori in Paris: Deconstructing the French Connection or the
     Legend's Satori." *Comparative American Studies.* 11.3 (2013): 290–299.
     Print.

> The deconstruction of Kerouac's trip to France in search of his family
> name and lineage as described in *Satori in Paris,* published in 1966, is
> examined, and consideration is also given to the very process of redefining

French connections. The novel—a voyage to the end of the night trying to decipher, redefine, and blur the French signs that Kerouac had scattered his Duluoz Legend with—is riddled with many deconstructing elements, which allow for better insight into both the quest Kerouac had set for himself and the meaning of French connections throughout the Legend. "What's in a name" could precisely be the question and possibly the answer. (General abstract)

Sperber, Michael. "Journey of the Traumatized Hero: Kerouac's *On the Road* and Gandhi's Railroad Ride." *Psychiatric Times*. 30.6 (2013): 11-13. Print.

In this essay, Sperber compares the journeys taken by Jack Kerouac described in *On the Road* to the one of Mohandes K. Gandhi related in *My Autobiography: The Story of My Experiments with Truth*. They are vastly different but in one important respect remarkably similar: each marked a turning point in the respective individual's life. The turning point for both occured at the "Abyss" in a schematic representation of the journey Joseph Campbell described for the traunatized hero. The essay explores these traumas as well as the resilience required to complete the journey. (*JBS* Editorial Staff)

Spikes, Mike. "Haiku and Ockham's Razor: The Example of Jack Kerouac." *Modern Haiku*. 44.2 (2013): 58–66. Print.

This essay presents the attributes and classifications of haiku. It offers information on how haiku evolved productively in different directions and how the distinguishing trait of haiku is its linguistic pronounced economy. Moreover, it presents an overview of the Ockham's Razor philosophical principle. (General abstract)

Allen Ginsberg

Bellarsi, Franca. "'Alien Hieroglyphs of Eternity' and 'Cold Pastorals': Allen Ginsberg's 'Siesta in Xbalba' and John Keats's Great Odes." *Comparative American Studies*. 11.3 (2013): 243–364. Print.

Examining the poetry of Allen Ginsberg in the light of that of John Keats, the possible connections between "Siesta in Xbalba"—a long poem by Ginsberg that received much more critical attention in the eighties than today—and Keats's so-called Great Odes are investigated. "Siesta" is here read as a composite mainly recycling "Ode on a Grecian Urn" and "Ode to a Nightingale," whose themes and motifs Ginsberg both preserves and subverts. This is the first attempt to conflate "Siesta" with Keats's Great Odes. (General abstract)

Dandeles, Gregory, M. "The Laurel Tree Cudgel: War and Walt Whitman in Allen Ginsberg's 'America'." *Journal of American Culture*. 36.3 (2013): 221–229. Print.

The article presents a critique of the poem "America," by the 20th-century American poet Allen Ginsberg. Focus is given to the theme of war and the influence of the earlier poet Walt Whitman on Ginsberg's literary output. An overview of Whitman's war poetry is given, identifying major features. Specific instances of Whitmanesque language in "America" are identified. Conclusions are given regarding reference to Whitman's "laurel tree cudgel." (General abstract)

Ferris, William R. "Trading Verses: James 'Son Ford' Thomas and Allen Ginsberg." *Southern Cultures*. 19.1 (2013): 53–60. Print.

The text is the transcription of a conversation between Beat poet Allen Ginsberg and Blues musician Thomas Ford. Recorded on video and film by Ferris, the conversation was witnessed after a written and oral literature panel at the annual MLA meeting. (*JBS* Editorial Staff)

Harris, Oliver. "Minute Particulars of the Counter-Culture: Time, Life, and the Photo-Poetics of Allen Ginsberg." *Comparative American Studies*. 10.1 (2013): 3–29. Print.

Recent exhibitions of Allen Ginsberg's photographs, which feature 1950s snapshots of his fellow-Beats Jack Kerouac and William Burroughs, have been dismissed by some as marketing exercises for the Beat myth that promote their biocentric image. Ginsberg himself invited comparisons between his work and Robert Frank's *The Americans*. However, a detailed material analysis of his work as a poet-photographer, paying close attention to his handwritten captions, recognises it as a complex hybrid that extends his prophetic poetics. In particular, contextualising his work in relation to the 1950s photojournalism of *Life* and *Time* establishes the ways in which Ginsberg and Burroughs responded to the attacks made on the Beats in those magazines on behalf of Henry Luce's "American Century." (General abstract)

Kearful, Frank J. "Alimentary Poetics: Robert Lowell and Allen Ginsberg." *Partial Answers: Journal of Literature and the History of Ideas*. 11.1 (2013): 87–108. Print.

Robert Lowell coined the famous distinction between cooked and raw poetry, but beginning with Joel Barlow's epic treat "The Hasty Pudding" there is a long tradition of American poetics sustained by copious and artful use of tropes of hunger, food, and eating. Allen Ginsberg's *Howl and Other Poems* and Lowell's *Life Studies* would be emaciated beyond recognition without them. Also taking other poems into account, the essay argues that Lowell and Ginsberg did more to enrich the American alimentary poetic tradition than anyone else since T. S. Eliot and Wallace Stevens. (General abstract)

Mead-Brewer, Katherine Campbell. *The Trickster in Ginsberg: A Critical Reading*. Jefferson, North Carolina: McFarland. 2013. Print.

This scholarly close reading of Allen Ginsberg's "Howl" considers the iconic poem through a four-part trickster framework: appetite, boundlessness, transformative power, and a proclivity for setting and falling victim to tricks and traps. The book pursues various different narratives of the trickster Coyote and the historical and biographical contexts of "Howl" from an interdisciplinary perspective. This study seeks to contribute to the current literature on the poetry of the Beats and of Allen Ginsberg, specifically his "Howl," and the ways it continues to expand in meaning, depth, and significance today. (McFarland)

Perloff, Majorie. "Allen Ginsberg." *Poetry*. 202.4 (2013): 351–353. Print.

A personal narrative is presented in which the author discusses her friendship with the American poet Allen Ginsberg, including the June 1993 conference of the U.S. National Poetry Foundation at the University of Maine at Orono, Ginsberg's poem "A Supermarket in California," and Ginsberg's relationship with art patron Stanley Grinstein. (General abstract, abridged)

Ramírez, J. Jesse. "The Ghosts of Radicalisms Past: Allen Ginsberg's Old Left Nightmares." *Arizona Quarterly: A Journal of American Literature, Culture, and Theory*. 69.1 (2013): 47–71. Print.

In a critique of thin contemporary analyses of Beat literature, Ramírez aims to give a richer, historicized, and more novel account of meaning in Allen

Ginsberg's work. Ramírez draws on Jacques Derrida's notion of "spectral" experiences of time and history to build a historical frame with which to read Ginsberg. In doing so, he hopes to disjoint the hegemonic interpretive paradigm of "pastlessness" applied in contemporary Beat analysis. To this end, Ramírez traces the connection between Beat writers and the "specter" of the Old Left. (JBS Editorial Staff)

Walker, Luke. "Allen Ginsberg's Blakean Albion." *Comparative American Studies.* 11.3 (2013); 227–242. Print.

Focusing on a selection of poems written during Allen Ginsberg's visits to Britain between 1958 and 1979, an attempt is made to show how Ginsberg's British poetry might productively be read in the context of William Blake's mythopoetic system, particularly insofar as it relates to the Blakean figures of Albion and Jerusalem. Ginsberg's poetic vision of a Blakean Albion is revealed to be more complex, and more problematic, than might be supposed. This is partly because Ginsberg's own position is conflicted: as a key representative of American Beat poetry and later of American counterculture, he is nonetheless engaged in these "British" poems in re-envisioning and reshaping Blake's Albion. Such nationalist tensions are not, however, restricted to Ginsberg's work; they can also be linked to similar conflicts between nationalism and internationalism which already exist within Blake's own vision of Albion. (General abstract)

Walker, Luke. "Allen Ginsberg 'Wales Visitation' as a neo-Romantic response to Wordsworth's 'Tintern Abbey'." *Romanticism.* 19.2 (2013): 207–217. Print.

The article considers the 1967 visit by American Beat poet Allen Ginsberg to the Wye River Valley and the Vale of Ewyas in Wales. As a result of the trip, Ginsberg was inspired to write poetry which paid homage to English poets William Blake and William Wordsworth. The reception of Blake and Wordsworth by the American counterculture of the 1960s is explored. Poems discussed include Ginsberg's "Wales Visitation" and Wordsworth's "Lines Composed a Few Miles above Tintern Abbey, On Revisiting the Banks of the Wye during a Tour. July 13, 1798". (General abstract)

William S. Burroughs

Cline, Kurt. "'Time Junky': Shamanic Journeyings and Gnostic Eschatology in the Novels of William S. Burroughs." *Tamkang Review: A Quarterly of Literary and Cultural Studies*. 43.2 (2013): 33–58. Print.

[No abstract availible]

Cran, Rona. "'Everything is permitted': William Burroughs' Cut-up Novels and European Art." *Comparative American Studies*. 11.3 (2013): 300–313. Print.

This essay suggests that during the 1960s William Burroughs was as much an avant-garde European artist as he was an American novelist. It argues that the nature of his cut-up novels requires readers to situate them within the context of twentieth-century European art—specifically collage—as well as American literature. Burroughs held the view that "if writing is to have a future it must at least catch up with the past and learn to use techniques that have been used for some time past in painting." This attitude towards his writing led him back into the rich, experimental half-century of European art which had gone before him, and into which his resulting cut-up work must be incorporated if its profoundly confusing and anacathartic effects upon readers are to be in any way tempered. (General abstract)

Davis, Stephen. *Williams Burroughs/Local Stop on the Nova Express*. Providence, RI: Inkblot, 2013. Print.

This is the long-lost interview with author William S. Burroughs, never reprinted since its first appearance in *The Real Paper* in 1974. The introduction treats Burroughs' life and work. Part 3 is an overview of the discussion between Burroughs and Jimmy Page printed in *Crawdaddy* in 1975. Author/interviewer is noted rock biographer and journalist Stephen Davis, known for his books on Led Zeppelin, Jim Morrison, The Rolling Stones, Bob Marley, and Aerosmith. (Amazon, abridged)

Lane, Véronique. "The Parting of Burroughs and Kerouac: The French Backstory to the First Beat Novel, from Rimbaud to Poetic Realist Cinema." *Comparative American Studies*. 11.3 (2013): 265–279. Print.

[See entry under Kerouac]

McFayden, Ian. *William S. Burroughs: Cut (The Future of the Past)*. Ed. Axel Heil. Amsterdam: Köln Walther König, 2013. Print.

This volume looks at the collages, scrapbooks, films and audio works made by Burroughs in collaboration with his mentor Brion Gysin (with whom he authored the book *The Third Mind*), London filmmaker Anthony Balch, and electronics technician Ian Sommerville—as well as his later collaborations with writers and artists such as John Giorno and George Condo. An interview with Burroughs conducted by Jean-Jacques Lebel in Paris in 1982 is included, published here for the first time in English. (Amazon, abridged)

Weidner, Chad. "Mutable Forms: The Proto-ecology of William Burroughs' Early Cut-ups." *Comparative American Studies*. 11.3 (2013): 314–326. Print.

This article explains the extent to which ecocriticism can engage the early texts of William Burroughs with their lack of coherent narratives and shortage of recognizably relevant environmental content. The suggestion that early cut-ups from *Minutes to Go* and *The Yage Letters* can be considered a move towards proto-ecological writing forms is explored. Fragments from Burroughs' early cut-ups "VIRUSES WERE BY ACCIDENT?" (1960) and "I am Dying, Meester?" (1963) are examined to establish whether there are any connections between ecology and Burroughs' cut-up method, and to illustrate the evolution of the cut-up method. *The Yage Letters* are shown to connect the cut-up method and ayahuasca as radical techniques of reality transformation, which means the undoing of Western assumptions about identity. The differences between Burroughs' methods and those of the Dadaist Tristan Tzara are also discussed. (General abstract)

Wills, David S. *Scientologist!: William S. Burroughs and the "Weird Cult"*. Beatdom, 2013. Print.

Scientology is largely overlooked in major texts about the life and work of William S. Burroughs, author of some of the most notorious literature of the twentieth century. Its importance in the creation of the cut-up method and Burroughs' view of language as a virus is undermined by the omission of details regarding his interest in the religion over the course of a decade —certainly the most creatively fertile period of his life. Now, for the first time, his life and literature are reexamined in the light of newly-uncovered information about Burroughs' fascination with this "weird cult," as he once described it. (Amazon, abridged)

Charles Bukowski

Clements, Paul. *Charles Bukowski, Outsider Literature, and the Beat Movement.* London: Routledge, 2013. Print.

> This book uses cultural and psycho-social analysis to examine the writer Charles Bukowski and his literature, focusing on representations of the anti-hero rebel and outsider. Clements considers the complexities, ambiguities, and contradictions represented by the author and his work, exploring Bukowski's visceral writing of the cultural ordinary and everyday self-narrative. The study considers Bukowski's apolitical, gendered, and working-class stance to understand how the writer represents reality and is represented with regards to counter-cultural literature. In addition, Clements provides a broader socio-cultural focus that evaluates counterculture in relation to the American Beat movement and mythology, highlighting the male cool anti-hero. The cultural practices and discourses utilized to situate Bukowski include the individual and society, outsiderdom, cult celebrity, fan embodiment, and disneyfication, providing a greater understanding of the Beat generation and counterculture literature. (Amazon, abridged)

Debritto, Abel. *Charles Bukowski, King of the Underground: From Obscurity to Literary Icon.* New York, New York: Palgrave Macmillan, 2013. Print.

> Charles Bukowski was a product of the small press movement, an unparalleled phenomenon in the so-called little magazines that proliferated in the United States during the 60s. His long journey through the "littles" and the small presses was finally rewarded after bitter battles in the back alleys of the American literary scene. This critical study offers a comprehensive picture of the literary magazines, underground newspapers, and small press publications that had an impact on Charles Bukowski's early career. Abel Debritto draws on archives, privately held unpublished work, and interviews to shed new light on the ways in which Bukowski became an icon in the alternative literary scene in the 1960s. (Palgrave Macmillan)

Vats, Smitri, Asta Bhargav, & Ritu Sharma. *Charles Bukowski's* Ham on Rye *and* Women: *a Study in Autobiographical Undercurrents.* Lambert Academic, 2013. Print.

> The book aims at discussing critically autobiographical tones in the fiction of Charles Bukowski with special reference to his two famous novels *Ham on Rye* and *Women*. An attempt has been made to examine how truly he could, through his characters and their peculiar situations, express his

autobiographical facts in these novels. Bukowski created a literary persona named Henry Chinaski as a vessel for expressing his alternative view of the world, to a large extent concerned with commenting on the role of the artist in the society, the stultifying dullness and conformity of the "day-job," the comic dimensions of sexual relationships, the often unpleasant realities of poverty and chronic drunkenness, and the constant struggle of the alienated individual to assert his non-conformist identity. The book traces the development of Chinaski's non-conformist personality from *Ham On Rye*, based on Bukowski's youth in Los Angeles during the Depression, to *Women,* where Bukowski focuses on relationships and sex. (General abstract)

Villines, Melanie, ed. *Bukowski: An Anthology of Poetry & Prose About Charles Bukowski (Volume 4)*. Los Angeles: Silver Birch, 2013. Print.

A collection of poetry, short stories, memoirs, book excerpts, interviews, and essays about Charles Bukowski as well as portraits of the author from over seventy-five writers and artists around the world. (Amazon, abridged)

Herbert Huncke

Holladay, Hilary. *American Hipster: The Time Square Hustler Who Inspired the Beat Movement*. New York City, New York: Riverdale Avenue, 2013. Print.

The first biography of the hustler/junkie/writer who turned the Beats on to the drugs, sex, and postwar counterculture that shaped their writing and radicalized American literature. (Amazon, abridged)

Gary Snyder

Bachinger, Jacob. "Gary Snyder's 'The Wild Mushroom'." *Explicator*. 71.1 (2013): 7-10. Print.

Gary Snyder's poem, "The Wild Mushroom" offers a vision of the wilderness in which binary opposites—work/play, food/poison—are reconciled and united. Snyder accomplished this via a perhaps not-so-likely candidate: the wild mushroom itself. Ultimately, the mushroom represents the ways in which wild nature provides for humankind. (Excerpt)

Philip Whalen

Giles, Todd. ""No Permanent Home': The Five Skandhas and Philip Whalen's 'The Slop Barrel'." *Philosophy & Literature*. 37.2 (2013): 405–420. Print.

Six months after the famous 6 [sic] Gallery poetry reading in 1955, Philip Whalen began working on "The Slop Barrel," a poem that is an interior examination of Mahāyāna Buddhist notions of impermanence, interdependence, and awakening. Giles argues that "The Slop Barrel" is an exploration of the Five Skandhas, or five aggregates of attachment, which collectively make one's personality. The poet-narrator comes to recognize, as he moves from being trapped in the world of objects and concepts to reaching the other shore of liberation, that suffering lies not in the aggregates themselves, but in his lack of understanding of emptiness. (General abstract)

Amiri Baraka

Bennett, Michael Y. "Dominance and Triumph of the White Trickster Over the Black Picaro in Amiri Baraka's *Great Goodness of Life: A Coon Show*." *Callaloo*. 36.2 (2013): 312–321. Print.

In the opening scene of Baraka's *Great Goodness of Life: A Coon Show* (1966), Court Royal—"a middle-aged Negro man, gray haired, slight" (156)—is urged, with a "Come on" from the Voice of the Judge, towards the center of the stage and into the "center of the lights" (157). Court states his unease and puzzlement: "I don't quite understand" (157).The

all-encompassing and pervading Voice responds, "Shutup, nigger" (157). Thus begins Court's "trial." He is isolated in the center of the stage, berated by the Voice throughout the entire play. Court is, phenomenologically, a defender on an island under attack. He has nowhere to run and no ground to stand on other than his own. He is dominated because there is no respite from the attack and there is no escape route in sight, other than going right through a more powerful attacker.

These paradigms of conquest, these modes of domination, are framed geographically, spatially, and physically. Baraka's satire becomes ironic, even for a satire, for he portrays the triumph of a white trickster over a black picaro. In a dominant-submissive relationship that mirrors the relationship of colonizer to colonized, the picaro is wiped right out of the African American. In such cases of domination, the only result can be a "coon show"— something vile that denigrates oneself and the community, ending in a self-negating, self-defeating violence. (Excerpt)

Pisano, Claudia Moreno. *Amiri Baraka and Edward Dorn: The Collected Letters.* Albuquerque, New Mexico: University of New Mexico P, 2013. Print.

These letters offer a vivid picture of American lives connecting around poetry during a tumultuous time of change and immense creativity. Reading through these correspondences allows access into personal biographies, and through these biographies, profound moments in American cultural history open themselves to us in a way not easily found in official channels of historical narrative and memory. (Amazon, abridged)

Willey, Ann. "A Bridge over Troubled Waters: Jazz, Diaspora Discourse, and E. B. Dongala's 'Jazz and Palm Wine' as Response to Amiri Baraka's 'Answers in Progress'." *Research in African Literatures.* 44.3 (2013): 138–151. Print.

This essay explores how Emmanuel Dongala's story "Jazz and Palm Wine" (1970) rewrites Amiri Baraka's story "Answers in Progress" (1967). Baraka's story calls for a black revolution based in futurist thinking and diaspora consciousness embodied in jazz. In rewriting Baraka, Dongala resists discourses of coherent and stable identity through a recasting of the aesthetic functions of futurism and jazz. Dongala's intertextual use of, and emendations to, Baraka's story suggest his discomfort with articulations of diaspora identity that, in the late '60s, were increasingly defined by cultural symbols. In transposing Baraka's futurist fable of the revolution to the African continent, Dongala stresses that while aesthetic objects, even ones as universally appealing as jazz, can be equally effective in different contexts, those contexts generate dramatically different effects. (General abstract)

Zygmonski, Aimee. "Amiri Baraka and the Black Arts Movement." *The Cambridge Companion to African American Theatre.* Ed. Harvey Young. Cambridge, England: Cambridge UP. 2013. 137–154. Print.

This Companion provides a comprehensive overview of African American theatre, from the early nineteenth century to the present day. Along the way, it chronicles the evolution of African American theatre and its engagement with the wider community, including discussions of slave rebellions on the national stage, African Americans on Broadway, the Harlem Renaissance, African American women dramatists, and the "New Negro" and "Black Arts" movements. Leading scholars spotlight the producers, directors, playwrights, and actors whose efforts helped to fashion a more accurate appearance of Black life on stage, and reveal the impact of African American theatre both within the United States and further afield. Chapters also address recent theatre productions in the context of political and cultural change and ask where African American theatre is heading in the twenty-first century. (Amazon)

Bob Dylan

Bell, Ian. *Once Upon a Time: The Lives of Bob Dylan*. New York City, New York: Pegasus, 2013. Print.

In *Once Upon a Time*, award-winning author Ian Bell draws together the tangled strands of the many lives of Bob Dylan in all their contradictory brilliance. For the first time, the laureate of modern America is set in his entire context: musical, historical, literary, political, and personal. Full of new insights into the legendary singer, his songs, his life, and his era, the artist who invented himself in order to reinvent America is discovered anew. *Once Upon a Time* is a lively investigation of a mysterious personality that has splintered and reformed, time after time, in a country forever trying to understand itself. Now that mystery is explained. (Amazon, abridged)

Black, Taylor. "Ballad of an Untimely Man: Bob Dylan at the Hollywood Bowl." *American Quarterly*. 65.2 (2013): 397–404. Print.

Unbeknownst to most of the very distracted and all-too-chatty members of the audience for Bob Dylan's Friday night show at the Hollywood Bowl on October 26, 2012, there was a moment when it became clear that the concert was something more like a war between Dylan and us. An untimely hero, Dylan has already predeceased himself; the man we heard that night was a man paving his victory trail into a world-to-come. As he spat and echoed his way through the always menacing "Ballad of a Thin Man," he had won. Dylan rose up from his seat behind the baby grand piano, where he had spent most of the evening tapping his toe and crooning his hits, to grab a microphone, proceeding to prowl around the stage with a devilish grin . . . (Excerpt from Project Muse)

Hampton, Timothy. "Tangled Generation: Dylan, Kerouac, Petrarch, and the Poetics of Escape." Critical Inquiry. 39.1 (2013): 703-731. Print.

[indexed under Kerouac]

Maxwell, Grant. "'An Extreme Sense of Destiny': Bob Dylan, Affect, and Final
   Causation." *Journal of Religion and Popular Culture*. 25.1 (2013): 146–162
   Electronic.

Bob Dylan has explicitly suggested on numerous occasions that he
possessed "an extreme sense of destiny," which has been the primary
driving force in the development of his music and his identity. This
article traces Dylan's and his milieu's articulation of final causation in its
various inflections and demonstrates that this causal mode is intimately
connected to an affective epistemology in Dylan's experience. Through
abstract philosophical reflection (shown here to parallel closely the ideas
of philosophers like William James and Henri Bergson) and the relation of
particular occasions of final causation, Dylan suggests a worldview that
offers an alternative to what he perceives as the "madness" produced by
"pure materialism" (2004). (General abstract)

Frank O'Hara

Girard, Didier. "Frank O'Hara's Anti-Disciplinarian Discipline." *Journal of
   Cultural Poetics* (Zeitschrift für Kulturgeschichtliche Literaturwissenschaft).
   13.1 (2013): 82–93. Print.

[abstract not available]

Klein, Scott W. "For Frank O'Hara: Morton Feldman's *Three Voices* as Interpretation
   and Elegy." *Modernist Cultures*. 8.1 (2013): 120-137. Print.

Morton Feldman's 1982 Three Voices,a large concert work for solo voice,
takes its textual materials from Frank O'Hara's 1957 poem "Wind," The
essay investigates to what degree (1) Three Voices can be called a "setting"
of O'Hara's 'Wind'? (2) a musical composition, typically understood as
an art free of semantic associations, can be claimed to be an interpretation
of a text, (and 3) a musical work can create a work of elegiac art in the
absence of clearly defined textual or formal allusions to established genres
of mourning or remembrance. (*JBS* Editorial Staff)

O'Hara, Frank. *Poems Retrieved* (*City Lights/Grey Fox*). Ed. Don Allen. San
   Francisco, California: City Lights, 2013. Print.

Originally published under Donald Allen's classic Grey Fox Press imprint,
Poems Retrieved is a substantial part of Frank O'Hara's oeuvre, containing
over two hundred pages of previously unpublished poetry discovered after

the publication of his posthumous *Collected Poems* in 1971. Featuring a new introduction by O'Hara expert and friend, poet and art critic Bill Berkson, *Retrieved* has been completely reformatted and is essential for any reader of twentieth century poetry. As Berkson writes, "The breadth of what Frank O'Hara took to be poetry is reflected in the many kinds of poems he wrote. . . . Turning the pages of any of his collections, you wonder what he didn't turn his hand to, what variety of poem he left untried or didn't, in some cases, as if in passing, anticipate." (Silver Light)

Perloff, Marjorie. "Meditations in an Emergency." *Poetry*. 201.5 (2013): 540–543. Print.

The article looks at the artwork of expressionist painter and printmaker Joan Mitchell. The author discusses poet Frank O'Hara, his poem "Meditations in an Emergency," and the metaphors in the works of O'Hara and Mitchell. The article also presents an image of the color lithograph "Meditations in an Emergency" by Mitchell. (General abstract)

Shaw, Lytle. *Frank O'Hara: The Poetics of Coterie*. Iowa City, Iowa: U of Iowa P, 2013. Print.

In this stimulating and innovative synthesis of New York's artistic and literary worlds, Lytle Shaw uses the social and philosophical problems involved in "reading" a coterie to propose a new language for understanding the poet, art critic, and Museum of Modern Art curator Frank O'Hara (1926–1966). (University of Iowa, abridged)

Young, C. Dale. "The Veil of Accessibility: Examining Poems by Frank O'Hara and Kenneth Koch in Light of Conrad's *Heart of Darkness*." *American Poetry Review*. 42.2 (2013): 25–29. Print.

This essay examines "Ave Maria" and "Poem," both by Frank O'Hara, and "One Train May Hide Another" by Kenneth Koch in light of the novella *Heart of Darkness* by Joseph Conrad. The notion of the accessibility of literature is addressed in relation to rhetorical simplicity. (General abstract)

Joanne Kyger

Kyger, Joanne. "A Wonderful Interpretation." *Jung Journal: Culture & Psyche*. 7.3 (2013): 7. Print.

Kyger, Joanne. "Conscious Reenactment." *Jung Journal: Culture & Psyche.* 7.3 (2013): 8. Print.

Kyger Joanne. "Finger Pointing at the Moon Is Not the Moon." *Jung Journal: Culture & Psyche.* 7.3 (2013): 10. Print.

Kyger, Joanne. "It's the Big Trip." *Jung Journal: Culture & Psyche.* 7.3 (2013): 4. Print.

Kyger, Joanne. "Kissing Ferrets." *Jung Journal: Culture & Psyche.* 7.3 (2013): 6. Print.

Kyger, Joanne. "Plum Blossoms on Evergreen." *Jung Journal: Culture & Psyche.* 7.3 (2013): 11. Print.

Kyger, Joanne. "Some Notes on the Poems." *Jung Journal: Culture & Psyche.* 7.3 (2013): 13. Print.

Kyger, Joanne. "Spring Time Babies." *Jung Journal: Culture & Psyche.* 7.3 (2013): 15. Print.

Kyger, Joanne. "Stoutly Maintain I Never Rewrite." *Jung Journal: Culture & Psyche.* 7.3 (2013): 12. Print.

Kyger, Joanne. "Wall Painting at Brighton Beach." *Jung Journal: Culture & Psyche.* 7.3 (2013): 5. Print.

Watsky, Paul. "A Conversation with Joanne Kyger." *Jung Journal: Culture & Psyche.* 7.3 (2013): 94-116. Print.

Call for Proposals or Essays for the *Journal of Beat Studies*

Seeking high quality criticism across the range of Beat writing, including fiction, poetry, drama, autobiography, life writing, travel writing, technology, and screenplay writing. The application of diverse critical perspectives is welcome in essays that address Beat literary production as both complex art and engaged cultural critique.

Topics might investigate:
- Studies of individual Beat writers (e.g., Kerouac, Ginsberg, Burroughs, di Prima, Waldman, Baraka, Kaufman)
- Connections between Beat writing and other schools, such as Black Mountain and the New York School
- International and transnational nature and impact of Beat writing
- Neo-Beat writers in the late twentieth- and early-twenty-first centuries
- Reception to Beat literature
- Beats and Technology
- Beats and Film, Popular Culture, etc.
- Beat Rhetoric
- Beats and Philosophical Perspectives
- Eco-criticism

Please consult style guidelines published in this issue and posted on the Beat Studies Association web site: http://www.beatstudies.org/jbs/index.html.

Essays can be submitted at any time, but if the author is interested in possible publication in Volume Four of the *Journal of Beat Studies*, submit essays no later than July 1, 2014, and proposals no later than June 1, 2014. Submit simultaneously to Ronna C. Johnson (ronna.johnson@tufts.edu) and Nancy M. Grace (Ngrace@wooster.edu).

Notes on Contributors

Maria Damon is chair of the Humanities and Media Studies Department, part of the School of Liberal Arts and Sciences at the Pratt Institute in New York City. Prior to that she taught for twenty-five years at the University of Minnesota—Twin Cities. Damon is the author of several scholarly books, including *Post-literary "America": From Bagel Shop Jazz to Micropoetries* (2011); *Poetry and Cultural Studies: A Reader,* which she co-authored with Ira Livingston (2009); and *The Dark End of the Street: Margins in American Vanguard Poetry* (1993). Her poetic work includes *Literature Nation*, the first book-length hypertext poem on the Internet (2003), which she co-authored with frequent collaborator mIEKAL aND in 1998.

Todd Giles is an assistant professor of Contemporary American Literature at Midwestern State University in Wichita Falls, Texas, where he teaches a wide range of undergraduate and graduate courses, including postmodern American literature, nature writing, and the Beats. His scholarship, which appears in *Philosophy and Literature, Texas Studies in Language and Literature*, the *Willa Cather Newsletter and Review*, and *American Literary Realism*, focuses on the cross-fertilization of American literature, music, philosophy, and the visual arts. He is associate editor/ book review editor of the *William Carlos Williams Review*.

Dustin Griffin is professor emeritus of English at New York University, where he specialized in eighteenth-century British literature. He is the author of *Authorship in the Long Eighteenth Century* (2013), *Swift and Pope: Satirists in Dialogue* (2010), *Patriotism and Poetry in 18th-Century Britain* (2002), *Literary Patronage in England, 1650–1800* (1996), *Satire: A Critical Reintroduction* (1994), *Regaining Paradise: Milton and the 18th Century* (1986), and *Alexander Pope: The Poet in the Poems* (1978). He is the recipient of a Guggenheim fellowship, an American Council of Learned Societies fellowship, and a National Endowment for the Humanities grant.

Oliver Harris is a professor of American Literature at Keele University in Staffordshire, England. He has written on and edited numerous works by William S. Burroughs, including *Queer: 25th-Anniversary Edition* by William S. Burroughs (2010), *Naked Lunch@50: Anniversary Essays* (2009), *Everything Lost: The Latin American Notebook of William S. Burroughs* (2008), *The Yage Letters Redux* by William S. Burroughs and Allen Ginsberg (2006), *William Burroughs and The Secret of Fascination* (2003), *Junky; the definitive text of "Junk"* by William S. Burroughs (2003), and *The Letters of William S. Burroughs 1945–1959* (1993). He is founding president of the European Beat Studies Network and sits on the editorial board of the *Journal of Beat Studies*.

Marian Janssen is head of the International Office as well as an independent researcher at Radbound University Nijmegen in the Netherlands. She is the author of *Not at All What One Is Used To: The Life and Times of Isabella Gardner* (2010) and *The Kenyon Review, 1939–1970: A Critical History* (1990).

David Sterritt is professor emeritus of theater and film at Long Island University; adjunct professor, Columbia University, School of the Arts Film Studies Faculty/Graduate Film Division; chair of the National Society of Film Critics; chief book critic for *Film Quarterly*; and a member of the editorial boards for a number of scholarly journals including the *Journal of Beat Studies*. He is the author of numerous books on film, literature and popular culture, including *Screening the Beats: Media Culture and the Beat Sensibility* (2004) and *Mad to Be Saved: The Beats, the '50s, and Film* (1998).

Matt Theado began teaching American Literature in 2014 at Kobe City University of Foreign Studies in Japan. Prior to that, he was a professor of English and chair of the Department of English Language and Literature at Gardner-Webb University in Boiling Springs, North Carolina, where he taught for eighteen years. He is the author of *The Beats: A Literary Reference* (2002) and *Understanding Jack Kerouac* (2009).

Essay Abstracts

John Wieners in the Matrix of Massachusetts Institutions: A Psychopoeticgeography by Maria Damon

Beat writers were among the first U.S. writers who took on the city as a serious site of ambiguous magic in which subjectivity could undertake its own experiments and undergo those imposed upon it. To explore this phenomenon, Damon foregrounds the poetry of John Wieners as well as aspects of his Boston biography; these are coupled with Damon's own memories of growing up in the area. She focuses on the north and south slopes of Beacon Hill to illustrate the sharp class divides of the early 1970s and the ways in which such cultural realities affected Beat aesthetics. Escape comes in the form of unexpected textual malformations, if one is open to falling through their holes into other worlds, rather than altered external conditions. Her exploration reveals that one's movement into textual rather than social and political freedom is Wieners's version of the apolitical, post-HUAC nature of Beat writers' resistance.

Entering the "Gate of Nondualism": Gary Snyder's "On Vulture Peak" and Mahāyāna Shūnyatā by Todd Giles

This essay presents the first full critical analysis of Gary Snyder's early poem "On Vulture Peak," which he wrote soon after he left the United States to study Zen Buddhism in Japan. The poem eventually was revised and expanded into *Mountains and Rivers Without End*. The essay argues that "On Vulture Peak" presents some of the most complex and allusive concepts of Mahāyāna Buddhism that we find in Snyder's poetry. Giles details the contents and form of the poem, the types of ancient poetic and sacred texts upon which Snyder drew to construct the poem, and Snyder's manipulation of these forms for mid-twentieth-century aesthetic and cultural purposes. In addition to providing readers with an accessible entrance into Mahāyāna Buddhism, the essay reveals a point of genesis for Snyder's life-long engagement with the intersectionality of poetry, philosophy, and spirituality.

The St. Louis Clique: Burroughs, Kammerer, and Carr by Dustin Griffin

Drawing upon unpublished letters from and to David Kammerer, Griffin creates a fresh historical overview of the St. Louis lives of three of the main figures in the creation of what we know as the Beat Generation. The essay presents a vivid portrait of St. Louis, pre-World War II, as well as detailed portraits of the early years of William S. Burroughs, David Kammerer, and Lucien Carr, following them to New York City, where Carr stabbed and killed Kammerer in August 1944. The essay reaches no definitive conclusion about Kammerer's or Carr's sexualities, but does complicate the images we have of them, as well as that of Burroughs. The focus on Kammerer's life, heretofore undeveloped in Beat Studies, grounds the essay, which ultimately argues that at the time of the killing, Kammerer showed as much promise to develop into a major writer as did Carr and Burroughs.

The Enigmatic Relationship of Poets Isabella Gardner and Gregory Corso by Marian Janssen

Janssen is the author of the biography of the poet Isabella Gardner, the grand-niece of art collector Isabella Stewart Gardner and the cousin of poet Robert Lowell. At the height of the heyday of Beat-to-Hippie culture in the United States, Gardner and Gregory Corso knew each other in Boston and Cambridge. Their relationship began, as Janssen writes in the essay, with a fan letter from Corso to Gardner and ended years later as both their lives spiraled into addictions, disappointments, and indiscretions. Janssen's essay reveals nuances of the intersections of their lives, Corso as a much-lauded Beat poet and Gardner as an overlooked poet of traditional rhymes and meters. To this mix, she weaves in relationships among Beat writers and the more conventional but powerful writers and editors Allen Tate and Paul Carroll. The essay reveals that, contrary to recalcitrant myth, Beat writers and writers of more traditional forms interacted a great deal, often supporting each while simultaneously rejecting each other's aesthetic principles.

Theorizing Breast Cancer: Narrative, Politics, Memory

Guest Editors Mary K. DeShazer & Anita Helle

Tulsa Studies in Women's Literature
Vol. 32, No. 2 / Vol. 33, No. 1
Fall 2013 / Spring 2014

College **Literature**

a journal of critical literary studies

Graham MacPhee, Editor

West Chester University
201 E. Rosedale Avenue
West Chester, PA 19383
Tel: 610.436.2901
collit@wcupa.edu

College Literature publishes innovative scholarship from across the various periods and fields that comprise the changing discipline of literary studies. The journal aims to scrutinize the theoretical parameters and assumptions underlying contemporary critical practice, and to examine the political and institutional limits that define the discipline.

http://www.wcupa.edu/_academics/sch_cas.lit/

Policy

The *Journal of Beat Studies* invites articles on the works of Beat movement writers and their colleagues, especially New York School, Black Mountain School, and San Francisco Renaissance writers, as well as those connected to these movements, in the United States and globally. The *Journal* intends to represent the breadth and eclecticism of critical approaches to Beat Generation writers, and welcomes new perspectives and contexts of inquiry.

Articles that are deemed appropriate are sent for review anonymously to a member of the Editorial Board and at least one other reader. Manuscripts should not be under consideration elsewhere, and we do not publish previously published work. It is strongly advised that those submitting work to *JBS* be familiar with the journal's content. Among criteria on which evaluation of submissions depends are whether an article demonstrates recognition of and thorough familiarity with scholarship already published in the field, whether the article is written clearly and effectively, and whether it makes a genuine contribution to Beat studies.

Preparation of Copy

1. Articles are typically between 25 and 30 pages, and do not exceed 9000 words, including notes and works cited. Inquiries about significantly shorter or longer submissions should be sent to the editors.

2. A separate page should include the article's title, author's name, address, telephone & fax numbers, and e-mail address. The author's name and identifying references should not appear on the manuscript to preserve anonymity for our readers.

3. All submissions must include an abstract of no more than 250 words.

4. The manuscript should be in Times New Roman 12, double-spaced, and should adhere to the most recent MLA style.

5. Submissions may be sent by email as word documents ("doc" only, not "docx") to Ronna C. Johnson (ronna.johnson@tufts.edu) and Nancy M. Grace (ngrace@ wooster.edu) simultaneously. Mailed submissions may be sent to Nancy M. Grace, Department of English, 400 E. University Street, The College of Wooster, Wooster, Ohio 44691. For mailed submissions, please send three copies of the article and abstract.

6. Submissions may also be sent via the online submission form at http://www.
beatstudies.org/jbs/submission_guidelines.html.

7. Authors of accepted manuscripts are responsible for any necessary permissions
fees and for securing any necessary permissions.

8. All editorial, review, and advertising inquiries should be addressed to ronna.
johnson@tufts.edu and ngrace@wooster.edu.

9. Inquiries concerning orders should be addressed to PaceUP@pace.edu.